M.T

FOOLISH PRIDE

19/02/14

ANNE SKELLY

To Nicky,
With all my best wishes
and thanks for taking such
good care of me.

Anne Skelly

PUBLISHED BY ANNE SKELLY, 2012

ISBN: 978-1-907221-32-3

The paper used in this book comes from wood pulp of managed forests.
For every tree felled, at least one tree is planted, thereby renewing natural resources.

A CIP catalogue record for this book is available from the British Library and the Irish Copyright libraries.

Foolish Pride

Anne Skelly

DEDICATION

I WOULD LIKE to dedicate *Foolish Pride* to Mike, the love of my life, now and always, whose unwavering belief in me kept this book going even when it seemed like all the words in my head had dried up.

PROLOGUE

It is a truth universally acknowledged that a single woman, of a certain age, must be in want of a man.

So when a prospective husband is sighted on the horizon, mothers, friends and the entire community rally round to be of service.

As the first tentative rumours of a male addition to the staff at St Colmcille's National School sweep through Carrigmore, imaginations billow into overdrive and the busy wings of speculation begin to flap.

The idea that he is destined for one of their own takes root, and is nurtured. Until it flowers into certainty. However, at times, even deep-rooted certainties can contain a degree of foolish pride.

CHAPTER ONE

I SLOTTED THE key into the ignition, clicked in the seatbelt, and peered through the mud-spattered windscreen. Dark rain-bearing clouds were moving across an expanse of sky the colour of wet cement. A couple of magpies rose into the air, cawing hoarsely. My head was pounding, it was 9:15am, and I was just pulling out through the gate. After a frantic scramble from the shower to a rushed mug of coffee, only half drunk, there'd been no time to make the healthy option tuna and sweet corn salad I'd planned. It would have to be one of Miss Maloney's sandwiches. And her repertoire extended to ham or cheese. Stodgy white bread. Slathered with full cream butter. Just when I'd been getting serious about my pre-Christmas diet. Damn that snooze button!

As I swerved into the parking area outside the village shop, I could see through the glass door the gaunt figure of Miss Maloney in her charcoal tweed skirt, grey head nodding devotedly at her sole customer, Fr Flannery. If there was one thing the aging shopkeeper-cum-postmistress hated, it was being dragged away from a conversation with those whom she deemed the pillars of society. And Fr Flannery was up there next to God himself. Getting this sandwich could take a while.

I pushed open the door, setting off the tinkle to alert Miss Maloney to a new customer, almost enjoying the look of annoyance that twitched across her features. She subconsciously licked at the fringe of wiry grey hair that adorned her upper lip.

'Morning, Beth.'

The priest's voice boomed with a heartiness that betrayed his relief.

'And how are you on this fine day?'

'Grand, Father,' I lied. 'And yourself?'

'No use complaining, Beth. Sure who'd listen to me?' His plump fingers reached out for the newspaper and obligatory bar of Cadbury's chocolate he bought every morning. 'Anyway, must be off. A priest's work, you know… God bless, now.'

In a whirl of black soutane flapping like crows' wings, he angled his way out through the standard sized door.

'Have a good day, Father.' Miss Maloney's high-pitched whine floated after him before she grudgingly turned her attention to me.

'Well, Beth?' Sourness seeped from her tone. Having just put an end to her little chat with the parish priest, undoubtedly the highlight of her day, I was about as welcome as an army of cockroaches.

'The *Independent* please, Miss Maloney. And I need something for lunch. Would you have a ham sandwich?'

Her thin lips pursed tightly in further censure. I had just created more inconvenience for her. 'I'll have to go inside and make one up for you, dear. It'll be a few minutes.'

I sighed quietly. Now there was even less hope of making it on time. Thank God I wasn't on early playground duty.

The bell tinkled again to announce another customer. Fonsie Kelly was a bachelor farmer in his late 50s with thinning sandy hair in a basin cut, and a round florid face. In spite of having been rejected by just about every female in the county at some stage, he had never quite given up believing in his manly charms. His dogged persistence, combined with the whiff of silage that clung to him like a damp overcoat, tended to alienate most of his potential targets. Even Miss Maloney had not escaped his attentions in the past.

'How're ye, *Beth*, are ye well?' He was jovial by nature, but his tone bordered on the lewd when addressing any woman under 40. Something to do with the emphasis he put on names. And he always stepped just that bit too close, enough to invade your personal space. This time, it wasn't just silage, more like the sour smell of unwashed flesh under layers of grimy winter clothes.

'Great, Fonsie,' I shifted back slightly. 'In a bit of a rush, but sure, what's new?'

'That's the problem with you young ladies. Always rushing round.' He drew his lips back in a smile that showed pointy teeth, like those of a fox terrier. I agreed that yes, the world had become a busier place, and that we should all take a leaf out of his book.

'And did ye hear about the goings on in Ardmore?' His bloodshot eyes were dancing.

'What was that, Fonsie?' I shifted from one foot to the other, trying to contain my impatience. Bad enough that I was going to be late for school but having to listen to this little ferret's blether while I waited was stretching my tolerance just a bit.

'Didn't Delaney's wife up sticks and go off to live with her fancy man! What do ye think a that, hah?'

This, of course, was manna from heaven for the local gossips. Mossie Delaney had turned a blind eye for years now to the vagaries of his erring wife, 25 years his junior. A development like this would expose the poor man to unbridled ridicule.

'Is that so, Fonsie? Well sure maybe he's better off without her.'

'You mark my words, he's a ruined man.' Fonsie chuckled with delight. 'Not able to hold on to the woman who promised to love, honour and *obey* him! What's the world coming to at all at all?'

By now, I was dancing with impatience. If there was one thing that really exasperated me about Carrigmore, it was this sense of glee which greeted another's misfortune. It was probably the downside to what people considered the 'close-knit community' so warmly spoken of by the likes of estate agents and social workers. Everyone saw it as their right to be involved in everyone else's business. And as so little of any consequence happened in the village, anything that might be construed as a story was a major event and could generate excitement for weeks. God knows, I'd had my own share of being on the receiving end of it! Mercifully, Fonsie's tirade was cut short by the curtains parting and Miss Maloney shuffling back out, complete with ham sandwich wrapped in cling film. I handed over a five euro note, grabbed the newspaper, wished them both a good day, and fled.

I'd somehow got through morning classes without any further setbacks and was in our tiny staff room, making coffee to have with my now limp ham sandwich. The door swung open. Marie navigated her considerable bulk through the narrow space.

'Heard the news yet, Beth?'

Her breathing was even more ragged than usual, eyes gleaming with the importance of what she had to convey. The exuberance of the 70 children shrieking in the playground outside could hardly compete with hers.

'Go on.' I resigned myself to the deluge of information coming my way.

'It's a man!'

'No way!' I answered sarcastically though my curiosity was piqued.

Marie eased herself carefully into the sagging armchair that filled a corner of the room. Undaunted, she plunged on.

'Name of Andrew McKay. A Scotsman, no less. Can you just picture a fella in a kilt around here?'

Now she had my undivided attention. With her maternity leave starting in January, curiosity had been running high about her replacement. But of course we'd all assumed it would be a woman. Carrigmore National School had never, in its 85 year history, employed a male teacher. And a Scotsman to boot! What on earth was bringing a Scotsman to Carrigmore? While the place had its rustic charms, it could hardly be described as a hub of excitement. A sleepy village situated in the vast brown expanse of bogland in the north midlands, it attracted no more than the occasional tourist in search of heritage sites, or maybe a spot of fishing. Hardly the place for a Scottish teacher in search of adventure.

'He's probably a balding, middle-aged widower with a paunch and bad breath. A guy on the verge of retirement, looking for some peace and quiet.'

'Well, apparently, he has Lanesborough connections. Jennifer said his mother came from there.'

'Oh, yeah?'

'Yeah. Sure there had to be something behind it. His ending up here, I mean.'

'Hmm, suppose so. Pretty unusual isn't it?'

Marie shifted to accommodate more comfortably the vast expanse of her belly and patted it knowingly.

'Mark my words, this will shake things up around here.' Her eyes crinkled in amusement. 'Don't forget I'll be expecting regular news bulletins.'

I cringed. Here we were off on the treadmill again. It was one thing that my mother constantly nagged me about my single status, but now Marie was at it too. The way people round here were going on, you'd think being unmarried signified a social blight, that every single woman was a lonely spinster eking out a loveless existence. I still had plenty of time. One thing I didn't need was the whole 'close-knit community', God bless them, matchmaking on my behalf. I attacked my ham sandwich with a vengeance.

'WELL HELLO, BETH, so pleased to meet you. The name's McKay, Andrew McKay.'

A vision in heavily-starched jeans and an open-necked shirt towers above me, the soft Scottish burr caressing the words. He stretches out an immense hand. Long tapering fingers, nails immaculately manicured. As I extend mine, he swiftly raises it to his lips. A tingling sensation, the brush of velvet. The air fills with the scent of Blue Stratos, conjuring up images of bronzed, rippling muscles on surfboards. His piercing silver-blue eyes bore into mine. The roof of Carrigmore National School slides back as sun-drenched highways roll out in a shimmering vista before me, open-top Ferrari at the ready. My stomach flips over and the strains of *For Your Eyes Only* start pounding through my head.

'Miss, Miss!'

15 upraised arms waved frantically as 15 pairs of eyes sought to attract my attention, their owners clearly wondering if I had finally lost it. In the middle of rehearsing their Nativity scene, I had vanished into dreamland, leaving them to their own devices.

'Miss, wasn't the innkeeper supposed to come in there?'

The indignant tones left me in no doubt as to how

seriously these eight-year-olds took their Christmas production. No method actor could have outdone them in getting into their parts. I really would have to concentrate. Things must be worse than I thought if the prospect of a male substitute teacher was enough to send me hurtling into fantasy land. With all the energy I could muster, I rejoined my young charges in their stable at Bethlehem and brought the recalcitrant innkeeper back into the picture. Joseph and Mary knocked once again on the door and this time were told emphatically there was no room at the inn. Back on track, the story proceeded in its familiar groove. Outside, the December afternoon closed in under slate-grey skies.

'THANKS, BETH. JUST leave it there, will you?'

In her little curtained-off alcove, surrounded by a forest of paperwork, Jennifer Muldowney, school principal, was working her way through end-of-term reports when I dropped in with the daily register. Her work environment seemed to mirror the narrow contours of her life. She had never married, and lived in one of the old workers' cottages that bordered the Tullyruane estate, in the company of at least a dozen cats. She had taught in Carrigmore National School for close on 40 years, watching successive generations grow up, move on, and establish themselves. I still had a vivid memory of my first introduction to the alien world of the classroom and her kindness to me, almost 30 years ago, when I'd been left at the door by my mother, shivering with nerves. She'd taken me by the hand, given me a lollipop, and in no time had me convinced that school was all about having fun. In her younger days, her love of travelling had taken her abroad each summer, North Africa, Mexico, Canada, but these days, her world was beginning to shrink. Now approaching 60, her main concerns were her failing health and the welfare of her cats.

Since the lunchtime revelations, my curiosity had been gathering pace. Surely Jennifer could supply a few more details. I decided to see what else I could find out.

'I believe you've found a sub for Marie.'

The shrewd grey eyes narrowed in amusement. She signed another report and added it to the pile on her left.

'Doesn't word travel fast around here? Yes, A man from Edinburgh. Looking for a change, apparently. Comes highly recommended.'

Not exactly the kind of information I was looking for. I tried again.

'It'll certainly make a change to have someone like that around here. Probably shake things up a bit. Broaden our perspectives and all that, eh?'

Another flicker of mirth lit the grey-flecked eyes before they returned to the pile of reports, dismissing me with an apologetic smile.

'Yes, I suppose so. Well, I'd better be getting on with these.'

I drew the curtain back across the little recess and went to collect my things. It looked like I'd just have to wait. All of a sudden, January 7 seemed like a long time away.

'Is that you, Elizabeth, dear?'

Who the hell did she think it was? Jack the Ripper?

'Yes, Mam. It's me.'

'Come and see this, dear.'

Her voice quivered with excitement. The clicking of nails on the pine floorboards signalled that Amber was on her way to greet me. Our Labrador, at least, could always be relied on to welcome me home. She sauntered lazily out from the warmth of the kitchen, her tail swinging in a circular rhythm and presented herself for her customary pat. She was now 12 years old and her frantic greetings of the past had slowed down to this a more sedate ritual.

I dumped my bag and pushed open the living room door. There was Mother at the bureau, poring over a letter, the horn-rimmed spectacles she used for reading perched on the end of her nose.

'Look, dear. It's from Fr Brian. He'll be home with us for a whole week, please God. Isn't it great?'

My younger brother Brian was the golden child of the family. The one who had fulfilled his mother's dearest wish the day he was ordained five years ago. Having worked on the missions in Zambia since then, he was due back home for a couple of weeks leave, or whatever they call it, but until now, we weren't sure if he'd manage more than a day or two with us. Of course, news of his imminent arrival was enough to set Mother's world dancing. As for me, while I would be delighted to see him again, I didn't quite view his visit as the monumental event of the decade.

'When's he coming?'

'December 26. A whole week. Just think. He'll have time to do the rounds. Catch up on things here. I must tell Fr Flannery he's coming. He might want to...'

She was off, seeing herself in a radiant light — the mother of Fr Brian, a Man of the Cloth. For one shining week, she would parade him around, basking in the reflected glory, heart pulsating with family pride. No doubt she'd want him to accompany her to daily Mass, even cajole Fr Flannery to allow him to concelebrate it. I could see the plans taking shape inside her head.

'I wonder would we ever get time to paint his room. You'd give a hand, wouldn't you, dear?'

Here we go, I thought. The last time he came home, it was just the same. As if we were expecting the Pope. After all, *Fr* Brian was entitled to some respect, wasn't he? The funny thing was the poor guy was always mortified by her insistence on what she considered his due, especially when she made a big deal of it in public.

'Oh, I suppose. Next week some time. Didn't Rosemary say she and David were coming down? There's her perfect opportunity to get in some practice with home décor.'

I couldn't resist the dig. My sister Rosemary had spent the duration of her last visit home wittering on about their new semi-detached house in the ever-expanding and anonymous world of Dublin 4. We had been treated in minute detail to the colour schemes and coordinating features of each room, the scatter cushions that matched the swagged velvet curtains, not to mention the chiming doorbell with it's *Frère Jacques* motif. She'd be only delighted to give us the benefit of her expertise!

'We'll see if they have time, dear. Remember they're on their Christmas holidays.'

And what about me, I wailed inwardly. But of course, now that Rosemary was married, she was above being roped into such menial chores as painting rooms. My 24-year-old kid sis had achieved what I was missing.

'And do get that dog out of here. We'll have hairs all over the carpet.'

A look of displeasure tightened across her face, making it look even more pinched than usual. Amber had followed me in from the kitchen, and was settling herself comfortably on the fireside rug, forbidden territory as far as Mother was concerned. It gave me the perfect excuse. With her on her favourite hobbyhorse, I needed to get out for a while, anywhere I didn't have to listen to her singing the praises of the son and daughter who had got it so right.

'Well, I'd better take her out while there's still some daylight. See you later, Mam.'

'Yes, dear. Wrap up well. There's a wind out that'd skin you,' her voice floated after me, already devoid of interest in my doings. Of course, Fr Brian was always going to be the shining star of her world. By contrast, I had failed her in every way. Still single and living at home when the only path to respectability, in her eyes, was the married state. Still not even a sniff of a prospective husband on the horizon when she herself had been married with three children at my age. And still the subject of village gossip over the disaster that had engulfed me all those years ago. Was it any wonder I sometimes felt like damaged goods?

Ten minutes later, I was battling my way through the northerly gale whipping up the canal water, blowing flecks of sleet into my face. Amber panted along behind me, nose to the ground, stopping every so often to sniff out new treasure along the moist, boggy track. The undercurrent of my mother's ecstasy swirled and eddied around in my head, rippling into ever-widening circles.

THAT NIGHT, THE dining room of the Longford Arms Hotel was a sea of balloons, and crepe party hats. Multicoloured streamers swirled in curls from the ceiling and blinking fairy lights glittered on every wall. I followed my fellow writers through the maze of already-seated party-goers pulling crackers and blowing hooters. Our table awaited us, wine glasses filled with crimson serviettes. Neatly arrayed cutlery gleamed in the light of squat red candles. Our Christmas night out was under way. The Golden Nib writers' group had decided to push the boat out this year since we were celebrating both our 10th birthday and the launch of our first anthology. We had reserved a table for the 'Gala Dinner followed by Disco'. We were doing things in style.

'So, Beth. Any wild plans for Christmas?'

This was Laurie, my friend since we were both four years old and went to each others' birthday parties in little pink party frocks with pink socks to match. We'd sat together in school, united immediately in our dislike of a bullying teacher with pursed-up lips and a limp. We'd swotted together for exams, taken our first foray into underage drinking together with cans of Harp, and been there for each other through all the ups and downs of adolescence. When she married Keith Fitzpatrick 13 years ago, I'd been her bridesmaid. And she had been the one who had gotten me through the worst time of my life. Now, with three children under 10 and a husband who had never really taken to joint parenting, her Christmas was going to be pretty lively.

'You know how it is, playing happy families, as usual. Oh yeah, and painting my brother's room, if Mother has her way. He's coming back for a week and she's wired.'

'Brian's coming home? That's great, Beth. It'll be really good to see him again.' Laurie had always got on with Brian, in fact I think had even been sweet on him once, back when we were teenagers.

'Yeah,' I grimaced. 'If Mother doesn't hijack him. I can just see her parading him around the village like a film star.'

Laurie smiled. 'I suppose you have to make allowances for her being proud of him and all that. It *is* his first time home since the ordination. Anyway, I'm sure you'll be able to drag him off for a pint.'

'I'll sure as hell do my best.' Just the thought of being stuck at home over the festive season was enough to send me into solitary confinement. I stabbed the air with the little fork for spearing melon balls. 'You've no idea, Laurie. Each Christmas is just a replica of the last one, the same arguments over dinner, the same presents, the same boring jokes. Dad getting sozzled and Mother spitting fury. Some day, I swear I'm going to put it all into a book. *The Real Irish Family Christmas*. Think it'll be a bestseller?'

'Course it will, honey!' She beamed. 'Look at *Angela's Ashes* and all that miserable Irish childhood stuff. You could do the miserable Irish adult still living with parents scenario. Wouldn't the publishers snap it up?'

She made crocodile snapping gestures with a finger and thumb to illustrate her point, sending me into fits of laughter. By now, the wine had arrived and we were all swilling it merrily around our balloon-shaped goblets in a mock attempt to look like connoisseurs. A toast was proposed to our amazing writing skills and crystal clashed in mid-air as we chanted the words happily with total conviction.

'To our anthology!' we all yelled, buoyed up already with wine-fuelled enthusiasm.

SEVERAL HOURS LATER, in the back of the taxi bringing me home, my mood suddenly dipped. The elation of a great night out with my friends evaporated in a moment, leaving me in a greyer, colder place. Most of the others had husbands/partners/boyfriends collecting them from their revelries, while I was once again on my own. But it hadn't always been like this. Memories of past Christmas parties tugged at me painfully. The old regrets filled my head, pounding like a dozen sledge hammers, pulling me back down the path of 'if onlys'. If only I'd trusted my gut feeling. If only I'd had the courage to stand up to them all. If only we'd talked it through properly. But now, it was too late.

CHAPTER TWO

'Of course, you know we're doing quite a bit of entertaining these days. It's expected of us, now that David's been promoted.'

My sister's voice was high and metallic, and just as soothing as the clamour of a pneumatic drill. It was Christmas Eve, and we'd all converged on the local. Rosemary was holding forth on her husband's meteoric career path. David worked for an insurance company in Dublin and had just moved another rung up the ladder. This promotion was the icing on her cake. Of course, Rosemary would fit in to a tee with the whole social scene it would involve. If it wasn't corporate entertaining, it would be coffee mornings, or bridge nights, or maybe the golf club. She'd have gone down well in the colonies. I could just see her lording it over the natives, like the obnoxious British wives in *A Passage to India*.

'Good, good.' I was making an effort to nod in the right places while my mind roved around more engaging pastures. The as yet unknown Andrew McKay was continuing to preoccupy me, a flickering light that now and again flared up like a match being struck. In spite of my gut feeling that he had to be balding and middle-aged, I couldn't help hoping for something better. God knows we could do with a new face around here, I mused, looking at the line-up of crusty bachelors seated along the counter. There was old Matty Doran, wisps of grey hair drawn over the egg-shaped dome of his head. Nodding sagely in agreement with whatever platitudes emanated from the cracked lips of Jemsy Malone. Both were septuagenarians, each locked into his own isolated existence, farming his pitifully small holding with a tenacity born of land hunger. Seven nights a week, they were to be seen on the same stools at the bar, no doubt exchanging the same opinions on the same topics. On the corner stool, where he could keep an eye on who came in with whom, sat Fonsie Kelly, bloodshot eyes performing an automatic scan of the premises every few minutes. And then there was the village drunk. A podgy little man with a sagging beer belly and a passion for céilí music. Jeremy McCann knew his jigs from his reels all right. The only trouble was, the more Jameson he drank, the more enthusiastic he became to demonstrate his talents to a less-than-willing audience. The entertainment was complete when he ended up on his back on the floor. And that was what my local pub boasted in the way of eligible men.

An icy blast of night air rushed in as the door swung open and Marie pushed her way through, followed by her husband, Sean. I have to say she looked great, dressed in a flowing burgundy dress that flared out over her bump, with an off-white hooded chunky cardigan. She raised her eyebrows, enquiringly if we were okay for drinks. I tipped back the last of my Heineken, and went to join her at the bar.

'Thank Christ you've arrived!' Relief poured from my tone. 'I've had Rosemary wearing my ears out for the last hour. Going on and on about how *wonderful* married life is! She now feels *totally* fulfilled. She would *definitely* recommend it.

'Poor Beth,' Marie grinned. 'What you need is more drink, and plenty of it. She won't seem so bad after another few pints. Here, get that down you.'

By now, the pub was starting to hum with the babble of various conversations, the volume rising in tandem with the amount of alcohol being consumed. Holly grew from every wall, strings of coloured lights flickered and artificial pine trees glittered. Even the bar staff wore Santa hats. A load of commercial claptrap really, but you couldn't deny the festive atmosphere it created. My spirits were definitely on the rise as we threaded our way back to the alcove where Rosemary was chatting to a captive David about the guest list for their New Year's Eve party.

'Marie, Sean, good to see you again!' she purred, standing to deliver the socially requisite peck on both cheeks. 'I see congratulations are in order.'

Marie's hands cradled her belly, and her smile broadened.

'Yeah, another six weeks or so. We still can't believe it's happening, after so many years of trying. You never know what's around the corner, do you?'

'Perhaps you can let us in on your secret.' Rosemary smiled surreptitiously at David. 'We're trying too, aren't we, sweetheart? We don't really go for all this 'career first' business. I intend to enjoy motherhood while I'm still young.'

Oh great, I thought. Rosemary Maguire Richardson is socially acceptable, married and on the brink of motherhood — unlike her older sister who's been left on the shelf and who's going to end up a sour, twisted old hag. Waves of self pity lapped around me, buoying me back to another place, another time. Ten years back. To the first night I met him.

It was the birthday party of an old school friend in Ballymartin. I'd been cornered by some computer nerd with jam-jar glasses who was boring me to death. Then, while he was extolling the virtues of the latest software from some photo explorer package, over his shoulder I noticed someone else moving into my field of vision. Close-cropped sandy hair, Clarke Gable style moustache. Slight gap between his front teeth. Looking directly at me. I half-smiled and he moved closer. And closer. Until Computer Nerd looked around.

'Ah, Sam. Do join us. This is, eh, sorry, what was it again?'

Jerk. He'd been so busy prattling on about his bloody computers he'd forgotten my name.

'Beth.'

'Ah, yes, Beth. This is Beth. Sam.'

'How do you do, Beth?'

The clipped tones immediately betrayed his class. Definitely not from peasant stock. Had to be one of the gentry. But there was something in his eyes that sent an ache of longing through my guts.

'How do you do, Sam? Nice to meet you.'

Oh, Lord! Could I come up with nothing better than worn out platitudes when I'd just met the man who'd turned my insides to liquid fire? At that point, the gods did their stuff and Computer Nerd spotted another guy he simply had to catch up with. Leaving Sam and I alone together.

'Would you like to dance, Beth?'

He held his hand towards me as if we were at an 18th Century ball. And smiled. And that did it. I'd never really believed in all that 'love at first sight' crap, but this hit me like a gust of warm air. *Hey Jude* was playing, and by the end of it, the party going on around us had faded into the background. All I was aware of was the wonder of feeling his arms moving down my back, and the earthy smell of tweed jacket mixed with something like linseed oil. And the look in his eyes when…

'*Beth*, what planet are you on?'

'Sorry, Marie. You were saying?' Yanked back to the present, my mind went spinning into confusion.

'Just that Carrigmore is waiting with bated breath for its latest recruit to the teaching ranks. Nothing to get worked up about.'

I grinned maliciously. 'This is the bald guy with the paunch we're talking about, right?'

'They're bringing in a guy?' Rosemary's awed tone spoke volumes. 'Into the *school*?'

'You see,' smirked Marie, winking at me. 'Bald or not, he's going to raise a few eyebrows.'

From the far corner, the first sing-song of the evening got under way as discordant voices swayed unevenly into the raucous chorus of *Feed the World.* Christmas had arrived in Carrigmore.

'Of course he'll be delighted to come and see you. You know how he likes to keep up with all the goings on around here.'

My parents' house. 1.00pm. Christmas Day. The lounge full of smoke and whiskey-swilling neighbours, all at pains to spread good will in every direction. Rosemary was perched prettily on David's knee, one arm around his neck, crowing about the delights of matrimony and how it made her feel like a complete woman, and so on. Just for good measure, my mother was in 7th heaven about the imminent return of Fr Brian. Wherever she could find an audience, she was making arrangements for him to come and visit. She had just collared Yvonne Glennon, one of her bridge associates.

'Yes, yes, we'd love to have him over. Any time he can fit us in.'

Yvonne's voice sang with amusement. With a tilt of her elegant throat, she knocked back her gin and tonic and flashed a sideways grin at her barrister husband. It was one of those 'come and rescue me' sort of looks. My bloody mother never knew when to stop. Over the years, she had regaled anyone who would listen with the full account of Brian's devotion to his altarboy duties, his progress through the seminary, and his subsequent appointment to the missionary post in Zambia. 'Of course, he was always heading in that direction, you could see it even when he was in school, wasn't he the most devout boy in his class?' No wonder poor Yvonne wanted to be rescued.

'Care for some prawn toast there Frank?' I decided to do a little circulating with the finger food Rosemary had insisted on. All the rage, apparently, in Dublin 4.

'Well, I shouldn't, but it is Christmas after all.' The portly GP with the hook nose crunched into the calorie-laden snacks.

'How is life with you, Beth? Any excitement?'

His beady little eyes, like glowing embers, burned into me for gossip. Since the death of his wife several years ago, his chief solace seemed to be in meddling in other people's lives. He was always on the look-out for titbits of scandal to embellish and pass on, his golden nuggets to be treasured and stored.

'Afraid not, Frank. What would I get up to?'

'No word from that Sam fellow, then?'

The blood rushed into my face. Trust him to dredge that up from the past. The old rat must have a better memory than I'd given him credit for.

'No, no,' I replied smiling insincerely. 'Still in the States, I believe. Anyway, must keep going with these.'

Was there no getting away from my muddied past being constantly dragged up, pulling me back into unwanted memories. Surely after all this time, I was entitled to forget him. I *had* forgotten him. If only people wouldn't keep bloody reminding me.

The next to arrive was Miss Maloney. Her greying hair that was normally pinned up in a tight bun now hung in limp strands around her shoulders, and her cracked lips were streaked with crimson. This must be the one day in the year she abandoned her tweed skirts and shapeless jumpers for 'the good dress'. The same emerald green party frock that had hung in her wardrobe for the last 35 years peeped out from under her grey woollen coat. Her thin face was stretched into a smile to greet her hosts.

'Mrs Maguire, a very happy Christmas to ye. Isn't it grand to have everyone together like this? Y'are great to keep up the tradition.'

Armed with a bottle of cheap sherry, she extended a delicate hand to my mother.

'You're very welcome, Miss Maloney.' Mother took the proffered hand between her thumb and forefinger. 'If we can't have a few neighbours around at this time of year, when can we? You'll take a little something?'

'A brandy and port'd be lovely, Mrs Maguire. The old tummy's been a bit out of sorts lately, and that's just the thing that'll put it right.'

'Beth, a brandy and port for Miss Maloney.' Mother had just spotted me circulating with the prawn toast and saw her opportunity for a quick getaway. As hostess, she had more important duties to attend to than listening to the symptoms of a hypochondriac.

'Merry Christmas, Miss Maloney.' I breezed over with the drink while casting around for someone I could pair her off with. Frank Moran would just about fit the bill. Not only would he pronounce a qualified opinion on her ill health but the two were perfectly matched in their insatiable hunger for village gossip.

'Marvellous woman, your mother, Beth. It's not everyone would think of a lonely old soul on her own for Christmas Day,' she sniffed. Now we were heading off down the poor 'lonely creature' road. I needed to locate Frank fast.

'You know, Miss Maloney, I think Dr Moran was enquiring about you a few minutes ago. Most solicitous, he was.'

'Dr Moran, dear, oh dear. And how is the poor man? Dreadful business, his poor wife being taken like that.'

Miss Maloney never failed to refer to Frank as anything other than the grieving widower. Was it some kind of Freudian thing that she was just waiting for him to get over the loss of his wife to notice her waiting in the wings? Whatever the motivation was, it was going to serve my purpose right now in offloading her. I steered her in the direction of the living room.

'Beth! Phone.'

My Dad's intervention was never more welcome. I flashed him a grateful smile and made my escape to the receiver in the hall. Laurie's voice on the other end was like a symphony to my ears.

'So, how are things going? What's the craic?'

'Well, the lap dancers have just arrived, and the men are about to do the full Monty. Oh, and Leonardo di Caprio said he'd drop in later. Apart from that, it's business as usual. How about you?'

'Ah, you know. Just the usual chaos.' She sounded exhausted. 'Eoin's hammering the hell out of his new drum kit. The other two are laying into one another over whose turn it is on the Playstation. It's doing my head in! As if that's not enough, Keith's in one of his moods. And his parents are on their way over for dinner. That'll just make my Christmas!'

My heart went out to her. Her parents-in-law had always regarded her as some low-life hussy who trapped their only son into marriage. She had long ago given up trying to please them. But Christmas was Christmas, and Keith insisted on having them over. And once Keith laid down the law, that was it. For the sake of a quiet life, she would do her best to paper over the cracks that, once opened, could plunge them all into a minefield of barbed comments and counter-reactions.

'Sounds like you're the one who needs rescuing. Fancy a stroll later? We can walk off the dinner.'

'I'll hardly get out of here before dark, but thanks anyway. Talk to you soon.'

There was something about her tone that was off. We'd have to get together in the next couple of days for that long overdue chat.

CHRISTMAS DINNER EVENTUALLY got underway around 3.00pm with all the usual fuss and ceremony. By this time, Dad was swaying on his feet, eyes slightly glazed, and Mother was sending filthy looks in his direction, muttering about not having her efforts appreciated. Nothing much changed in our house. For as long as I could remember, the stress of playing happy families for Christmas had driven Dad to seek release by getting sozzled. His way of coping, I suppose. Most of the time, their relationship pottered along well-worn tracks with Mother steering him in what she considered the right direction. There would be an occasional blip when he stood up to her and a major row would erupt, and then the inevitable war of attrition before the status quo would resume. And although he'd scaled down his work in the estate agency to a few hours a day, even that was enough to provide a release valve when he needed it. But over the Christmas break, when he was more or less grounded, all of the underlying tensions gathered momentum and it took very little to shatter the smokescreen of respectability presented to the outside world. I often wondered what had brought them together in the first place. Whatever they must have once felt for one another was now only a memory and had long ago given way to a resigned acceptance of the indifference that now characterised their relationship. Their marriage was probably a replica of a thousand others of their generation, the type that trapped its victims, wrapping them up them in a kind of emotional inertia. Maybe there was something to be said for staying single.

ST STEPHEN'S DAY dawned grey and misty. The blustery winds and sleet showers of the past few days had given way to low granite skies and persistent drizzle; the kind of weather that would suggest cuddling up in front of a blazing fire with a hot port. But with Brian due in a couple of hours, Mother was like a tornado, swooping on every speck of dust she could find. I thought the best option would be to retire to my room and do a general tidy-up. At least there, I'd have sanctuary from her ravings for a while. I set about trying to impose some kind of order on my bookshelves, a task I always enjoyed as it conferred unlimited freedom to immerse myself in the pages of my favourite books. I was assembling all the contemporary Irish fiction together when the old leather-bound diary I used to keep caught my attention. It dated back to when I'd first joined the writers group, and we were all encouraged to 'write something every day'. Jotting down my thoughts in diary form seemed to be the easiest way to keep this up. 1999. The year I joined the writers group, yes, but also the year I met him. I couldn't stop myself from leafing through the pages.

Sunday, April 11

Can't believe I'm writing this, but last night, IT finally happened. In the words of some poet, like 'a hail of diamonds showering into my life'. One minute, I'm bored out of my tree stuck with some computer geek who won't stop talking at me, and the next, HE appears, and there's manic excitement racing through me and my stomach is churning, like there's a rush of air swirling round inside me.

Just can't stop thinking about him. Replaying it over and over in my head. The touch of his fingers moving across my back. The slowness of Hey Jude drawing us closer and closer. His eyes chocolate brown with golden flecks. Oh Christ, I'm beginning to sound like a love-crazed teenager talking in clichés. But it's WONDERFUL! Can't wait for next weekend. My first riding lesson. Imagine, me up on a horse with HIM showing me what to do. Roll on Saturday!

Saturday, April 17

I'd never have believed the smell of horses could be so erotic. And the velvety texture of their coat and way they nuzzle you, looking for treats. Mine was called Bessie. A very broad dapple grey mare they used to keep for hunting, but now in semi-retirement. Gentle as a summer breeze. Sam showed me how to ease the bit into her mouth and slide the headpiece over her ears. And she just stood there, patient as a saint while I hauled myself up onto her back. We started off on a lunge line with Sam in the centre keeping her in a placid walk while I got the feel of her stride. Then he showed me how to keep her going forward with even pressure from my legs, and to close my fingers on the reins to bring her to a halt. Half an hour later, I was off the lunge and pottering round on my own. The feeling of all that power rolling around beneath me, moving whatever way I asked was just amazing. We even tried a very sedate trot. A bit bumpy but I managed to hang on to the mane and keep in some kind of balance with her. Yeah, I'm definitely hooked. And to crown it all, he's asked me out for dinner tomorrow evening. Only 24 hours before I see him again! Can't wait!

Monday, April 19

Just when I thought things couldn't get any better, for three hours last night, the dining room of a Mullingar hotel was transformed into paradise. Sitting across the table from a man I just couldn't get enough of. We relived the riding lesson and I was praised all over again for my 'natural empathy with horses'. I'm floating along in a bubble of euphoria. Until I got home and Mother laid into me. As soon as she twigged that my date was none other than Samuel Butler from 'The Big House', all hell broke loose. Apparently, I was disgracing the family by associating with 'one of that sort'. And I might as well give it up now. There was no future in it. He was different from us. From a 'different breed'. The breed of landlords that had almost 'destroyed our country'. How could I even think of betraying our cultural heritage by consorting with his kind! And so on... But I was still counting down the days until our next meeting. Next Saturday. My next riding lesson.

Saturday, April 24

Another trip to paradise AKA the Butler estate. This time Sam focused more on what he called 'my seat'. He tried to get me to feel the movement of the mare beneath me and go with her. And he was more exacting about my position. Getting the weight down into my heel, and sitting straighter. By the time we'd finished I was stiff and sore all over, but still somewhere up on cloud nine. And then, back in the stable, while I was untacking Bessie, an austere looking woman in a pencil skirt and knee-high leather boots appeared in the yard. Sam had vanished in the direction of the barn

> *to get some more hay bales so I thought I'd better introduce myself. The cheery 'Hello' froze in my throat when she gave me an icy look and turned away. Clearly Mrs Butler was no more kindly disposed towards me than my mother was towards Sam. Not a great start to the fairytale I'd been living in for the last couple of weeks. The bubble of euphoria I was floating in began to sag ever so slightly.*

I'd been so happy back then, even though I'd had the odd sliver of doubt. I'd been buoyed up by an implicit, overpowering belief that Sam and I were meant to be together. That no force on earth was strong enough to prise us apart. Not his mother and her haughty airs and graces. Not my mother and her narrow-minded bigotry. Oblivious to it all, Sam and I carried on. Even when our engagement threw the whole village into flurries of consternation, we shut our ears to the uproar, blindly ignoring the signals that were like flaming beacons, plain for all to see. Until they couldn't be ignored any longer.

My musings were brought to an abrupt halt when the crunch of tyres on the gravel driveway plunged the Maguire household into a whirlwind of excitement. I got to the window in time to see the blue Ford Escort Brian had borrowed from the order pulling up at the front door.

'Elizabeth! He's here!'

My mother's voice resembled the screech of an abused violin. I replaced the diary on its shelf and made my way downstairs to greet the homecoming hero. The scene before me was nothing short of comical. Poor Brian was being waltzed around the hallway by our enraptured mother. Dad was following close on their heels, trying to find a free hand to shake, pretty much overwhelmed at having his only son back in the bosom of his family. Rosemary was oohing and aahing over the blessings of having an ordained priest under our roof. As I caught his eye, it closed in an exaggerated wink of complicity. He was still our Brian, still able to see the ridiculous in all this obsequiousness. Being close in age, we had shared many secrets throughout our childhood years. And right now, we were both amused observers of this farcical show of reverence.

He was propelled into the front room where the fire was blazing and the Welcome Home Cake was waiting. Rosemary was dispatched to the kitchen to make the tea. Mother sat herself down on the couch and patted the vacant space beside her for him to occupy. It was now time for her to launch into the matter closest to her heart.

'And of course everyone's been asking if you'll do a House Mass — just for friends and neighbours. Wouldn't it be nice, dear?'

Of course it had been Mother's idea but it hadn't taken her long to convince herself that it was the wish of the entire community. Soaring on the crest of her own exuberance, she didn't see the flicker of anxiety in his eyes before Brian resumed his more familiar, jocular expression.

'I can see this is going to be some holiday! Does a fella not get to take a break over Christmas?'

'But this is the chance for you to see everyone again — and for them to see you!'

Of course, what she really meant was for them to marvel at the son the Maguire family had produced. The woman was so transparent. If you looked closely, you could almost see the ideas forming in her head.

What she didn't see was Brian's backward glance in my direction, whispering of storms gathering on the horizon.

CHAPTER THREE

THREE DAYS LATER and the Maguire household gleamed from top to bottom. Every surface had been polished to within an inch of its life. Mother had supervised the operation, and needless to say, Rosemary and I had been conscripted into service. Dad had been given the most severe warnings to be on his best behaviour. The local florist had been prevailed upon to rise to the occasion, and the sweetness of freshly cut hyacinths and honeysuckle filled the air. The front room had become our chapel, complete with improvised altar. The time was fixed for 7.30 that evening, and invitations had gone out to everyone in the parish.

Since Brian hadn't had the foresight to bring all his paraphernalia with him, Mother had gone to Fr Flannery to borrow the robes, chalice and wafers he would need to celebrate Mass. His protests that these were not strictly necessary went unheard. She was in full flight. This would be a House Mass to be remembered! No effort was to be spared. The green chasuble of the Nativity with its gold embroidery hung in readiness along with the alb, while the chalice rested on the white tablecloth covering the altar. The whole apple cart had come close to being up-ended when the two neighbours Mother had invited to do the readings had been asked to stand down in favour of the aging Sr Philomena and her cousin who happened to be visiting. (Apparently, she'd been one of my mother's teachers back in Belfast a million years ago.) However, the scene was now set in readiness and the very household seemed to be holding its breath in anticipation.

'RIGHT! I THINK that's it. At this rate, we'll have enough to feed the whole county.'

Brian and I were loading up my Fiesta with the 'one or two last-minute things' Mother had asked us to get in Ballymartin in case we ran out. Things like more cocktail sausages, more vol-au-vents to be filled with egg mayonnaise and salmon, more chicken and ham for sandwiches, and a couple of bottles of Jameson 'for the men folk' (specially requested by Dad). At this rate, our fridge would be crammed with leftovers for the next month!

'Oh, you know Mother. Never one to let the side down. Especially when she's showing off her darling son,' I grinned.

Brian flinched, as if I'd punched him in the stomach. When he spoke, his voice had tightened, each word coming slowly, like he was thinking aloud.

'Beth, how do you think she'd take it if...'

He trailed off, leaving the sentence unfinished.

'If what, Brian?' I hated that. When someone leaves you guessing about what they're leading up to. 'Come on. I'm not a mind reader.' His gaze remained troubled, staring into space. He seemed to be searching for the right words. Now I was getting anxious. 'What on earth are you planning to spring on her?'

His expression suddenly cleared. 'Ah sure, it mightn't come to anything. Probably just a phase I'm going through. Nothing to worry about.'

I knew Brian well enough to pick up the warning signs. Something was wrong. But he obviously wasn't ready to talk about it. I didn't want to nag him, so I let it go, and sat into the car, gazing at him curiously, as he chewed his bottom lip, staring into space.

'ROSEMARY, CAN YOU take over with these vol-au-vents while I help Fr Brian with his preparations?'

It was 'get the last-minute stuff ready' time, and our kitchen was a maelstrom of activity. Plates were piled high with assorted sandwiches sprinkled with chopped parsley and Pringles, (Rosemary's idea) and Victoria sponges waited on the table for their jam and cream filling. The aroma of the brown soda bread still in the oven competed with that of the roasting honey-glazed chicken wings. Dad had been given the job of greeting any early arrivals and was stationed in the hallway while Mother was flitting around from one task to another like a demented bee, and had just decided that her services would be better employed helping 'Fr Brian' to don his priestly vestments.

'But I was just about to get ready myself.' Rosemary moaned. 'I can't be seen at Mass looking like this.'

She didn't look too bad to me, in her cream cashmere jumper, chocolate-brown velvet trousers and soft brown leather ankle boots. But obviously, that wouldn't be good enough for the sister of the main attraction. I had no choice but to step into the breach.

'It's okay, Rosemary. You go ahead. I'll look after things here.'

I applied myself assiduously to ladling the egg mayonnaise into the vol-au-vents, almost singing with relief at the luxury of having the kitchen to myself. There was a limit to my patience where my mother and sister were concerned, and I had only just managed to keep a lid on all the irritations the day had brought. Now, my conversation with Brian came drifting back, igniting flares of anxiety. 'Just a phase he was going through.' What the hell was going on in his head? I'd often wondered what life was like for him out in Zambia. I could only imagine from his letters that it was a strange world of steaming heat, vibrant colours, pungent smells, and direst poverty. He'd spent the last five years there working closely with the famine relief trust. I wondered if he had any regrets about choosing the missionary order. Would he be happier working in a parish back in Ireland?

A movement at the door caught my attention. It was Dad following his nose in search of a snack. The poor man was all trussed up in his Sunday suit, his stomach straining against the buttons of his shirt. He made straight for the vol-au-vents.

'Mmm, they look good. Maybe I'll just try one for tasting purposes.'

'Hey, Dad! What about the cholesterol?' His last check-up had revealed a level of 7.5 and he'd been warned in the strongest language.

'Ah, come on Beth. You wouldn't begrudge your old Dad a thimbleful. My stomach thinks my throat is cut.'

Looking at his portly figure, I had my doubts on that, but I didn't have the heart to stop him. Brought up in the 40s in the days of rationing and general scarcity, his philosophy now was to make up for lost time and cram as much as possible into his stomach. There was no point in lecturing him, so I decided to change the subject.

'Dad, I don't suppose you've noticed anything odd about Brian. He doesn't quite seem himself to me.'

'If you ask me, it's all this fuss your mother goes on with. The poor chap isn't getting much of a break, is he? Being dragged off to visit everyone in the parish! No wonder he's out of sorts.'

'I just wondered if there was something else. You know, if he's happy out in Africa. He seems kind of preoccupied. As if his mind is elsewhere.

'Can't really say I've noticed.' He brushed off the flakes of vol-au-vent that had crumbled onto the shoulders of his navy blazer. 'But sure maybe we could drag him out for a pint before he goes back. If he wants to talk about it, he'll be more inclined to without your mother there. That woman has his head done in with all her *Fr* this and *Fr* that!

I had to smile. Dad would avail of any excuse for a visit to the tavern.

THE TINKLING OF the little bell Mother had bought specially for the occasion announced the arrival of Brian in all his finery. Approximately 30 friends and neighbours were crammed into our parlour, several of them spilling out into the hall. They stood in a semi circle, three deep, around the room and all crossed themselves as my brother made his appearance. He looked around nervously, clearly ill at ease, and in spite of Mother's exhortations about sanctity and keeping a distance, began by walking around the circle, shaking hands and greeting everyone individually. Then he positioned himself behind the home-made altar and, in an expansive hand movement, welcomed the congregation. The 'House Mass of the Century' was under way.

'My brothers and sisters, to prepare ourselves to celebrate the sacred mystery of the Mass, let us call to mind our sins.'

The older folk cast their eyes down in soul-searching manner, while the younger ones shifted in embarrassment from one foot to the other. Mother ostentatiously lowered herself onto one knee, hands joined like a child making her

First Communion. At Brian's exhortation to praise the Lord, her voice launched into the hymn she had asked Rosemary to lead. When we were prompted to offer one another the sign of peace, she threw her arms around everyone within reach, thanking them all for being there to rejoice with her in her son's homecoming. Her every action was designed to draw as much attention to herself as befitted the mother of the celebrant, while of course ensuring as much embarrassment as possible for the rest of her family. Every moment brought fresh discomfort as I willed my brother to speed things up. But the seconds crawled by as, against the backdrop of our floral wallpaper and china ornaments, the age-old Catholic ritual followed its course.

'A WONDERFUL OCCASION. You must be very proud of him, Mary. What a blessing for all the family.'

Dr Moran, beady little eyes darting around the room, was conveying his congratulations through a mouthful of vol-au-vent. Fragments of creamed salmon laced with his saliva landed on the carpet. I could see the look of disgust on my mother's face wrestling with her reluctance to offend our GP. After all, with a priest in the family, the Maguires were pretty much of the same social standing as the doctor. It wouldn't do to fall out. Might upset her bridge nights!

'Thank you, Frank.' She beamed at him 'Yes, I thought an occasion like this might be nice. Give Fr Brian the chance to catch up with everyone.'

I couldn't miss Frank's amused grin at the use of Brian's title. The little boy whose measles and chicken pox he had treated and whose cut knee he had stitched, had morphed into 'Fr Brian'. What was it with my mother that she always had to keep up this nonsense? I grabbed a plate of cocktail sausages and made for the other side of the room, fingers of red rising from my neck up into my cheeks.

'Beth! What a spread you've put on. This is better than the Hilton.'

Good old Laurie. My embarrassment evaporated with the warmth of her greeting. Here was a place I could take refuge. I gratefully slid onto the vacant stool beside her, balancing the plate of sausages on my knee.

'Oh Christ, am I glad to see you. I've had some day of it. I swear she couldn't make more of a fuss if Brian was proclaimed Pope. Just look at her now.'

Mother had just cornered Paddy O'Connell, the Principal of the secondary school in Ballymartin we had all attended. She was yapping away about Brian's academic merits and how intelligent a boy he always was. At least Paddy was nodding in all the right places. A born diplomat, God bless him.

'Ah, she's just doing the proud mother-hen thing.' Laurie speared a sausage with a cocktail stick and popped it into her mouth. 'Doesn't it brighten up her life to show him off like this? And she's not really bothering anyone.'

'No, but she sure is providing them all with a good laugh. You wouldn't get better in a circus,' I muttered darkly. 'Anyway, where's Keith tonight?'

'Off at a soccer match with the kids. And only too glad of the excuse. He's not what you'd call an avid Mass-goer, if you know what I mean.'

Keith had spent several years in England, and had shaken off the indoctrination of his childhood which threatened eternal damnation for missing Sunday Mass. This had grown into an issue between them as Laurie felt they should be setting an example for their kids. But Keith had even less regard for Laurie's wishes than for the dictates of the

Church, and made no secret of his disdain for what he called "servile craw thumping".

'Can't say I blame him for giving this one a miss.' I nibbled on another sausage. 'It's not exactly his scene, is it?'

'Hallo, Beth!' Annafrid, our German neighbour advanced on us and threw her plump arms around me. 'You haff done a brilliant job with all this food. Enough for half the county, I think.'

'Thanks, Annafrid.' I hugged her warmly. Good old Annafrid. She was one of the few inhabitants of Carrigmore who didn't judge by appearances, had no interest in village gossip, and never had a hidden agenda. She ran a sort of unofficial dog shelter in the rambling farmhouse she and her Swiss husband had bought and restored, and devoted herself to the care of up to twenty stray dogs who found their way to her on their quest for a permanent home. She had never surrendered a dog to the pound, always finding room for the hapless creature until she managed to re-home it.

'We must go walking while you are on the holidays from school, yes? We both together.'

Having come from the industrial Ruhr Valley, there was nothing Annafrid liked more than soaking in the glory of nature trails and the frenetic birdsong to be found in the woodlands behind her home.

'I'd love to, Annafrid. Walk off all the Christmas pudding, huh?'

She beamed, passing her hands over her rolls of belly-flesh. 'Ja, we walk it all off. And then, it creeps back on again, no?'

I couldn't help smiling. Annafrid was too fond of her food and too little concerned about public opinion to let her rotund figure bother her. She reached out and speared a couple of cocktail sausages as if she already had a dispensation thanks to all the walking we were going to do. Just then, her eyes dilated with pleasure as she spotted Rosemary emerging from the kitchen with a tray of glistening honey-glazed chicken wings.

'Maybe I help with bringing more food out, Ja?' Off she pottered, kitchen-bound, clearly intent on helping in the tasting department. Laurie grinned at me.

'Nice to see all your culinary efforts appreciated anyway.'

Across the room, Mother was deep in a one-sided conversation with Sr Philomena. The ancient nun had forgotten to bring her hearing aid and was cocking her head to one side like a sparrow in her attempts to manage without it. Her small bony hands, mottled with liver spots, curled around the top of her walking stick like claws. Just then, Brian reappeared, minus all the traditional garb, and managed to steer his way towards us without being waylaid.

'How do you think that went, Sis?' There was a hint of trepidation in his question that surprised me. I mean he was the star of the show, and all that.

'Come on, Brian! You know it was great, what more could they ask for?'

'Too right! You should be up for the House Mass Celebrant of the Year Award,' Laurie grinned at him. 'Don't know when I've been at a better one!'

'Ah, would ye give over.' Brian's natural good humour returned. 'Don't mind me. I'm just a bit edgy on home ground, you know? Anyway, how're things, Laurie?'

'Not so bad, considering we're just over the mayhem of Christmas. Though I must say I could do with the kind of celebrity status you're enjoying. Long may it last, eh!'

'God forbid.' He flinched visibly, jabbing a cocktail stick into the remaining sausage. 'All I want is some peace and quiet. Some holiday this is turning into.'

By now, Mother had detached herself from Sr Philomena and was bearing down on us, her face arranged into an expression that combined deference to the Cloth and maternal pride.

'There you are, dear.' Since the day of his ordination, she had never called him by name. 'I was wondering where you'd got to. Sr Philomena's been singing your praises. You must come and meet her'

As Mother steered Brian in the direction of the ancient nun, I spotted Dad over by the drinks table, helping himself to the Jameson. Not such a bad idea. I could use one myself at this stage. With Laurie in tow, I manoeuvred my way through the packed room to join him. He tipped a liberal amount of the amber liquid into our glasses, not missing the opportunity to refresh his own. Now that the more formal part of the proceedings were over, the rest of the evening was beginning to take on a softer glow. In spite of my mother's heroic efforts to expose our entire family to the derision of the parish, the welcome burn of the whiskey trickling down my throat was having its desired effect. Another one of these, and I might even begin to see the funny side of her antics. Anyway, wouldn't they have something new to talk about tomorrow? One thing you could be sure of in rural Ireland, there was always some fresh bit of gossip ready to leap hot off the presses of wagging tongues. I supposed the next morsel they'd be feasting on would be the new man in town. As my thoughts drifted once again towards the tornado that was about to hit Carrigmore National School, the knot of curiosity began to once again uncoil. No matter what January 7 had in store for us, it would be a change from the everyday humdrum of village life. I tipped back the rest of my whiskey and held out my glass for a refill, my head swirling with images of swashbuckling Scotsmen in kilts, arms raised in the air, dancing the Highland Fling over a pair of crossed swords. Yes, the evening was definitely beginning to glow.

CHAPTER FOUR

MONDAY, JANUARY 7 finally arrived, a clear, freezing morning with veined ice patterns scrawled across the puddles and an azure sky. The Christmas break had dragged on through two weeks of sodden days and overcast skies, and everybody was worn out trying to keep alive the seasonal goodwill. And then there was the atmosphere. Mother was still treating Brian like a little God and continuing to parade him around the parish. No wonder he was pissed off! In spite of all my efforts to draw him out, he wasn't ready to talk about whatever was on his mind. Any time I thought I was getting somewhere, his face would assume a vacant, impassive expression, like a coat of armour and just as difficult to penetrate.

In spite of my certainty that he'd have a paunch and bald head, thoughts of the Scotsman kept intruding. Now at last, I was facing the moment of discovery. I pulled into the parking area with not quite the usual resignation that characterises the first day back at school. Something more akin to anticipation. Even enthusiasm.

'Morning, Beth.' Jennifer hurried past, a whirl of business, laden down with new copybooks.

'Morning.' I moved forward to share the load with her. 'Have a nice break?'

'Oh, you know,' she half smiled. 'Mainly catching up on things. Nothing spectacular.'

Our attention was drawn to the smooth purring of an engine in the distance. And to its increase in volume. And finally to the splash of colour that invaded the waterlogged landscape as a crimson BMW swung through the concrete pillars and pulled in beside my Fiesta. The door opened to reveal an immense pair of shoulders in a sand-coloured

Italian leather jacket. Our new substitute swung himself out of the low seat and advanced to greet us.

'Good morning, ladies.' The Scottish burr was soft but audible. He was about 40. Well over six feet tall. Thick, wavy hair the colour of wheat. So much for the paunch and bald head.

'Andrew, I presume.' Jennifer stretched out her hand. 'Good to meet you. Jennifer Muldowney.'

Was that a degree of warmth I heard in those normally clipped tones?

'And this is Beth Maguire. She teaches third and fourth, so you'll be next door to her.'

His eyes swivelled in my direction.

'Beth, delighted to make your acquaintance.' The enormous hand enveloped mine.

'Yeah, you too, eh Andrew,' I stuttered.

'Right, Andrew, let's go through and I'll show you around.'

In immaculate control as always, Jennifer led the way into our prefabricated schoolhouse, which seemed even smaller when accommodating a man of Andrew McKay's proportions.

10.53AM, AND MY storytelling session was drawing to a close. There was another seven minutes until break time. Through the glass panels, I had a full view of Mr McKay holding his charges in thrall. Their attention was absolute, as if he had sprayed them with some kind of immobilising gas.

At 11.00am on the dot, the strident clanging of the bell pierced the room, an old-fashioned metal type being rung with gusto by a child in the corridor. My curiosity flared again. 20 minutes in the confines of our pocket-sized staff room with a new male presence. Interesting times ahead.

'So, Beth. How long have you lit up the lives of the kids around here?'

How about that for an opening gambit. I teetered around, searching for the right response.

'I hate to admit it, but I suppose it's 12 years, give or take.'

Now he has me down as a middle-aged spinster stuck in a rut.

'Well, well, well! You must have been a child prodigy. Started teaching when you were ten, eh?'

I smiled back. This guy had pizzazz. So far at least, I hadn't been disappointed.

By the end of the break, I had established that he played rugby, liked Indian food, and was renting a cottage on the canal line. His mother was originally from Lanesborough, so he had Longford connections. He in turn now knew that I was still living at home, liked Abba, and was currently unattached. A real femme fatale, huh! He was bound to be impressed.

That afternoon the steel-grey clouds rolled in again and the wind picked up. I was just back from a more-than-bracing walk with Amber when the phone rang. Laurie. Her voice trembling.

'Beth!'

'What is it?'

'Oh, Beth.' She half-sobbed, half-hiccoughed. 'I'm in such a mess.'

This was serious. I don't think I'd ever heard that wobble in her voice before.

'Laurie, pet, just sit tight and I'll be straight over.'

Ten minutes later, I was sitting in her kitchen listening to her version of the latest row she'd had with Keith. Apparently, he'd invited his business associates over for dinner last night, and in spite of the culinary masterpiece she'd pulled off at short notice, (roast duck with some kind of raspberry coulis) he'd embarrassed her in front of them with tactless comments about married women letting themselves go and paying more attention to their children than their husbands. Then later, he'd had a go at her about her appearance and accused her of not making any effort. For once, she'd retaliated with some barbed retorts that cast aspersions on his performance in bed, at which point he'd stormed out with a parting shot that he didn't get too many complaints in that department.

'He's never happy with what I can give,' she gulped, screwing a damp tissue into a ball. 'He always wants more. Typical Mammy's Boy! Sometimes I wonder what I ever saw in him.'

'Come on, Laurie, he's just letting off steam. He knows damn well there's no-one in the world who would put up with his shenanigans the way you do.' I put my arms around her as her shoulders started to shake with the next wave of sobbing. I knew I'd said the wrong thing. Damn that asshole and his screwing around. The entire county was aware of his 'weakness for the fairer sex' as it was euphemistically referred to. Even Laurie herself must have her suspicions. But right now, that wasn't what she needed to hear.

'Look, honey. This'll all blow over. He's probably regretting what he said right now. I'll bet he arrives in with a huge bouquet, or chocolates, or something,' I trailed off lamely.

'He never has before.' Her voice wobbled again. 'He's never really thought enough of me. That's the problem.'

She was right, of course. Keith had never seen her as an

equal, probably an attitude he'd absorbed from his parents. It went back to the 'there's no woman good enough for my son' fallacy. With that message coming from his mother, and his father worshipping the ground he walked on, was it any wonder Keith had such a high opinion of himself? Poor Laurie was left with the job of massaging his ego and pandering to his needs. Word on the street had it that his latest bit on the side was some young one from his department. Tall and willowy. Surely it could only be a matter of time before Laurie saw him for the gobshite he really was and sent him packing. She'd be left to bring up three kids on her own, but no marriage was worth putting up with the treatment she got from him. And God love her, she didn't deserve it. I didn't want to be the one to encourage her to take that route, but I had stopped believing in any kind of happy-ever-after for herself and Keith. At that moment, I felt worse than useless, like a bystander at the scene of an accident with no knowledge of even simple First Aid. All I could do was be there for her and hope for the best.

'WELL, LADIES.' OUR second day of term, lunchtime in the staffroom, just Andrew, me, and Julie, the special needs resource teacher we shared with three other schools. Newly engaged and flashing a white-gold solitaire, she had managed to display some immunity to his charms. Even so, she threw a dazzling smile in his direction that made the most of her glistening white teeth.

'I was hoping you two could fill me in on the social scene around here. All the wild and wonderful things you folks get up to.'

'Wild and wonderful!' Julie chortled. 'Well now, let's see. There's the two pubs, the bridge club, the GAA, and, oh yes, the village choir, if you feel really adventurous.'

For a second, I caught a flash of contempt in those sea-green eyes. His riposte was immediate.

'Looks like we'll have to shake things up a little, doesn't it? Maybe I could start up Highland Fling classes. Or run gate-crashing tours to Balmoral during the Royal visits. Think that'd go down well?'

'Yeah, why don't we introduce a village lap dancing club while we're at it?' Julie collapsed into laughter.

'Now ye're talking! We could transform Carrigmore into a real hot spot. Dancing at the crossroads, 21st century style with a pole in the middle! How about it, Beth?'

Was I seeing things or was that a glint of invitation in his eyes? It wasn't exactly a wink, nothing that blatant. More of a 'do you want to come out to play' expression, with a quizzical arching of the eyebrows. Like the spurt of a lit match, the beginnings of desire flickered in my stomach. Even though it was now ten years since Sam and I had broken up, there was still a well of misery deep within me that hadn't yet drained away. But maybe now was the time to fully move on.

'Lead on, Macduff!' I offered a mock salute. 'We'll be your faithful retainers in the crusade. Right, Julie?'

'Aye, aye, Captain.' Julie sashayed across the room with an exaggerated rotation of her hips. 'Beth and I can be your first lap dancers.'

Throughout the afternoon, notions of Andrew McKay kept zigzagging through my head. Was he showing signs of interest? I tried to tell myself not to be ridiculous, but a tiny voice kept whispering what I wanted to hear. After all this time, was I going to get a second chance at love and finally dispel the ghosts of the past? The world was suddenly spinning with questions.

CHAPTER FIVE

As THE DAYS went by and rolled into weeks, Andrew McKay charmed all those he came into contact with. In school, the kids were mad about him. Probably due to a combination of the Scottish accent and the novelty of having a male teacher. Although he must have been around 40 years old, he retained all the vigour and enthusiasm of a graduate fresh from college. In the wider community, he was seen at Sunday Mass, which pleased the devout; he attended matches, Gaelic, soccer or rugby, which impressed the sporting fraternity; and perhaps the most important, he was to be found in the Village Inn several nights a week, which delighted everyone. Having said that, I wasn't really making much progress in getting to know him any better. While he was happy to engage in light-hearted banter, I always had the impression that he was holding something back. As if he wasn't quite ready to reveal the real Andrew just yet.

'So, YOU RECKON things are still a bit dodgy between you?'

Laurie and I were having a girls' night out, mainly for a women-bitching-about-men chat. She and Keith had partially patched up their differences, but an undercurrent of rancour still bubbled between them, the kind that gradually corrodes the trust needed to hold a relationship together.

'Yeah, we're kind of tiptoeing round each other a lot. You know, not venturing into shark-infested waters. And that seems to include so many areas now. He just takes offence so easily. Any time I try to really talk to him, he always finds something else to claim his attention.'

Worry tightened her brow, deepening the creases.

'I suppose it's just the petty irritations that build up when you live with another person. But they're getting blown out of proportion. And he's so tense all the time, like an elastic band that's pulled too tight, ready to snap.'

'Maybe the two of you just need a break. Even a long weekend away. Leave the kids with his mother. Could work wonders.'

'Do you think?' Her face cleared. 'You could be right. Time on our own could be just the thing. I'll say it to him tomorrow. See what he thinks.'

'Good eeevening, ladies.'

My stomach flipped over. The lengthened vowels betrayed the speaker immediately, as did the huge shadow looming over our table.

'Laurie, let me introduce my colleague, Andrew McKay. Andrew, my oldest friend Laurie.'

'Delighted to make your acquaintance, Laurie. Would you ladies allow me to buy you a drink?'

I looked at Laurie, who was looking at the floor.

'That would be lovely, Andrew. Thank you. A Heineken and a Budweiser, please.' The words came out in a rush in an effort to cover my friend's rudeness. I knew it was meant to be a girlie night but she could have shown a bit more enthusiasm. He was, after all, the man the whole village was talking about.

'May I join you ladies?'

It wasn't really a question. He was already moving the table aside to squeeze his way into the circular seat in our booth. With bad grace, Laurie shifted over to make room.

'Cheers, Andrew.'I raised my fresh pint to his.

'Yeah, cheers!', muttered Laurie, clinking her glass while looking straight at the wall opposite her.

'Here's to your very good health, ladies.' He flashed me a smile that sent my mind spinning off in all directions.

'Well, Laurie. Beth's oldest friend, eh? I'll bet you could tell some tales about her.'

Laurie's eyebrows arched dangerously. He barrelled on, impervious to her body language.

'I'm sure the two of you must have broken a few hearts in your time at the local clubs.'

Now her upper lip had pulled into a scornful curl. 'Maybe we just weren't into 'breaking hearts' as you so delicately put it.'

'Oh, come on.' He still hadn't read the signals. By now, I was squirming in my seat. 'Two such attraaactive young ladies as you. Sure wouldn't any man be swept off his feet.'

'Maybe you should be a little more careful about who you throw compliments at.' Her lip curled even further as she flashed her wedding ring. 'Attraaactive, married ladies might not be so impressed.'

'Christ, that's me told off.' He held his hands up in a backing-off gesture. 'I meant no harm, ladies. Ye'll not take any offence, I hope.'

'Of course not, Andrew.' I cut in before Laurie could insult him further. 'So, how do you like Carrigmore? Bit of a change from Edinburgh, I guess.'

'Och, it's a bit on the quiet side all right, but I'm sure it has its compensations.' Another flash of that brilliant smile with a half wink. My stomach flipped again.

'Well, we could always run a village talent competition, just for your benefit. Only open to attraaactive young ladies.' Laurie's tone was acidic. I shot her a murderous look.

'Well, if you need anyone to show you around, just give us a call. We're always happy to help, aren't we Laurie?' My foot connected with her ankle in a sharp kick.

'Sure. No problem at all.' Her lips curved in a Cruella de Ville smile that never reached her eyes, a bit like a wolf baring its fangs.

'Much appreciated, ladies. I'll take you up on it sometime.' He looked directly at me, excluding Laurie. He had obviously by now deleted her from his list of possibilities.

After that, we managed to confine the conversation to the fairly safe backwaters of small talk for a while until Laurie, who seemed to be in a particularly foul mood, took exception to what she called Andrew's patronising tone. He was talking about the simple pleasures of life to be enjoyed in quiet country retreats, and she let rip at him for belittling rural dwellers. This time, he couldn't ignore her rudeness.

'Do accept my heartfelt apologies.' His look was withering. 'I didn't mean to intrude. I'll take my leave of you.'

As we watched him take his pint to the bar counter, my embarrassment over Laurie's behaviour spilled into annoyance. She had gone too far.

'Did you have to be like that?' I hissed. 'He was only being friendly.'

'Friendly, my arse,' she spat viciously. 'He's only out for what he can get! I know his type. Pushy and overbearing! Just look at the way he imposed himself on us.'

'Ah, come on Laurie, give the guy a break.'

'You're into him, aren't you?' Her look was like an iron door slamming shut on the glimmer of hope I'd found myself nurturing. 'Ah, Beth! He's a waster! I'll bet he's left a string of broken hearts behind him. And I don't want to see you getting hurt.'

The phrase bulldozed its way into my consciousness. Getting hurt. Yes, I could write the book on it. But that was all in the past. This time it would be different. If it amounted to anything at all. So far, I had no idea how he felt about me. But one thing was becoming clear. That tingling through my veins every time I saw him was unmistakable!

I spent the remainder of the evening glancing

surreptitiously in the direction of the bar in the hope of catching his eye. All in vain. He wasn't into giving second chances

ONE OF MY mother's major preoccupations around this time was Brian. She'd noticed him being somewhat moody over the holidays, and kept on at me in an effort to whittle out any disclosures he might have made. It seemed like her whole life revolved around her three offspring. If she wasn't trying to pair me off with someone she considered suitable, or advising Rosemary about some aspect of 'good housekeeping', she was worrying about Brian and what she termed the 'thornier side of priesthood'. No wonder she and Dad didn't enjoy doing things together. She was too busy playing mother-hen to her three *adult* children.

She had by now of course heard all about Andrew and was badgering me daily for updates on 'how he was getting on'. Of course, what she really wanted to know was if I was making any impression on him. Having a daughter of 34 still single was beginning to make her feel ill at ease. It didn't quite measure up to what was expected. In my more bitter moments, I couldn't help feeling she deserved whatever aspersions the neighbourhood chose to heap on her. If she hadn't been so adamant all those years ago, things might have turned out so very differently. Sam and I could have sailed off together into a glorious future. We did have our problems. He had let me down badly when he was the one person who should have stood up for me. Should have shown some loyalty. But we could have worked things out, if it wasn't for the whole parish sticking their noses into our business and throwing eyes up to heaven at the 'unsuitability' of the match. And the champion nose-sticker-in was who? My blessed mother.

Looking back on the storm that erupted, I find it hard to believe that attitudes could have been so entrenched. I mean we're talking about the late 90s here, not the Dark Ages. Ecumenism and all that? Wouldn't you imagine mixed marriages were becoming more common? Apparently not in Carrigmore! Then there was the whole class issue. Although somewhat fallen from the grandeur of the past, Sam's family would always be Anglo-Irish gentry. The ones who used to lord it over us indigenous Irish. Who used to drive into their estates in their carriages expecting the gatekeeper to come running. After all, we were only a couple of generations removed from the IRA activists who burnt down several of the Big Houses in the area in the 1920s, and rural dwellers whose attitudes were largely shaped by the dictates of Eamon DeValera and John Charles McQuaid have long memories.

That first time I mentioned his name at home, you'd think the world was about to end. When I brought him over for tea, my mother's tone with him was bitterly cold. He wasn't two minutes gone when she launched into a diatribe against 'Dirty Protestants' and their pernicious influence across the land.

'Are you out of your mind, Elizabeth, consorting with the like of him?' As always when she was angry, the slanted vowels of the Belfast she had left behind rose to the surface. 'Is this what so many good people gave their lives for? My daughter getting mixed up with our colonisers? What have their kind ever done for Ireland, except bleed it dry, and treat us like slaves? Take our butter while we ate dry bread?'

And so on. Her outrage gathered force as I went on seeing Sam and she never lost an opportunity to taunt me about betraying my cultural heritage, etc. I really tried to make allowances for her Belfast origins, with the distrust of the entire Protestant population that comes with the territory, but there was no talking to her. Sam Butler was the devil incarnate and there was 'nothing more to be said on the matter'.

My Dad, having come from farming stock, was more tolerant, but even he had reservations.

'Don't get too involved, pet. You're from two separate worlds and there's no bridge across. He's not the man for you. You're my little girl and I don't want to see you get hurt.'

And that's how it went on. Until the day we announced our plans to marry and our world turned into a jagged, screaming universe with steel rivets of accusation flying in all directions, both from his family and from mine. They gave the feuding Capulets and Montagues a run for their money in the bigotry department. This was the background against which our engagement was played out. No wonder things fell apart.

'SO? TELL ME all.'

Laurie was just back from her 'romantic' weekend away with Keith. She'd persuaded him to splash out on the full works in Ashford Castle, the ultimate in honeymooner's heaven on the shores of Lough Corrib, hoping to re-ignite whatever flame had once lit up their relationship.

'Let's just say it wasn't an unqualified success.' Her slumped shoulders told the tale.

'But there must have been something about it you both enjoyed?'

'Yeah,' she admitted glumly. 'The king-sized bed. Loads of room in between us.'

'Ah, Laurie. What went wrong?'

'Well for one thing, he never stopped complaining about

the price of everything. I mean when you go somewhere like Ashford Castle, you know you're going to be paying over the odds. That kind of pampering doesn't come cheap. But Keith went on and on about it. I ended up sorry we hadn't just brought a tent and camped outside on the grounds.'

'And what about the food? Or did you go to the local chipper?'

She grimaced. 'Oh, yeah. We went to this really classy restaurant the first night. Ever heard of Nouvelle Cuisine? Portions a three-year-old child could demolish in the blink of an eye. We were so hungry an hour later we did resort to the local chipper. Spice burgers and onion rings. Full of grease. The kind that smears all over your chin.' She grinned. 'So, in the immortal words of Forrest Gump, "That's all I have to say about that."'

I laughed at the Southern drawl, but inwardly, my heart bled for her. This was her last shot at resurrecting what was left of their marriage. And no matter how flimsy the sinking ship may be, when you're on it, clinging to the rails for survival, you'll do anything rather than see it go down.

THE WEEKS WERE rolling by, and it was lunchtime on a Friday about a month into the term. Jennifer had called a meeting to update us on new safety procedures to be implemented. It was a bright, frosty day and the windows of the tiny staff room steamed with our collective breath. With all five of us squeezed around the table, physical proximity was a given. Andrew was sitting next to me. I could smell the lemony tang of the fabric conditioner he'd used on his Fair Isle sweater and feel the occasional bump of his thigh against mine. Throughout Jennifer's talk, I kept wondering if he was as keenly aware of me as I was of him.

'And now, to move on to more pleasant topics,' Jennifer adjusted her steel-rimmed varifocals further up on her nose. She had just begun wearing them full-time and was still trying to get used to switching from reading mode to making eye contact. She produced a letter from the back of her folder.

'I'm delighted to say that Belinda Duncan and Caroline O'Shea have both been shortlisted for the Young Leinster Poet Competition.'

They were both in my class. I'd started them off on that as a creative writing exercise. I grinned proudly.

'So, I'd like to say very well done, Beth. I know how much you encouraged them.' Jennifer was leading a round of applause for me. Andrew stamped his feet in raucous approval.

'Hear, hear! I think we should nominate Beth for Teacher of the Year.'

'If there was such a thing,' Jennifer smiled, her eyes betraying a faint glimmer of scepticism at such naivety.

'Well, let's at least treat it as a cause for celebration.' Andrew continued unabashed. 'Why don't we head out for a wee drink tonight? It is the weekend, isn't it? What do you say, Beth?'

With my heart hammering against my chest, I managed to agree that it wasn't a bad idea.

'Anyone else?' Andrew looked around expectantly.

'Well, we might join you for one, but we've got this football thing in Ballymartin later. You know the fundraiser thing?' Sheila, the Infants teacher, was going out with the trainer of the local Gaelic team, and so her social life pretty much hinged on football fixtures and socials.

'Julie?' I ventured, knowing that she'd have planned something with her fiancé.

'Thanks, Beth, but we're actually driving down to

Connemara this evening. We've a pre-wedding meal tomorrow. Friend of Mick's.'

At least this time, the prospect of yet more nuptials didn't bother me unduly. It looked like for once, the gods were smiling on me. A wave of anticipation tumbled through my stomach as my mind raced ahead, fashioning the scenario into the most desirable shape. As Sally Bowles once said, 'Maybe this time I'll win'.

FEELING A BIT like a teenager before a first date, I finally emerged from my room after nearly an hour of trying on five or six different outfits. I'd settled on a pair of tight jeans, even tighter now with the extra pounds still wobbling around my waist since Christmas, and a cream silk blouse just low-cut enough to make it 'interesting'. While I wanted to make the most of my first real opportunity to impress him, I wasn't going looking like a tart. After all, it was just a get-together among colleagues, wasn't it? And I still hadn't decided whether this was what I really wanted. I'd just wait and see.

At exactly 9.05pm, I pulled up outside the Village Inn. It would have been hard to miss the flamboyant crimson BMW with its metallic sheen parked just across the road. A few proverbial butterflies started dancing a tango around my stomach as I made my entrance.

With all the Christmas lights and decorations taken down, the lounge looked much more spacious. An open fire blazed in the corner, orange sparks flying from the logs. The subtle lighting cast a warm glow over the red upholstery. At the counter sat all the usual suspects, the familiar line-up of bachelor farmers who came in to hear the latest news and to escape the numbing isolation of their daily lives. In their midst was Andrew, perched on a barstool, chatting easily about the prices fetched at yesterday's cattle mart. He seemed to blend in with any company. Pint in hand, he was nodding vigorously in agreement with whatever judgement had been pronounced on the auctioneer's handling of proceedings.

'Ah, the lovely Beth!' He had me spotted, and was moving in my direction. 'So, how's the Teacher of the Year?'

'Give over', I hissed. 'It's not that big a deal.' I was conscious of the entire farming community of Carrigmore gazing mystified at me. A rush of heat spread up my neck and into my cheeks. I beat a hasty retreat into the corner booth, away from the staring faces. Not seeming to notice anything amiss, Andrew sauntered over with the drinks and slid in beside me. In spite of my annoyance, a tingling of desire surged through me. Maybe he just wasn't tuned into the level of gawping curiosity you get in a small village pub. I had a feeling he was going to learn pretty fast.

'Well, Beth, looks like I have you all to myself. Lucky me, eh?'

I have to admit I positively simpered.

'Oh, well, sure I suppose we'd better make the most of it.'

I couldn't believe what I'd just heard myself say. Here I was, behaving like a starry-eyed teenager who finally strikes gold. It hadn't gone unnoticed. He was looking at me curiously, almost like a cat toying with a field mouse. I had to distract him.

'So, Andrew, what was it that brought you to Carrigmore?' I ventured. 'Hardly the nightlife!'

'There's not much wrong with the nightlife from where I'm sitting.' He turned slightly to face me. 'In fact, I'd say it was one of its main attractions.' He shot me a playful look.

'Ah, but seriously, I think I told you already my mother's originally from Lanesborough, so I'd been looking for an opening somewhere in the general area. Thought I might do a little research into the family history.'

'Research, eh?' He was becoming more interesting by the minute. 'Is it leading somewhere. I mean, are you planning to write about it or anything?'

'Hey, steady on. I'm only at the information gathering stage. Let's wait and see what happens.'

One of those happy flashes of inspiration came hurtling towards me. 'Why don't you join our writers group? We're always looking for new members.'

'Writers group? Well, well, isn't Carrigmore full of surprises. Tell me more.'

'Well, I suppose it's a fairly modest little group,' I backtracked, in case he had visions of the cream of the Irish literati gathering in our local pub. 'There's eight of us and, well we just sort of scribble, mainly,' I tailed off unconvincingly.

'Ah, but you have a novel in you just waiting to come out, right?'

He'd hit on my secret ambition. For about a year now, I'd had a couple of main characters swimming around in my head along with the wobbly thread of a plot. I just hadn't got them down on paper yet. But I would, someday soon.

'Oh, sure,' I replied. I just have to sit down at the computer for a couple of hours tomorrow and I'll dash it off. Where do you think we should have the launch?'

'Oh, the biggest theatre in Dublin, of course. And then on to the West End for the British market. Hey, maybe we can double up. My family history and your novel, how about it?'

By now, we were both doubled up all right, but with

laughter.

Just then, Sheila and Steve arrived. A new couple, they were still at the hand-holding stage, and almost soppy in the way their eyes locked into one another. In fact it took them a while to spot us in the corner. With a definite what's-going-on-here look, Sheila came to join us.

'How're ye doing, lads? Ye look well settled in anyway.'

Her Cork accent lilted its way through the greeting with its obvious implication. Andrew was on his feet immediately ushering her to a seat.

'Ah, sure, the night is young yet. We're just gettin' started. Right, Beth?'

'I can see this is going to be a good night,' Sheila said as she eased herself in to the far corner, leaving space for Sean. 'So, guys, going to let me in on whatever it was?'

We only had to look at one another to dissolve into more laughter. The kind that draws two people into the private world of co-conspirators.

AN HOUR LATER, it was just the two of us again. Sheila and Steve had abandoned us for their football thing in Ballymartin, and by now, we were both nicely mellow. On his return from the bar with more drinks, Andrew had moved in a bit closer, and I could feel his damp breath on my forehead. The bluish flames rising from squat candles on every table began to dance.

He was talking about the last book he'd read when I noticed his arm travel down my back. I leaned into him. Whatever that aftershave was, I just couldn't get enough of it. I tilted my head slightly and his lips closed on mine while his massive hand curled around my waist. I went limp all over, yielding to the ache of desire travelling through my body, beyond caring that we were in practically in full view of the locals at the counter.

'Beth.' His voice broke the spell, urgent and hoarse. 'I've been wanting to kiss you for so long.'

Tiny sparks of fire went zigzagging through me, heightening further the shivering sensations his touch was creating. He was kissing me again, and the old familiar joy of being with someone who wanted me roared through my veins. He really wanted me. One thing was for sure, this time, *nobody* was going to interfere.

THE NEXT MORNING, I was lying in bed, reliving every moment of the previous night when the phone rang. It was Marie's husband, Sean, his breath coming in short gasps. Marie had gone into labour. She was 'a bit uncomfortable but doing nicely' according to the staff nurse on duty. It would be 'a while yet', they said. I skipped down to the kitchen, grinning to myself.

'Like some toast, love?'

In the kitchen, Dad was ambling around, dropping two slices of thick-cut white bread into the toaster. A scribble of telltale egg-stain decorated the front of his shirt. Mother had been at him and at him to cut down, but to no avail. Even our GP's words of warning at his last check-up had made no impact. One of the few pleasures he had left, I suppose.

'Thanks, Dad. Yeah, why not? Might even have marmalade. It's Saturday, isn't it?' I shot him a conspiratorial grin. Mother was obviously out on an early shopping trip so we had guilt-free access to the contents of the fridge. I piled the Dairygold and Seville orange marmalade onto the toast.

'So, what's new?' The perennial question, stemming from the insatiable desire for whatever titbits of gossip might add spice to the day, for once opened a treasure trove.

'Marie's in labour. That was Sean on the phone. Sounds like it's going to happen today.'

'Well, isn't that just grand! I suppose she'll be giving up the teaching, eh? Sure how'd she manage with the little babby?'

'Ah, come on, Dad! Haven't you ever heard of a crèche? Marie'd be climbing the walls stuck at home with a baby all day.'

'You wait till you have one of your own and you'll understand.' He patted my shoulder knowingly, nodding his bald head, shiny as a Granny Smith apple. 'You have to be a mother yourself to really know what it's all about.'

Oh, sweet Jesus, if anyone else told me I need a man or a baby to make me complete, I'd throw up all over them.

'Yes, Dad. I'll bear that in mind.' I chewed my way viciously through the remains of the toast, flinging the crusts at Amber, who was drooling at my knees.

CHAPTER SIX

THE OVERSIZED LIFT, designed to carry trolley beds and reeking of disinfectant, whirred its way up to the third floor and St Joseph's Ward. The profusion of tulips in my arms, along with the enormous pink teddy, announced to my lift companions where I was heading so I was regaled with delighted smiles. I followed the directions signposted on the corridor and turned into a room filled with blue and pink balloons and huge cuddly toys. The conflicting smells of baby powder and antiseptic rose on the air. Facing each other along the length of the walls were six beds, each with a cot beside them. At the bed in the corner by the window, a nurse was adjusting an intravenous drip. Directly opposite her, Marie was asleep, with Sean dozing in a chair by her side. Two of the other bedside chairs were similarly occupied by comatose husbands, their heads nodding onto their chests. The poor bastards had probably been up all night. Still, their wives must have gone through a lot more. So much for solidarity.

As I approached the bed on tiptoe, Marie's eyes opened and she beamed in delight. I leaned over to give her a hug, and caught my first glimpse of the miniature creature balled up in a fluffy white bedspread in the adjoining cot. All I could see was a little pink face with a snub nose and the tiniest fingers curling over the blanket. Her breath was coming in gentle puffs through a slightly open mouth. As I watched, the mouth opened wider in a peaceful yawn. I was gobsmacked. Not all the baby books in the world could have prepared me for the sense of wonder that overwhelmed me.

'Meet our daughter, Kylie,' Marie half whispered the name, as if not quite believing she was real.

'Marie she's beautiful! So perfect! You must be ecstatic. Just look at her.' The infant had shifted slightly and brought one tiny fist up to her mouth. Marie reached out a finger and touched the little cheek. The eyes opened briefly, closed again, and she snuggled herself further in under the coverlet.

'Well, yes. We are pretty amazed. I mean, in spite of all the blood and gore, this has to one of those champagne moments in life, doesn't it?' She winced from the effort of moving in the bed. 'Although I'm not so sure I'd have gone along with that last night. I was convinced I was being torn asunder by a host of devils with red-hot pitchforks,' she smiled ruefully. 'Don't ever let anyone try to tell you childbirth is a piece of cake.'

'But just look at what you have to show for it.'

Roused by the two of us oohing and aahing, Sean jerked awake, and gazed adoringly at his wife. She closed her hand over his and a jolt of private communication flickered between them.

'We'd like to ask you something, Beth.' A glimmer of apprehension crossed her brow. 'I don't want to impose or anything, but Sean and I were wondering... well, we'd love you to be her godmother.'

'Yes, Beth. It would mean a lot to us. You're so good with kids. You'd be the perfect godparent.'

I was dumbfounded. A warm blanket of euphoria was wrapping itself round me. It was the next best thing to having a child of my own. I was going to have a god-daughter. A little girl to buy ice-creams for. To bring to the circus. To fuss over on her birthday. To share the excitement of Santa with. My mind went galloping away to the land of candy floss and flying carousels with pink and blue hobby-horse heads bobbing up and down just like in *Mary Poppins*, with the blare of carnival music ringing in my ears. For the first time since I was about six, I began to believe in the magic of childhood again.

'AND NOW LET us offer each another the sign of peace.'

The monotonous drone of Fr Flannery tailed off giving us a few seconds respite while we all shook hands and invoked peace on each other. It gave me the chance to look down the aisle towards the rear of the church where I was sure Andrew would have taken up position. 11:00am Mass on a Sunday was the one event of the week where you were bound to meet everyone in the parish. 9:00am was for the pious ones who wanted to impress others with their early rising, like my mother. Saturday Evening Mass was for those who were anticipating a hangover on Sunday, like my father. But 11:00am, that was for us normal folks. Like me and Andrew. And yes, there he was, beside old Matty Doran, the sheep farmer with the stray wisps of grey hair pulled over a balding crown. And just look at the earnest expression on his face as he proffered his enormous hand to Matty's little wizened one. No wonder he was the talk of the parish.

The Mass trundled its way to an end punctuated by ragged coughing which rose and fell in different parts of the church. Suddenly, the wailing cry of a bored infant pierced the rhythm of invocation and response. Like a reel of film, pictures of me standing at a baptismal font with my new god-daughter in my arms unrolled in my brain. I couldn't suppress a fleeting smile of delight. My mind took flight into the land of baby clothes, talcum powder and cuddly toys. Meanwhile, back at the church, the rancid smell of damp overcoats and unwashed human flesh was contributing to the general gloom of people who just wanted to get to hell out of there and home to an open fire and dry clothes. Or in some cases, into the local pub with its open fire and copious amounts of hot whiskey. As Fr Flannery finally reached the parish news and informed us of Bingo sessions, a fundraiser for the Old Folks, and Open Day for the Missions, feet began to shuffle and the sporadic unease in the back rows turned to a more concerted movement towards the doors. Like a demented crab, I scuttled along the bench, made a hasty genuflection and joined the throng proceeding down the aisle.

In the cold mizzling rain blowing from the north, churchgoers stood around in knots huddling under giant umbrellas, discussing the events of the week. This was where the weather, the week's prices at the cattle mart, and whose health was failing, were all thrashed out. The sisterhood of respectable married women flapped around lamenting the latest misdemeanours of their men folk, and speculating on who was 'carrying on' with whom. The latest misfortunes of Mossie Delaney whose wife had absconded with her 'fancy man' were dwelt on with glee.

'Ah, Beth, there you are!' Frank Moran, with his fleshy jowls that drooped like those of a Basset Hound, was bustling over in my direction. 'And how are all the Maguires?'

'Grand, Frank. We're all grand, thanks. No complaints.' By now, I could feel every nerve in my body tightening in my anxiety to locate Andrew, and really didn't want to get drawn into a protracted conversation with this inquisitive little man about the health of all our family. I shifted uneasily from one foot to the other.

'And how are things in that school of yours? I'm hearing wonderful things about the new fellow, what's his name?'

'Andrew,' I said faintly, my mind racing to find a way out of the inquisition. The last thing I wanted was to feed this gossipmonger's ever-smouldering little brain, always hungry for fresh crumbs that could be twisted to give them a more salacious flavour.

'Yes, Andrew.' A smile spread across his lips. 'Doing well, then, is he?'

I spotted the subject of our conversation striding purposefully towards us. In a fawn Crombie overcoat, he stood out from the crowd.

'Ah, the lovely Beth, I thought I might find you here.' I could see Frank's bushy eyebrows raise by two inches as Andrew drew me into a hug. I needed to set things straight here.

'Frank, this is my colleague, Andrew McKay. Frank Moran, our family doctor.'

'Delighted to meet you, Andrew.' Frank's eyes travelled up and down, measuring the worth of the man the whole of Carrigmore was talking about. 'You're very welcome to Ireland. And how are they treating you here?'

'I've never had it so good, Frank.'

Did I catch a lightning wink there?

'Sure aren't I spoilt for choice with all the beautiful women in these parts?' he grinned companionably.

'Ah, a ladies' man!' Frank couldn't have asked for better. This was the news that would take wings around the parish before nightfall. 'And is there a particular young lady in question?' The eyebrows had shot up again. I sent Andrew a warning look, but our signals weren't finely enough attuned for him to pick up on the danger.

'Let's just say I'm living in hope.' His meaningful look in my direction threw the doors to speculation wide open. By tomorrow, it would be all over the village that Beth Maguire had bagged the Scotsman. It was time to get the hell out of here.

'Well, nice talking to you Frank.' I put a hand on Andrew's elbow to steer him away. 'I'll tell Mam and Dad you were asking for them.'

Walking away, I could feel his beady little eyes boring into our backs with the penetration of a Stanley drill, his mind churning around the treasure trove he had unearthed, processing all the details to be regurgitated and no doubt embellished to his willing audience.

3.00 PM THAT afternoon, and the rain was now tumbling down in sheets from a leaden sky, rippling the puddles in the driveway. Book in hand, I sat at the window watching the silvery needles splashing off the pane, little rivulets streaming down onto the sill. I had just started to re-read *Jane Eyre*, and the no-possibility-of-taking-a-walk-that-day sort of depression was beginning to get to me. Andrew had accompanied me as far as my car after Mass, and then just pissed off without so much as a reference to Friday night. I was beginning to wonder if I'd dreamt the whole thing. Although I suppose he *had* gone on with all that guff about 'living in hope' to Frank Moran, so it must have meant something to him. But why hadn't he asked me out? Now I was really confused. What was he playing at?

'There you are, Elizabeth.' My mother's intrusion into my reverie was not overly welcome. 'I was wondering where you'd got to.'

She settled herself down, plumping up the cushions on the settee, obviously gearing up for one of her woman-to-woman talks. Of course she knew I'd been in with Marie last night, and was thrilled I'd been asked to be godmother.

'And what name are they giving the little one, God bless her!'

'I think it's going to be Kylie, Mam.'

'Kylie? Bless us and save us, sure there was never a saint called Kylie.' She sniffed. Wouldn't you think they'd at least give her a Christian name? I never heard the like of it.'

I let her witter on and retreated back to my musings. The inevitable observation came at me like a slap in the face.

'You know, Elizabeth, if you're ever going to have one of your own, you'd want to get a move on with finding a husband.' She frowned at me accusingly. 'It's not that I'm trying to put pressure on you, dear, or anything like that. But remember the body clock, tick-tock, tick-tock.' She swung her forefinger like a pendulum to drive home her point. 'And you know how happy your father and I would be to see you settled.'

'If that's the case, maybe you should have let things be when I *was* "settled" as you put it.' The words came out like a gush of water from a burst pipe. 'But no, you couldn't leave well enough alone, could you? You and your bloody meddling.'

'Well, really, Elizabeth. There's no call for that. I only did what I thought was best for you. You know that.' Her voice quivered with hurt.

'Do I?' I let the question linger in the air.

'Oh, come on, Elizabeth. What's the point of bringing it all back up again? It wouldn't have worked out anyway. Let it go.'

'You don't know that,' I turned on her. 'In fact, you know nothing about how we really felt about each other. All you were concerned about was what the neighbours would say. How it might affect *your* respectability.'

By now, I was close to tears and beyond caring what I said to her. Until I saw her turn away, head bowed and shoulders starting to shake. God damn that woman! She'd done it again. Made me feel guilty for the part she'd played in wrecking things for me and Sam. Right then, I'd willingly have swopped places with little Jane Eyre locked in the cellar by the cruel Mrs Reed. At least she finally got her revenge on the old bag!

THE ATMOSPHERE OVER dinner that evening was glacial. Mother was playing the wounded victim to perfection, her looks loud with accusation, her voice bright and shrill as a tin bell. My head was ringing with the reawakened anger that any discussion of the topic inevitably brought on. The air vibrated with tension. Poor Dad was doing his best to act normal and negotiate his way through the hostility all around him, throwing in the odd comment about what had happened in the office that day. When the phone rang, I jumped to get it, relief pouring through me.

'Beth, can you come over? Something's happened.'

'Laurie, are you okay?' She sounded like a child lost in the woods with darkness about to fall and wolves howling in the distance.

'Not really. Just come over, please.'

On the way to her place, I went through all the possible scenarios that could have unfolded, anxiety clawing through the base of my stomach. Could something have happened to one of the kids? Possibly, but I thought it far more likely that this related to Keith. Had she just discovered his latest infidelity? Had she finally decided enough was enough? Or had he made the decision for her?

Finding the door on the latch, I carried on through to the kitchen, steeling myself for whatever disaster had rocked her world. She was sitting at the pine table, huddled over a mug of coffee.

'He's left me.' Her voice was tight with misery. 'Gone off with some young-one from his department. Can you believe it?'

Only too well. But now wasn't the time to tell her just how badly and how often he'd betrayed her. She'd been so wrapped up in her kids and her homemaking she'd never noticed — or maybe had chosen not to see. The foundations on which she'd built ten years of her life were crumbling into dust.

'Come here, sweetheart.' What she needed now was a hug and a stiff whiskey. Her body shuddered into great racking sobs as her grasp of the situation sharpened. I held her in silence until the spasm of grief had subsided. Until she was ready to talk. My raid on the drinks cabinet produced a half-full bottle of Jameson, most of which I poured into two tumblers. Several gulps later, the details began to emerge. Apparently, he'd waited till the kids were at a friend's party to tell her. This afternoon, he'd returned from the golf course and blasted her world apart. And the new object of his affections? A pert little madam Laurie had met in passing at a work party. Skin-tight jeans and strappy sandals with red painted toenails. Some kind of floaty, turquoise chiffon knotted around her size eight waist. And of course available. Very available. Poor Laurie. After the initial shock, her emotions were see-sawing between ferocious anger and the searing humiliation of being rejected by the person who mattered most in her life.

'And you know the worst of it? I never saw it coming!' Bewilderment clouded her face as her chin wobbled, presaging another onslaught of tears. The whiskey glass rocked between her hands. All I could do for now was put my arms around her and let her grief exhaust itself. And to think Laurie was the one I'd envied, the one that seemed to have so much going for her. But even knowing what kind of a womaniser Keith really was, I never really believed he'd walk out on her. If this was the reality of marriage, maybe life on the shelf mightn't be so bad after all.

I thought back to the 25 compositions on 'My Christmas' I'd set as homework when we came back after the holidays. In spite of the statistics you hear so often of the demise of the traditional family unit, every one of these kids had penned a description of a Christmas day glowing with aunties, grandparents, visiting relations, and of course their Mammy and Daddy at the centre of their world. I couldn't help wondering what next Christmas would be like for Laurie and her kids. Certainly different to this one. Although there might be one or two advantages. At least she would never again have to put up with those obnoxious in-laws making their own of her home and treating her like a servant. In fact, once she managed to pull herself out of this morass, I could see her life taking a distinct turn for the better. No more running around after Keith, worrying about not having everything just right for him. She still had a lot ahead of her with all the hassle of a legal separation, assuming she wanted to go down that road, but surely in time, she'd come to appreciate her new-found freedom. In all the years I'd known her, she'd shown an inner resilience that I was certain would see her through this and move her on to a life away from the constant scrutiny of an over-critical sod.

I thought of the relentless bickering that went on between my own Mam and Dad, and wondered if they too had made the decision to separate years ago, would they both have led happier lives. I supposed times were different back then. With my mother's religious convictions, she'd never have allowed such a scandal to taint the family. So they had chosen to live with tension always simmering between them, ready to detonate into open confrontation on the slightest possible grounds for offense. The day after the House Mass of the Century was a classic example. Dad had made some innocuous remark about Brian managing to cope well with the celebrity status and Mother had hit the roof.

'What do you mean celebrity status? He's a priest, for God's sake! Not a rock star! And as such, perhaps entitled to a little more respect from members of his family.'

She sniffed audibly to underline her point. Maybe it was that sniff that really got to Dad.

'Oh, would you ever listen to yourself, woman! Going on and on about 'respect' for *Fr* Brian! You have the poor boy driven demented. Isn't he still the same Brian that lived under our roof for 18 years. You and your *Fr* Brian!'

'Well I never!' Outrage roared in her cheeks. 'With the likes of you around, it's no wonder the Church is facing a crisis.'

'You're dead right there!' Dad snorted. 'A crisis of its own making! With an army of paedophile priests destroying children's lives left, right and centre, withering its very heart. And then the bishops covering it all up, *protecting* those criminals! And you think they deserve 'respect'? Respect be damned!'

With that parting shot, he'd stormed off, leaving Mother muttering furiously about disrespect and irreverence.

ANOTHER WEEK PASSED with very little to get excited about. There was a bit of occasional banter between Andrew and I in the staff room, and now and again, I'd catch him looking at me intently. But all in all, it seemed as if what had passed between us in the Village Inn was an isolated episode. Maybe it hadn't meant anything to him. Maybe he was just a 'get them interested and then leave them hanging' sort of guy. If that was the case, I was better off without him. I'd just play it cool and let him wonder.

Then, the following Monday morning, it all clicked into place. I was drilling the kids in their usual Monday spellings while through the glass panel, Andrew was obviously engaged in something similar with his lot. In spite of my resolutions, I found myself stealing the odd glance at him, before I could look away, he caught me at it. This time there was no mistaking the wink. Once again, electric jolts of desire zigzagged through me, and I began counting down the minutes to break time. Overflowing with surplus energy, I waltzed around the classroom, encouraging, drawing out, and praising my pupils in textbook fashion. They were suddenly the best class in the world, and I must surely be the best teacher.

Finally, the bell rang. The kids filed out to the yard where Sheila was on break duty. Without looking through the glass panel, I gathered my stuff and made for the staff room. Being first in, I filled the kettle and snapped down the switch. The gentle hum was just increasing in volume when the door opened and I got the whiff of Blue Stratos.

'Well, my lovely. Alone again.'

The guttural tones did it every time. My legs wobbled as I turned towards him. Immediately, he took my face in his hands and ran his thumbs down my neck, setting every nerve in my body quivering.

'We have to stop meeting like this. Anyone could walk in.' His fingers were now running lightly down my back, moving in circles that rippled outwards.

'Yes, and probably will,' I muttered. 'This is hardly the place for...'

'For what?' he teased. 'For this, and this, and this...' He was dropping moist, velvety kisses on the back of my neck.

'Andrew, for God's sake! They'll be in any minute.'

He had me pinned against the counter, arms still moving down my back and reaching down towards my bum.

'I'll stop if you promise to go out with me.'

My breath caught in my chest. My wildest fantasy had just collided with reality. 'I suppose if you put it like that...' I trailed off, trying to look nonchalant.

'Tonight?' His hands closed around the contours of my bum, drawing me in closer. 'How about a trad session in Ballymartin?'

'Sounds good.' I knew the group he was talking about. They played in Molloy's every Monday. Uileann pipes, banjos, guitars and a bodhran. They were usually the best of craic. Especially if you happened to be in the company of the most sought after man in the parish. The feel of his arms around me conjured up lakeshore hotels and walks through moonlit forests. Reality cut short the fantasy with the tip-tap of high heeled boots in the corridor, an abrupt reminder of where we were, giving us barely enough time to disengage from one another before a hassled-looking Jennifer, laden down with her trademark copybooks, appeared in the doorway.

CHAPTER SEVEN

'ISN'T THIS WONDERFUL?' The recent row forgotten, my mother was dancing around the kitchen at the thought of me going on a date. 'I'm sure you'll get on like a house on fire.'

'It is just a first date, Mam. Let's not get too excited.' I could see her mind racing ahead. If Andrew and I made it to a second date, she'd be out looking for The Wedding Hat.

'Well anyway, have a lovely evening, dear. And be careful on the roads. It's going to freeze tonight.'

'Yes, Mam. See you later.'

'And make sure you give Andrew our regards.'

She'd never even met the guy and was already sending her regards? That was my mother all over!

Once I was in the car, my mind took wings. Soon all the petty irritations of my home life were fading into the distance. It was my first real date with the man I couldn't stop thinking about. What more could I ask for? I sang tunelessly along to *Rhinestone Cowboy* on the radio, beating out the rhythm on the steering wheel. After the heavy rain of the weekend, the skies had cleared and needles of starlight pricked the inky blackness. If I was looking for an omen, surely this was it.

In Ballymartin, the crimson BMW gleamed under the streetlight, blazing like a comet among the somewhat grubby-looking cars around it. It commanded just about as much attention as its flamboyant owner. After some final adjustments to my hair and a splash of Estée Lauder, with every nerve tingling, I stepped out of the car. The strains of the Uileann pipes capturing the haunting melody of *She Moved Through the Fair* reached my ears as I pushed open the door.

As expected, there he was up at the counter, Guinness in hand, surrounded by a group of locals, chatting as easily as if he'd known them all his life. This time, the topic was football. Longford had lost their game yesterday, and the post match analysis was in full swing, with all the recriminations and abuse of the referee that entailed. As he caught my eye, he immediately detached himself from the group and came to meet me. It seemed the eyes of the entire pub were on us as he guided me towards an empty booth.

'At the risk of breaking into song, I have to say you look wonderful tonight'. His eyes lingered on the sapphire pendant hanging round my neck, just over the more-than-usual depth of cleavage I was showing. He reached out a hand to finger it. 'It's as beautiful as you are' he whispered, gently pulling me towards him. I inhaled deeply as his heady scent surrounded me, and my stomach clenched in delicious anticipation. This guy had it all. Natural charm, great looks, pulsating sex appeal, and a way with words. You don't get much better than that. For once, the script was going according to plan. Our drinks arrived as the final notes of *She Moved Through the Fair* with its poignant evocation of young love, died out to a scattered applause.

'Here's to Ballymartin and its nightlife!' Andrew raised his glass to mine and clinked with gusto.

'To Ballymartin!' I echoed, 'and all who sail in her.'

'And to all its beautiful women!' he clinked again. 'Especially the one I'm looking at. Tell me something, Beth,' he looked quizzically at me. 'How come I'm lucky enough to find you here waiting for me?'

The puzzlement must have shown in my face. He went on.

'I mean, how come you're not already spoken for?'

'Ah, that.' My brain whizzed into overdrive as I wrestled with the decision to tell him about Sam or not.

'Yes, that,' he smiled. 'Are you a lady with an intriguing past? Or have you spent all your life waiting for a handsome Scot to sweep you off your feet?'

It was the mischievous gleam in his eye that did it. This was a man I could tell everything to. Suddenly, my murky past didn't seem quite so murky. After all, it was just a romance that didn't work out.

'Well, now that you mention it, there was someone.'

'What happened?' He sounded genuinely concerned.

'Oh, it just kind of fizzled out in the end. Too much opposition from too many quarters. Maybe we didn't have enough faith in each other, I don't know. Anyway, it ended.'

'I guess it wasn't meant to be. You know we have a saying in Scotland, there's never an ill wind that doesn't blow some good. Here's to us.' He clinked my glass again.

'Right, that's my confession over with. What about you?'

'Oh, my past is even shadier,' he grinned. 'A real Pandora's Box.'

'Oh, yeah? I'm all ears,' I grinned back. 'Let's have it.'

'My dear, I have a dreadful tale to tell,' he said with a melodramatic flourish of his arm that would have done Victorian opera proud. 'I come to you fresh from the divorce courts.'

'Oh my Lord!' I went along with the histrionics, trying my best at a southern belle drawl while waving an imaginary fan at my throat.

'Yes, Ma'am,' he continued, picking up the Louisiana accent from me. 'My wife didn't understand me. It just all went kinda pear-shaped in the end.'

And that's how, on this pretty serious topic, we were both clutching our sides with hysterical laughter. Although I did fleetingly wonder how my mother would react to my dating a divorcee. From there, it just got better. We went on to talk about my writing ambitions, and the book that was going to come out of his research. He told me about his background in psychology, and how he'd done the postgraduate conversion degree in primary teaching when he realised how much he enjoyed working with kids.

A COUPLE OF hours later, the crowd was thinning and the musicians were packing up to go. By now, Andrew was really in party mood and was bellowing encouragement for them to 'Give us one more'. He had just called for another pint, his fifth. While I too was keen to prolong the evening's entertainment, I was getting just a bit edgy about the amount of Guinness he'd put away. I'd switched to mineral water some time back, but we were both driving home. It had been a great evening. He made me laugh and laugh over the silliest things. My niggling concerns took a backseat as an inner drumbeat of exhilaration swept me along, whispering promises of a future that glimmered with those lakeshore hotels and walks through moonlit forests.

'SO YOU GOT on well then?' Laurie's muted tone spoke volumes. God knows why! I couldn't help feeling that even the bare kitchen walls, with their white rectangles where the wedding photographs used to be, looked disapprovingly at me.

'You could say that.' I smiled, still replaying the scenes

from last night in my head. 'I don't know when I last enjoyed myself so much. He must be the best thing that's happened to me since...'

I trailed off, not really wanting to go down that road. Laurie looked hard at me, one of those searching looks that ask questions you don't want to hear.

'Look, Laurie, I know, for some reason, he's not flavour of the month with you, but he really does make me happy. And, like I said, it's been a long time. Carrigmore isn't exactly overrun with eligible fellas you know.'

Another searching look. 'That's part of the problem, Beth. The first guy who comes along, and bingo, you're swept off your feet! Don't you think it smacks just a little of 'too good to be true?' I shook my head disbelievingly. It was as if she didn't want me to be happy. She was either jealous, or still holding a grudge against every man who walked the universe. It had only been a few weeks since Keith had walked out, leaving her standing there amid the ruins of their marriage. How could I trust her judgement when it was so obviously flawed? For the sake of our friendship, I'd play along but then follow my own instincts.

'Another thing, Beth.' Her tone had become more hesitant, more careful. 'I was talking to Miranda the other day. We happened to meet in the bank. She had some news.'

She waited for this to register.

'He's coming back, Beth. I just thought you should know.'

A stone came hurtling down from a great height and landed with a thud on my heart. Coming back? After ten years? She went on.

'Yes, it seems his father's had a mild stroke. They need

Sam back to manage the yard. At least until they can sort something out.'

Sam's father had been running the Butler's livery yard. It was mainly hunters and a couple of show jumpers, although I'd heard the number had dwindled a bit in recent years. He was probably no longer able to cope with the hard slog involved in looking after horses. That could mean Sam would be around for a while. Ten years ago he'd disappeared from my life forever, and now, just as I was finally moving on, my past was coming back to haunt me. The stone plunged deeper, awakening a sea of turbulence that churned around inside me. The distance between Sam and I had grown and consolidated over the years. There was nothing in the world that could bridge that gap. At best, we would be distantly polite to one another. Worse even than strangers. In an instant, I was yanked out of the happiness I'd just found and sent hurtling down that all too familiar slope of regrets and recriminations. If only I'd had the courage to follow my gut instinct ten years ago, and risen above the prejudice of Carrigmore, everything could have been so different now.

THE NEXT DAY in school, I was on lunchtime playground duty, alone with my thoughts as 60 or more children orbited around me. It still hadn't fully sunk in. It was only a matter of time before I ran into him. I was dreading that first meeting. Like in a badly spliced reel of film, images of our last few weeks together came pulsing through my head.

Looking back, if it wasn't for that brick wall of hostility we met everywhere we went, and all the half-uttered snide remarks that gained momentum over time, our lives could have run an entirely different course. Now, the thought of all that lost happiness welled up in me, plunging me further into the grip of wretchedness. He was coming back, but now, we inhabited different worlds.

THAT AFTERNOON, I began the tidy-up process following the art session. On the other side of the glass panel, Andrew was stalking around, hands behind his back, stopping every so often to check on the progress of a particular child. He seemed to be miles away, locked into a private world the children had no part in. Suddenly, his attention was arrested by a copybook that, for some reason, displeased him, and in a flash, he'd flung it to the ground. The child looked up, more amazed than frightened. Just then, he caught my eye. He quickly bent down to retrieve the copybook and replaced it on the desk. The little girl continued to stare at him as he moved on through the rows of desks. I was surprised, but reckoned he must have had something on his mind. The kids all adored him. It was obviously a once-off occurrence. I returned to the sorting out of the crayons and coloured pencils.

'ANY WORD ON Marie and the little nipper, Beth?' asked Mother.

'Actually, she got home today. I'm going over this evening to see if I can help.'

The truth was, I was dying to tell Marie about Andrew, now that I was pretty sure we were an item. She'd be thrilled to hear I was officially dating again. Unlike Laurie, who had obviously developed a compulsive hatred of all men. She would be happy for me. We'd have a great natter. And I'd get to cuddle my little god-daughter.

'Well, isn't that grand, God bless her. Do give her our best.'

Mother's eyes were glistening and she that faraway

look— the one that spoke of a grandmother-in-waiting. I could sense another barrage of questions coming on.

'Why don't you invite Andrew over to dinner some night, dear? We need to welcome him to Carrigmore.'

Visions of Jane Austen's Mrs Bennett and her behaviour at the ball at Netherfield crowded my head. My mother would be just as capable as that good lady of wrecking whatever chance I had with my new boyfriend.

'Maybe we should just let him find his feet first, Mam. Anyway, I think he's kind of busy researching his book.'

'You never told me he was writing a book. Are we going to be in it?'

Her eyes gleamed at the prospect.

'I don't think so. It's about the Irish in Scotland.'

'Oh,' she sniffed. 'One of those biography things.' Her interest died like an extinguished flame and the conversation swung back to babies and the inevitable.

'You know, Beth, your Dad and I are beginning to worry about you.' Her face acquired an expression of heightened concern. 'Remember that chat we had the other day?' She'd obviously forgotten the explosion it had triggered. 'Body clocks and things? Us women don't have forever, dear.'

Dad's gruff tones came to the rescue, slicing through my mother's dark warnings.

'Would you leave the girl alone, Mary. Isn't she doing all right as she is?'

I felt like hugging him. He saw me as a complete person, not just potential wife/mother material. As far as Mother was concerned, the marriage of her eldest daughter would reaffirm her social status, whereas Dad didn't really give a hoot about that sort of thing. All he wanted was a quiet life, and no-one trying to badger him into playing a role he didn't fit. God love him, he'd had to struggle long and hard against her efforts over the years to turn him into the country squire. I think she only gave up on him when she had Brian steered firmly in the direction of the cloth. The prospect of having a priest in the family was enough to divert her attention from the rest of us, for a while at least. Unfortunately, it seemed I had now taken over as the object of her ambitions. Maybe she wouldn't have that long to wait. I might surprise them all yet.

'SHE'S ADORABLE, MARIE. So perfect!' I was sitting in my friend's kitchen with Kylie nestled on my lap. I watched her suck the end of my little finger, cooing over her as if she was the first baby ever born. Her tiny fists were balled up as if closed over some precious treasure, and her legs curled round in an arc, like those china dolls I used to play with long ago, only softer.

'Yeah, she's pretty amazing, isn't she?' Marie's voice was hoarse with love. The birth of this child had changed the focus of her life and now filled all her visions of the future. A familiar twinge of envy shot through me. Maybe my mother was right after all. Maybe I should start making things happen.

'So, what's all this I'm hearing about the most eligible bachelor in Carrigmore?' Her eyes crinkled up at the sides, betraying her amusement at the impact this guy was making.

I filled her in on the progress to date, taking care not to overstate the case. We were still in the very early stages. I didn't want to put a hex on my budding romance. Marie, however, expert at reading between the lines, concluded that this was 'it.' I'd met Mr Right, and we were on course to go galloping off into a golden sunset together, etc. She was an incurable romantic. I thought at this stage, I'd better let her know *all* my news.

'Actually, Marie, there's something else.'

My sense of unease must have penetrated the armour of her euphoria. She stopped in her tracks, eyes narrowing with concern.

'Guess who's back in town?'

The look on my face left her in no doubt.

'You're joking.'

'No. Laurie just told me. His Dad's had a stroke and he's come home to take over running the livery business.'

'Well, well, well. So what now?'

'What do you mean, what now? It's over, Marie. Ten years is a long time.'

'Anyway,' her eyes glinted with mischief, 'looks like he might meet with some competition now. It never rains but it bloody pours.'

I grinned back. 'Yeah, sure. Can you see the pair of them fighting a duel at dawn over me?'

'Let's just wait and see, shall we?'

Maybe she had a point. After ten years of a barren landscape on the relationship front, it was finally beginning to look as if fertile pastures were beckoning me.

CHAPTER EIGHT

As THE TERM progressed and the annual scatter of snowdrops starring our front lawn gave way to clumps of early daffodils, my life zigzagged between a comfortably safe routine within the confines of my classroom and the gut-wrenching uncertainties of what seemed to be an on-off romance.

Andrew and I had been out on several dates, most of which were just a night out in the pub, but we'd also taken in visits to local beauty spots. Belvedere House had particularly impressed him with its Jealous Wall and gruesome history of the imprisonment of wives for suspected infidelity. He'd jokingly remarked that that was how women should be treated, and that if he suspected his girlfriend was making a fool of him, he'd have her locked up too. I had to admit there was something thrilling about a man who felt such passion in his veins.

Even so, I was mildly puzzled by the fact that each date had ended with a goodnight kiss and a nonchalant 'See you around.' Even though attraction sizzled like a live wire between us, we still hadn't gotten to the ripping the clothes off one another part. One would think that the cottage he was renting would provide us with the perfect love nest, but he still hadn't invited me in. I must admit I found this a bit unnerving. It did raise doubts as to whether he really thought of us as a couple. He always seemed to be holding something back, as if he was acting out a role. He was also quite reticent about his life in Scotland. I knew his mother had come from Lanesborough, had married a Scottish doctor, and that he was their only child, but beyond that, he wasn't very forthcoming. I supposed that having just been through a messy divorce, he was hardly going to talk to me about it, but I would have liked to know more about what was going on in his head. However, I didn't want to jettison my chances by appearing too eager, so I was taking the casual line. After all, maybe he was one of life's real gentlemen, and was treating me with old-fashioned respect. Whatever it was, I reckoned he was worth waiting for.

All the same, I couldn't help thinking back to those early stages with Sam, when he had wanted to shout from the rooftops that we were officially dating, in spite of the adverse reactions all around us. The day we first had a formal meeting with his family, I could hear pride trembling in his voice when he introduced me as his girlfriend. In contrast, his mother's icy reserve couldn't have been more pointed.

'Delighted to make your acquaintance, I'm sure.'

The limp hand that was extended to me had all the warmth of a dead fish. Her austere features, complete with Roman nose and high cheekbones, were frozen into permanent disdain.

'And what line of work are you in, dear?'

Of course whatever I said, it wouldn't be good enough for her son, but when the words 'primary teacher' reached her ears, a wall of disapproval solidified the air between us.

'I see.' Her voice was like broken glass. 'Of course, we've always had a governess here for the children. Nothing like a private education, is there?'

And that was our first meeting. From then on, whenever I had the misfortune to run into her around the stable yard, I was greeted in the same aloof manner, made to feel like I was a speck of dust on the pristine carpet of her life.

But still, back in those early days, Sam's enthusiasm had blazed like a comet. It had seemed that no obstacles could stand in our way. We had both been glowing from the heady excitement of mutual attraction. Now, in hindsight, I can see how badly we underestimated the extent of the bigotry and narrow-mindedness all around us. My mother had been no more enthusiastic about our union than Mrs. Butler, so we had never really stood a chance.

ON A WINDY Saturday afternoon, in the middle of March, I found myself in Ballymartin. I was at the deli counter in Supervalu when someone coughed politely behind me. I turned slightly, and noticed Sam standing there, looking slightly sheepish. My stomach flipped over, knots of anxiety were coiling and uncoiling like snakes.

'Sam.' I eventually stammered, my voice hoarse with shock. 'Welcome back.'

'Beth…' He was clearly just as ill at ease, trying to look anywhere but at my face. 'What a surprise…'

'I— I heard you were back. How are you?'

'I'm fine.' His tone was measured, cold, uninterested. 'And you?'

'I'm good, thanks.' The silence stretched between us.

'Well, I'd better, you know…'

With my Stilton in hand, I backed away as if trying to escape from a psychopath. What a disaster; barely half a dozen words exchanged, and an Arctic coldness swirling up like poisoned mist between us. As I walked out into the blustery spring day, charcoal clouds gathered overhead in a huge rolling mass.

FOR THE REST of that day, I couldn't get him out of my head. He'd been so aloof. We had once meant the world to each other. The scenes of our early courtship danced around in my mind, taunting me. The day of our first major row replayed in my head. Hearing his words in my mind still drove a sliver of ice through my heart.

'You know, Beth, you can't expect them to change their whole way of thinking. They've always seen themselves as distinct from the Irish Catholic natives. It's in their blood.'

'That doesn't give them the right to look down their noses at "the Nationalist community" as your lot call us. In spite of all my efforts to be polite to her, your mother has never spoken a civil word to me. Are you so blind that you can't see that?'

'Oh, come on! That's an exaggeration. You're being paranoid.'

'Paranoid? What about that dinner party when she introduced me as "a friend of Samuel's from the village"? When we've been dating for the last three months, I'm just "a friend from the village." It's as if she was ashamed to have me in her home. How dare she,' I'd vented angrily.

And how the hell could he have just stood by and let her treat me like that? He just said nothing. He should have told her to shove her la-di-da notions up her arse. Stuck up cow.

I could still see that scene in the drawing room, with the glare of evening sunlight slanting in through the sash windows. It was the first time I'd been invited to dine with the Butlers and I'd really tried to make a good impression. But that woman had rejected every overture I made. No matter how friendly I tried to be, all I got in return was indifference. Even now, my eyes glittered with tears of frustration at the remembered humiliation.

Sam didn't even see it as an insult to me. In his eyes, his mother could do no wrong. Even when she did her utmost to make me feel like an outsider. With that chilly smile and the scratch of metal in her voice. Always so judgemental. As if every utterance was a pronouncement. I'd never felt so let down. After three months together, Sam should have shown a bit more loyalty. Instead of giving me the support I expected, he just shrugged the whole thing off.

'Well, you'll just have to make allowances, Beth. What about the way your mother treats me? I've never before been met with such suspicion and narrow-mindedness. She always manages to make me feel like an outsider.'

I'd stared at him aghast. Of course I was aware of my mother's distrust of anyone outside of the Catholic Church, but I hadn't realised it was that obvious to him. A blush of shame fingered its way across my cheeks.

'In spite of all her notions about her standing in the community and having an ordained priest in the family, she really lets herself down when it comes to mixing with "the other sort," as she calls us.'

His mocking echo of my words ignited a furnace of rage inside me. Although I knew he was right, I couldn't give in to him. Not after him taking his mother's side against me. And after several days of shutting each other out, we eventually drifted back towards a tentative reconciliation, but there was still an undercurrent of bitterness on both sides, ready to flare up again at the next provocation.

And so things drifted on with him never standing up to her. I guess he just never thought enough of me to go against her. Until a year later when he asked me to marry him. By then, we were so besotted with each other we were convinced that the whole world would be happy for us. In reality, our announcement was seen as a declaration of war. His mother and the Colonel closed ranks against me. The day we went to tell them, their faces were impassive, dead eyes staring straight ahead, her limp hand with its polished nails extended in my direction barely brushing my palm before being hastily withdrawn, as if my presence was infecting her world. Even then, the day of our engagement, the sparkle of my future with Sam was already beginning to dim.

The following Friday, I arrived home to another bombshell. A letter postmarked Zambia. A strong sense of foreboding rushed through me as I tore open the envelope.

St. Gabriel's Mission,
Kawambua
Luapula
Zambia
March 12, 2009

Dear Beth,

Just a few lines to fill you in on things over here. Hope all is well with you and the old pair. Anything new in Carrigmore? And how's that Scottish teacher working out? As far as I remember, the whole village was waiting for him with bated breath. Has he lived up to expectations?

I'm afraid things aren't going too well in this part of the world. At least in my corner of it. I didn't say anything at Christmas, but you knew something wasn't right. I just didn't want to worry you all unnecessarily, but the problem has escalated a bit since then. There's no easy way to say this, but I'm sure you can guess what's coming.

I've felt for some time that maybe I made the wrong decision in joining the order, and that I've spent years trying to fit into a life that just isn't right for me. I seem to be constantly going against the flow, disagreeing fundamentally with what I'm expected to preach. It's a bit like having to put on a Sunday suit when you'd rather be in jeans and a sweater. Only of course, it goes a lot deeper than that. When I'm up on the altar saying Mass and seeing at all the faces looking up at me, or in the confessional listening to a parishioner pouring out his troubles, I can't help feeling a bit of a fraud. I just don't see myself as a spiritual leader any more. I'm not even sure if I ever really have been. But of course that's how Mother saw me. I remember how assiduously she mapped out my future, even when I was just a kid. I'm beginning to wonder if it was really my decision in the first place. Maybe it was her dream I've been living all along.

Anyway, I have to work out whether I really do need to reassess my position, or whether it's just a temporary glitch. If I do end up walking away, what I'm dreading most is breaking the news at home. I'll probably be disinherited or outcast or whatever they call it these days. And then there's the whole issue of how I'm going to make a living. With Ireland in the middle of a recession, that's going to be a tough one. Anyway, like I say, I'm still not absolutely sure. I've got a lot more thinking to do, but I'll let you know as soon as I reach a decision.

Anyway, Beth, enough of my woes. I'm sure you've got your own concerns without me adding to them. Say hi to the folks, and do take care of yourself. Keep smiling.

God bless, and love, as always,

Your Bro, Brian

I stared blankly at the letter, struck dumb by this revelation. This was what they call an unmerciful pile of shit hitting a giant whirling fan. He was right about one thing. It would not be received well at home. Brian was the one who had made Mother's life glitter, who, as he said, had lived out her dream, and he was now about to blow the whole 'my son, the priest' thing to smithereens. All she'd see was the disgrace he was bringing on the family, the social backlash for her. When you thought about it, my mother always considered herself first. All of the high points in our lives — Rosemary's wedding, my graduation, Brian's ordination — represented opportunities for her to move a little further up the ladder of social standing. Whether it was as mother of the bride, graduate, or newly-ordained priest, she was the one at the centre of attention.

For a fleeting second and for purely selfish reasons, I found myself hoping that Brian wouldn't go through with it. Life wouldn't be worth living at home with a demented mother. But, I had to feel for him. He couldn't go on pretending to be something he wasn't. Whatever he decided, he'd have my support. God knows, he'd have enough people condemning him.

'Well, it's great things are going well for you, Beth. I'm really pleased.'

Laurie hesitated and looked away from me. She attempted to smile, but only got halfway there. Her tone was about as warm as the midwinter sun. It was obvious her antipathy to Andrew had increased, and I was at a loss to understand why. As far as I was concerned, my life was slotting nicely into the groove preordained for it. I suppose there were times when his natural ebullience unnerved me a bit, but hey, nobody's perfect. It was really good to be part of a couple again. I'd spent too long on my own.

'It's just that…' Whatever she wanted to say remained trapped in her head.

'Come on, Laurie, what is it?' My patience was starting to wear thin with her unease about me and Andrew.

'Can I ask you one thing?' She hesitated again. 'How involved with him are you?'

I looked hard at her. This wasn't following the contours of a comfortable girlie chat about boyfriends. Her voice was laced with concern.

'I'm sorry, Beth. I don't mean to pry. It's just that…'

Again, her intended sentence tailed off into thin air. Her unspoken words filled the silence between us. She stumbled on.

'I wasn't sure whether to tell you this, but I think maybe you should know.'

Now she had my full attention.

'I was in the launderette yesterday to pick up some dry-cleaning, and Andrew came in.'

'And?'

'He was looking a bit rough. Unshaven, smell of booze

off him. Anyway, he was kind of loud.'

'What do you mean, "kind of loud"?'

'Well, he was kind of annoyed that he had to wait his turn. He made a big deal of being in a hurry. Actually, he was quite abusive. He turned on Denise and told her she wasn't doing her "effin' job" properly, and a whole lot more besides.'

Denise was the teenage daughter of the launderette owner. She helped out there at weekends. A slow-moving, but obliging girl who would go out of her way to help you. I often met her at Annafrid's dog shelter where we were both helped out at weekends. I wondered what she could have done to upset Andrew.

'So, how did it end up?'

'She was pretty upset. Told him he could take his business elsewhere in future. Actually, she was in tears when he left.'

'I guess he was having a bad day.' I offered lamely. 'We can't all be Mr. Perfect a hundred per cent of the time.'

'He wouldn't want to have too many of those "bad days" with the job he's in,' she muttered darkly. 'It might not be viewed so tolerantly by Jennifer Muldowney.'

I thought back to the incident I'd witnessed when he'd thrown the child's copy book on the floor.

'Yeah, well, thanks for telling me, Laurie.' Giving her the clearest indication I could that the subject was closed, I picked up the coffee cups from the table and marched over to the sink.

'RIGHT, BETH. ON you go.'

I was at the Writers Group Corner in the snug of Sullivan's pub in Ballymartin where all of us wannabe novelists and poets were gathered to work on furthering our literary ambitions. One day, we would, of course, all be published authors, striking multi-million euro deals with agents clamouring to sell our work to Hollywood, but for now, we had to content ourselves with fortnightly meetings in our local where we applied ourselves to our task. I always enjoyed these evenings, bringing my work along to be appraised. Just getting together with others who shared my enthusiasm for the written word was a lifeline. While I'd been dabbling with short fiction for a couple of years, a more involved storyline was starting to take shape in my head and I was beginning to think I might have a novel in me, so I was eager to give it a go. For a while, I'd thought there would be an added excitement to the meetings, with Andrew set to join us, but in spite of my having dropped a couple of reminders to him, he'd kept coming up with excuses. He puzzled me; in fact, I'd even put it in writing. For this evening, we'd decided to do a piece on the theme of 'Crossroads' and it now fell to me to dazzle the company with my offering. I'd taken an idea from a James Joyce story, and gone down the 'crossroads in my life' route.

'Lisa sat at the window, watching the occasional passer-by through the patterned lace curtains, listening to the clacking of their footsteps on the pavement outside as they receded into the evening. Her thoughts drifted like a rudderless boat between the happenings of the last few weeks and the unexpected disclosures of her friend a few hours ago. Up until then, her world had been full of certainties. At last, after an eternity on her own, the glimmer of romance had once again trembled on the horizon. All the exhilaration of a new love had rushed over her, although, there were times when it was proving to be just a little unsettling, maybe because she'd spent so long on her own. But then, like a thunderbolt, a throwback from her past had swept in. Her ex-boyfriend was back in town. Now her mind whirred in confused circles, obscuring her vision of what lay ahead. Just when she was ready to move on, the road into the past had opened up again.

Outside the window, a small frenzy of birdsong erupted. The laurel trees planted at intervals along the pavement erupted into life with a beating of wings. The chitter-chatter of starlings broke through her reveries. If she was truly happy with Iain, why was she so unnerved by this latest turn of events? Layers of confusion piled up in her head like the thickets of an overgrown forest, each one more impenetrable than the last. Her doubts began to multiply, insidiously taking root. Maybe that was the crux of the matter. Maybe Iain wasn't all he seemed. Out of nowhere, a cloud of suspicion moved across the distant horizon. Locked into uncertainty, she no longer knew which way to turn. This was a crossroads in her life. A wrong decision could have disastrous consequences. But how was she to know? What was she to do?'

A stunned silence filled our little alcove. Then, like water from a burst dam, words of praise came hurtling towards me.

'Well done, Beth! You've got some great imagery there!' Jimmy, an English teacher from the convent school voiced his approval.

'Yeah, good stuff!' echoed Laurie. 'You dramatise a situation so many of us can relate to.' Her look left me in no doubt that she knew exactly what I was referring to.

'It all sounds so authentic, Beth. You really get inside this girl's head. All her confusion! You have us dying to know what she's going to do.' Yvette, our facilitator, was also impressed. She was currently doing a correspondence course on counselling and so was very much into confused minds. I couldn't help wondering if she recognised the thinly veiled autobiographical element. No wonder it sounded authentic; it was the crossroads of my life. Only thing was, it wasn't so much a crossroads for me, more of a cul-de-sac I'd chosen, and the car I was driving had no reverse gear. Sam had made it obvious he wanted nothing to do with me. The best thing to do would be just forget about his existence. Move on, as they say. So what was it that was holding me back?

CHAPTER NINE

April 3, 2009

Mrs Laura Fitzpatrick,
Lisnalee,
Carrigmore,
Co. Longford

Re: Fitzpatrick v Fitzpatrick
Ref: Ant Gar 101/FF

Dear Mrs Fitzpatrick,

Our client, Mr Keith Fitzpatrick, informs us that he was married to you on January 21, 1996, at St Mona's Church, Carrigmore, Co. Longford. Mr Fitzpatrick further advises that the said marriage has irrevocably broken down, to the extent that no marital relationship currently exists between you, and that he was left with no option but to vacate the family home eight weeks ago.

Mr Fitzpatrick is anxious to regulate all matters pertaining to the breakdown and in doing so he is desirous to cause as little as possible upset and distress to the children of your union. On his behalf we formally request that you enter into a marital separation agreement with him as soon as possible. As part of this agreement he requests joint custody and access to the issue of the marriage:

Keith Fitzpatrick Jnr (aged 9)
Eoin Fitzpatrick (aged 8)
Anna Fitzpatrick (aged 6)

Mr Fitzpatrick seeks a Judicial Separation and ancillary relief pursuant to the Judicial Separation and Family Law Reform Act, 1989, as amended by the Family Law Act 1995.

We recommend that you consult with your solicitors and further invite them, when on record, to confirm that you will consent to a Judicial Separation.

If no such agreement is forthcoming within 28 days of this letter we are instructed to issue proceedings and we reserve the right to exhibit this letter with any such proceedings.

Yours sincerely,

Garrigan Lloyd & Co

'So, that's what 13 years of marriage means to him?' Laurie's voice quivered with bitterness. 'After 13 years together and three children, this is what he's prepared to do to me.'

I was still trying to take in the implications of the letter she'd just shown me. A formal separation. The end of her marriage.

'Oh, Jesus, Beth, I could kill him for this. "Left with no option but to vacate the family home." When he walked out on me for that trollop!' She slopped milk from a carton into the two mugs of coffee she'd just set down on the table. 'And now he's going to parade our failed marriage to the whole world.'

'Listen Laurie, I know it's hard right now, but just think. Haven't things been bloody awful between you two for the past couple of years? You're so much better off without him. Even since he left, I can see the difference in you.'

She looked slightly flummoxed by this.

'You know he has always been trying to mould you into something you're not, into his version of what you should be. He's always wanted you to change. But why should you?'

'You really think so?'

'Anyone could see that, Laurie. He's always been a self-absorbed little prick.'

Now I hesitated. Could I go further or would that just hurt her unnecessarily? I decided to risk it.

'And those awful parents of his, walking all over you in your home. Don't you think you deserve better?'

She sipped at the coffee in front of her, weighing up what I'd said. I kept going.

'Laurie, this is the only way forward. Sure you'd never take him back now after this.'

Her lower lip wobbled. 'But Beth, it's the kids I really feel for. Their whole world's been rocked by this…' her hands heaved through the air, 'this mess!'

Of course, the kids were going to feel the impact of the whole drama of legal proceedings. They were already floundering, trying to understand why Daddy preferred not to live with them anymore. Little Anna in particular had taken it badly. She'd retreated into a lonely place filled with silence. The two boys seemed to be handling it in their own way, throwing themselves more frantically into school sports and in particular, pony riding, but they had to be pretty mixed up inside. Poor little things. At their age, they didn't deserve all of this.

'And then there's the practicalities to sort out.' She sighed. 'The mortgage and stuff. That'll all have to be regulated through our solicitors now.'

'Well that's good, isn't it? It means it'll be cut and dried. He'll have no option but to pay up every month. And maybe treat you with a little more respect than he has up to now.'

'Beth.' She was now teetering on the brink of tears. 'How did I not see this coming? With all the warning signs flashing like neon lights all around me!'

'Come on, pet,' I put my arms around her. 'It's not that easy to see things clearly when you're caught up in the middle of it. You know that.'

'Yeah, but I was probably turning a blind eye for a long time. Not seeing what I didn't want to see. Jesus, I've been such a fool.'

Not seeing what I didn't want to see. Wasn't that more or less what I was doing with Andrew? *Turning a blind eye* to those aspects of his character that were starting to bug me: his tendency towards flamboyance and the occasional signs of heavy drinking. Of course there were huge differences between how badly Keith had treated Laurie, cheating on her with anything in a skirt, and Andrew's minor deficiencies. No-one's perfect. And he did make me feel good about myself. And make me laugh. We were still in the early stages of the relationship. There'd be plenty of time to smooth out any rough edges and come to a clearer understanding of what kind of compromises were necessary to allow us to slot more easily into each others' lives.

'YEAH, THAT'S REALLY you, Beth. Not too formal, but classy. Clean elegant lines. Shows off your curves well.'

I wasn't so sure I wanted my curves on display, but had to agree that the sea-green flowing dress clinging to me did flatter my size 14 figure. Kylie's christening was next Sunday, and Marie and I were in a very swish department store in Athlone shopping for my outfit. It cost more than I'd normally spend on my wardrobe in a year, but, hell, I didn't get to see my god-daughter christened every day.

'You don't think it's too, well, revealing?' It had a plunging neckline that I wasn't convinced was appropriate for a church ceremony.

'Ah come on, Beth. It's perfect for you. It makes you look sensational! You'll be the belle of the ball.'

She'd convinced me. I shimmied my way out of it, took it to the check-out and thanked God for plastic money. On my salary, I'd be paying this off for a while, but it was a really special occasion. And I was going to look a million dollars. My god-daughter would look back at the photographs 20 years from now and appreciate the effort I'd made. Her little face with its dimpled cheeks floated into my vision and I got a sudden whiff of her baby smell, all talcum powder and milkiness. Like a blast of cold air, a sense of longing swept through me. I couldn't help thinking I'd make a good mother, but I didn't know if I'd ever get the chance to find out. Maybe this was the closest I'd ever come to rearing one of my own. I had to make the most of it.

ANDREW AND I were sitting in the front row of the tiny theatre in Ballymartin for the local amateur drama production of *An Ideal Husband.* Since Laurie's words about not seeing what she didn't want to see, I was more finely tuned to the little things about him that bugged me. While I still enjoyed being with him, and basking in his attentions, I was becoming more aware of how he liked to be in control. I'd dragged him along to the play because nobody else was free to come with me, rather than because I craved his company. The theatre manager was going through the safety routine and I was settling myself back to enjoy the performance when the distraction of a latecomer being admitted and shown to his seat caught my eye. I froze. There was no mistaking those broad shoulders and chiselled features. And he was alone. If only Andrew hadn't been my choice of companion. I'd always known that in small-town rural Ireland, the two would have to meet sometime, but here, in the confines of a tiny theatre with a bar the size of your average living room, there would be no room for escape. As the curtain rose to take us into the elegant world of Sir Robert Chiltern and his exemplary wife, with the stench of political corruption simmering just under the polished surface, my mind wrestled with how exactly I was going to handle the situation.

With the end of Act Two and Sir Robert's impassioned plea for the love of his wife, the anxiety was causing me to fidget. I was no nearer to finding a way to negotiate the minefield of introductions. The house lights came up and the theatre-goers needing to stretch their legs started shuffling out of their rows towards the bar upstairs. Andrew was one of the first up to the counter, ordering two glasses of red wine. I couldn't keep my eyes off the stairs.

When I saw Sam, I realised he was still alone. If he had fallen into conversation with an acquaintance, things might have been a little easier, but no such luck. Across the crowded room, as they say, our glances locked and he had no choice but to make his way over. I braced myself.

'Good evening, Beth.'

The stilted tone sent a needle of tension quivering through me. I knew this was his usual manner, but surely he could make some effort. Just then, Andrew settled his arm possessively around my shoulders. He had a dramatic sense of timing. Stiff with embarrassment, I blundered on.

'Sam, this is Andrew McKay, a colleague of mine. Andrew, my friend, Sam Butler, just returned from the States.'

The two exchanged limp handshakes, their fixed expressions confirming an instant mutual hostility. Desperate to engage them in conversation, I went for the obvious.

'Enjoying the play, Sam?'

For an instant, his eyes came to life before the veil came down again, just like the thick stage curtain, blocking out whatever lay behind. Before he had a chance to reply, Andrew cut in.

'It's not exactly the West End, is it? All overacting and loud gestures. Probably typical enough of these little country theatres, though.'

And so the curtain fell on whatever hope I had of a civil exchange of views. Not only did Sam now have evidence that I was involved with someone, but also that the guy I was dating was an arrogant sod who didn't hesitate to pour scorn over the local theatre company. I saw the faintest flicker of disgust cross his eyes.

'Actually, yes, I am enjoying it.' Sam's emphasis was pointed, his clipped enunciation like the chink of teaspoons brought down sharply onto gilt-edged saucers. 'We don't often get a period drama with such attention to detail in these "little country theatres." In fact, I'm pretty impressed with the direction too.'

'Yes.' I rushed in, not wanting to be associated with Andrew's remarks. 'I think the way Mrs Cheveley comes across as a champion of honesty works really well. Gives her more depth.'

I caught a gleam of admiration before his eyes went dead again, rejecting any further exchanges. In a room full of people all caught up in animated chatter, we three were marooned in a sea of silence. Finally, it was Sam who made his excuses, under the pretence of going outside for some air. In an instant, what had promised to be an enjoyable evening had disintegrated around me.

What really unhinged me was that flicker of admiration from Sam. That was what brought the memories rolling back of all the times we'd gone to the theatre together and the hours afterwards we'd spent discussing what we'd seen, highlighting for each other the subtle nuances of a particular performance. Andrew, on the other hand, wasn't interested enough to offer any comments further to his derisory ones at the intermission. He'd spent the second half itching to get to the pub and had remained surly and uncommunicative for the rest of the evening. Bit by bit, his less-than-attractive side was pushing through the super-cool James Bond image he had cultivated. The warm glow I got from being part of a couple was beginning to fade, and was giving way to irritation. If I were to be brutally honest, I had to admit that deep down, I reckoned that while I was with Andrew, Sam might pay me more attention. Like with the frenzied skidding of the glass beneath your finger on the Ouija board, it seemed there was some inner force regulating my actions, and all of its energy was focused in one direction.

IT WAS LUNCHTIME in the staffroom, and that Friday feeling was palpable. I was more or less sorted for the christening on Sunday, and was really looking forward to it. Marie had called in with little Kylie earlier that morning, and we'd all spent our break time exclaiming over her. Even Jennifer, normally quite reserved, totally melted when she snuggled her in her arms. Only Andrew, had remained unimpressed, which didn't go unnoticed by Marie, judging by her colourful comments on him afterwards. I was just finishing up my Pot Noodle while looking over the afternoon class plan when Andrew walked in, his face glowing from playground duty.

'Well, my beauty. Diligent as always, I see.'

'Oh, you know me. Just a last-minute check.'

'Och aye, but you know what they say about all work and no play. So, what are we doing this weekend?'

There it was again. His assumption that I was free whenever he clicked his fingers. And I was still miffed with him over the way he'd behaved with Sam.

'I've got Kylie's christening on Sunday, remember I told you?' I tried to suppress the irritation from my voice.

'So you did, so you did,' he sighed melodramatically. 'But sure this is only Friday. How about going out for an Indian tonight? My treat. I'll pick you up at home. Say about 8.00pm?'

My annoyance had obviously registered with him; his voice was now an odd mix of velvety seduction and little boy whining.

'Ah come on, Beth. You're not going to leave me on my own at the weekend?'

In spite of all my misgivings, the promise of Indian food was tempting after all of the Weight Watchers meals I'd had this week.

'Oh, go on. The Indian it is then. I'll see you at 8.00pm.'

Maybe I should have taken a stand, but hell, a girl has to have some fun. As long as I was fully aware that he was just someone to keep me amused in the short term, I wasn't really in any danger of a broken heart.

AFTER SCHOOL, I drove straight into Ballymartin for the appointment I'd made with the hairdressers. It was part of my new image for the christening. I opted for a cut which left my often lanky shoulder-length hair falling in soft fringy layers to frame my face, and was feeling a million dollars. I just had a couple of things to get in Supervalu before heading home. My mind had whizzed ahead to Sunday afternoon, playing out the scene where I was holding my god-daughter by the baptismal font, as I waltzed through the automatic doors and straight into Sam. This time, we collided physically. He stepped back immediately, clearly trying to put some distance between us, while I struggled to overcome the emotion welling up into my throat. The more cowardly part of me hoped he'd just walk away, when he suddenly took my arm as if to steady me.

'Okay, Beth?'

My heart heaved. I nodded dumbly, conscious only of his concern about me, his hand on my arm, the softness in his eyes. Something skittered around in my chest.

'So, how've you been?'

He wasn't walking away. He'd chosen to stop and talk to me.

'Oh, you know. Pretty much the same old scenario, still living with my folks, still teaching the same curriculum in the same school. Life in Carrigmore hasn't changed a lot since…'

I trailed off, awareness of my blunder seeping in too late. The last thing I wanted was to rake up the past, and the circumstances in which he'd left.

'Oh, I don't know. I see there's been at least one major change at St. Colmcille's.'

There could be no mistaking what he was referring to. I could feel the blush spreading up my neck.

'Oh, Andrew. Yeah, he's just temping for Marie until the summer.'

'Not exactly a supporter of amateur drama, is he?'

The blood rushed into my face. Of course Sam had taken note of Andrew's arrogance the other night. And no doubt the fact that we seemed to be an item. For the first time, I began to feel tainted by my association with Andrew McKay and resentful of having to defend him, but I had to try and come up with some excuse for his behaviour, however lame.

'Oh well, he's from Edinburgh. He's probably used to major productions there. Theatre festivals and all that. Pretty high standards, I suppose.'

'Getting on well in the school, is he?'

There was something about Sam's raised eyebrows that signalled a sinister undertone to the question.

'Oh, fine. It certainly makes a change to have a guy around the place! No more girlie talk in the staffroom.'

My attempt at levity drew a blank. Sam's face darkened, his lips drew together in a thin line.

'Be careful, Beth. There's something about him I — just be careful.'

While I was still trying to process this, he left. He'd sounded concerned. But I was gobsmacked that he was showing some interest in my welfare. I felt a small surge of optimism. I was committed to the Indian tonight, but maybe that was the perfect opportunity to call a halt to whatever was between Andrew and I. Clean break and all that. I had to let Sam know I wasn't otherwise involved. Make it clear to him that if he was interested, and it was still a big 'if', there might still be a chance for us.

CHAPTER TEN

'ELIZABETH! HE'S HERE.'

I was just putting the final touches to my make-up for our Indian night out when the BMW came rolling up the drive. With Mam on sentry duty, Andrew's arrival was well noted. The last thing I wanted was to have him grilled on the doorstep by my ecstatic mother. I scurried downstairs, grabbed my coat, and was out of the house before the Maguire welcoming committee had a chance to ambush him.

As I tumbled down the steps, he was already out of the car and opening the passenger door for me. Soft Italian leather jacket, light beige trousers, and camel-coloured boots. Impeccable as always. This super-cool image of his was starting to grate on my nerves.

'Well, my lovely. Is this a vision that I see before me?'

His arms reached around to help me into the passenger seat. I sank into its cushioned depths, overpowered by the whiff of Blue Stratos. From a state-of-the-art sound system, Barbra Streisand's *When a Man Loves a Woman* filled the car. I could already taste those succulent king prawns in creamy Korma sauce. Mmm. Might as well make the most of what would be our last date. And after that, well who knew what might happen with Sam.

The restaurant was dimly lit by a number of wall sconces, all giving off a soft golden hue. The serviettes folded into the wineglasses picked up the flicker of lighted candles on every table. The sallow-skinned Indian waiter greeted us joyously, as if we were the only customers he'd seen all week. The complimentary poppadoms with their various dips arrived while we were still poring over the menus. A bottle of Cabernet Sauvignon was uncorked with a flourish, approved by Andrew, and poured. We clinked our glasses together, as he loudly proclaimed a toast to happiness.

'More wine, Sir?'

The waiter emptied what remained of the bottle into Andrew's glass.

'We'd better have some more of that.' Andrew signalled to him. I felt I'd had enough, but we were only halfway through our meal. There was a prickle of anxiety nudging its way into a corner of my brain. Andrew might not be familiar with our drink driving laws here. 'Waiter!' He was signalling again, more impatiently this time. 'This wine is corked. We need a replacement bottle.' His tone was abrupt, imperious. I hadn't noticed anything wrong, but the waiter apologised profusely as he took away the bottle and our two glasses. A fresh bottle arrived, the cork pulled, and the two fresh glasses filled.

'You've got to keep these guys on their toes,' he grinned at me. 'Otherwise, they think they can put any kind of crap in front of you.'

I'd eaten here numerous times before, and never had any problems with the food or service, but I didn't want an argument and let it go. Maybe Andrew had a point. After all, we were paying restaurant prices. Everything should be just right.

'So, Miss Maguire,' he pushed a wedge of Naan bread around his plate to scoop up the last of the Lamb Biryani. 'Suppose we round off the evening with a little brandy? I think I noticed a very fine hostelry across the road.'

We'd already polished off two bottles of wine. As far as I was concerned, brandy on top of that would really be pushing our luck. If by any chance we did get stopped, the guards might not be impressed.

'Maybe we should be getting back?'

'It's only 10.30.' He sounded genuinely amazed that I would even contemplate ending the evening at such a time. 'Isn't the night young yet? Come on, Beth. A wee dram of brandy will help with the digestion.'

'Well, maybe just the one. You don't want to end up in the clink for drunk driving, do you?' He looked at me, finally seeming to take in my concerns.

'Tell you what. Just one brandy and we'll be off. How about that?'

Minutes later, we were threading a path through the throngs of revellers in The Jolly Fiddler, a lounge bar recently renovated to cater for the younger crowd. A Thin Lizzie track poured from the surround sound speakers, the volume well above comfort level. The number of 18 to 25-year-olds sporting tanned midriffs and size eight waistlines was making me feel distinctly old and unattractive. Andrew battled his way to the counter and tried to attract the attention of an overworked barman. Having waited the best part of 15 minutes to get served his good humour had given way to a general malevolence towards the 'crowd of wasters here' and he stormed off back to where I was sitting.

'Busy, isn't it?' I tried to head off the silence that was gathering between us.

'Wouldn't you think they'd hire enough staff to cope on a weekend night?' He said looking around in contempt. 'This is no way to run a pub.'

'Ah well, aren't we only staying for one?' My unease had escalated a couple of notches. The situation seemed to be skidding out of control.

'We sure as hell won't be staying in this kip anyway. Come on, we'll check out the hotel.'

It was time to take a stand. 'Andrew, I think we've both had enough, but if you want more drink, it'll have to be closer to home. Don't you have drink driving laws in Scotland?'

'Ah come on, girl, where's your sense of adventure? Just one more for the road. I'll even move on to soft drinks if it'll keep ye happy. Anything for you, my love.'

It was either go with him or find a taxi, a near impossibility at this time on a Friday night. I stood up leaving the heaving pub behind.

By contrast, the lounge of the Longford Arms Hotel was what you might call sedate, a few groups of middle-aged tourists relaxing after their day's excursion and a couple of commercial travellers sitting up at the bar. At least here, we could talk without having to roar at each other to be heard. I asked for a mineral water but he came back with an orange juice for himself and yet another brandy for me.

'Andrew!' I looked at him in dismay. 'I didn't want that. Why didn't you just get me what I asked for?'

He sat down heavily beside me, his breath just bordering on the offensive. 'But sure ye can't be drinking water in a hotel. Aren't we out for the night? You get that into you, girl. It'll do you good.' His mock brogue failed to amuse me. He was too much of a control freak. It was really starting to bug me. Yeah, maybe now was the time to call a halt to this.

'You know something, Andrew. I'm getting a little sick of you not listening to me. Maybe you should find someone who doesn't object to you doing her thinking for her.'

He looked at me astounded, ragged breaths coming heavily. 'Get on with ye! Just because I want ye to have a good time, ye get your knickers in a twist about it.'

My eyes narrowed in fury.

'Oh for Christ's sake! What is it with you and this male dominance thing? Are you so blinded by your own vanity that you think it's acceptable?'

His jaw dropped open. 'What the hell are ye talking about? Is it that time o' the month or something?'

If there was one thing that infuriated me beyond all reason, it was men making assumptions about women's 'time of the month'.

'Want me to spell it out? You and I are finished. It's over. End of story. Now, if you'll excuse me, I need to go and call a taxi.'

'Stay where you are!' His hand clamped over mine as I tried to stand up. 'No woman walks out on me.'

'I beg your pardon?' The words came out through clenched teeth. I extricated my hand from his, aware of several pairs of eyes swivelling in our direction.

'Just what the hell do you think you're doing?' I knew I had the upper hand. He wasn't going to risk a public embarrassment.

'Ah, would you just sit back and enjoy your drink.' His tone carried exasperation mingled with grudging concession. This time, I stood up, unimpeded.

'Like I said, I need to order a taxi.'

His face creased in disbelief as I picked up my bag and went out to reception. He made no attempt to follow me.

'I'm sorry, Madam, but it'll be at least an hour. Friday night, you know. You might do better to join the queue at the taxi rank.'

Outside, the drizzle had thickened to needles of rain blowing almost horizontally across the street. I looked over towards the rank where about 20 couples huddled under umbrellas or hoods. All I had was a light woollen cardigan. While I was deliberating about what to do, the revolving door of the hotel whirred, and out stepped Andrew, his huge form looming like a mountain beside me. There was something about his posture that caught my attention.

The belligerence of a few minutes ago had given way to a hangdog expression.

'Beth, I'm so sorry. I shouldn't have gone on like that. And you're getting drenched out here, you poor mite.'

That was a turn-up for the books.

'No, Andrew, you shouldn't have. What the hell were you thinking? Do you really expect me to put up with that kind of crap from any man?'

'Ah, Beth, come on. You know I didn't mean it. Sure don't you know I'm mad about you? You're all I think about these days. I just wanted you to have a good time.'

He reached out his hand and drew me towards him. The blaze of anger that had swept through me a few minutes earlier was extinguished as, in spite of myself, I responded to his touch.

'Come on, sweetheart. Let me drive you home.'

I tried to do a quick calculation. We'd drunk at least two bottles of wine between us. How risky was it? He read my thoughts.

'Beth, look at all the grub we got through.' His tone sang with earnestness. 'Sure that'll absorb the wine. I'll be grand, so I will. Don't you know what a good driver I am?'

Just then, as if on cue, the rain increased to a downpour. Within seconds, my hair hung in sodden strands and my cardigan was soaked through. He opened his jacket and drew me inside it.

'Let's go, Beth,' he murmured. 'You're shivering. We'll catch our deaths standing out in this.'

I couldn't deny he had a point. Whatever issues between us needed to be addressed could wait. Right now, all I wanted was to get home and dry off. The gentleness of his hand on my back was enough to convince me. We set off at a fast trot to where the car was parked.

Once inside, he pulled out a tartan rug from under the back seat and draped it around my shoulders. We clicked the seatbelts into position, and at the turn of the key, the engine roared into life. Andrew eased the car out into the stream of traffic and back up the main street. The windshield wipers rose and fell, swishing aside the rain that hammered against the windows. Streetlights gave way to the dim outline of hedges as we left the town behind.

'PLEASANT EVENING, WASN'T it?'

I looked at him. There was something different about his tone.

'Well, yes. The dinner was lovely,'

'Hmmm. Pity ye had to go and spoil it all, wasn't it?'

Now my mind was skidding toward anxiety.

'I beg your pardon?'

'Making a scene like that in the hotel. Didn't ye make a holy show of me.'

'*You* were the one who drew attention to us. How dare you try to stop me leaving like that!'

I should have chosen my words more carefully, but the outrage was shooting up through me, carrying the words out of my mouth.

'You won't be leaving so easily the next time, my girl. Like I said, no-one walks out on Andrew McKay.'

His words hit me like rocks, splintering whatever shreds of expectation I had that this was a normal situation; my boyfriend giving me a lift home. I froze with fear. How on earth was I going to get out of this?

The moments stretched on wordlessly until we approached the side road that led to my house, but he accelerated and kept going straight.

'Andrew, you've missed the turn.' My voice tightened as my fear spiralled towards panic.

'Dear, oh dear. So I have.' His voice had an edge to it I'd never heard before. The undertone contained shards of ice. 'Well, let's just see where this road takes us, shall we?'

'It takes us to the canal line, as you know damn well. Didn't I make it clear I wanted to go home?'

'Ah, home, yes, indeed.' His tone dipped. 'Yes, what we need is to go home for a wee nightcap, just to round off a perfect evening, don't you think?'

'Some other time, Andrew. I've had enough for one night.'

'What's wrong with you, girl? Afraid of having a bit of fun, are ye? Just wait till you taste the Glenfiddich I have stashed away. Only the best for you, my dear!'

The sour fumes of alcohol grew stronger. Revulsion took hold of me. As the BMW swerved into the driveway of the lock-keeper's cottage, the glare of its headlights invading the yard, pulses of terror began to throb in my head. Against the silence of the night, I could hear the rhythmic ticking of the engine as it shut down.

'Do come in, my dear. Welcome to my humble abode.'

He was over at my door, opening it with a flourish, his lips curved in a thin smile. He stretched out a hand and, in one swift movement, swung me out of the car. Exaggerating a drunken lurch with me in tow, he weaved his way across the yard, and fumbled with the key in the lock. Now paralysed with dread, I forced myself to sound calm.

'Andrew, I don't want to stay here.' I pulled my mobile from my bag. 'I'll ring for a taxi.'

'You don't want to stay here?' His mincing tones ridiculed

me. 'You've wanted nothing else since you first met me.' A loud belch interrupted his flow. 'You're gagging for it!'

I froze. Still gripping my arm, he pushed the door open and snapped on the hall light. He stumbled on into an icy sitting room with only the cold ashes of a turf fire left in the grate. In a desperate effort to keep a lid on the hysteria rising into my throat, I decided my best option was to play along for now. Okay, so he was angry with me, but surely he wouldn't hurt me. Not after the good times we'd had together. After the amount he'd had to drink, it couldn't be long before he passed out.

'Okay, we'll have a coffee. I'll put the kettle on.'

I left him prodding uselessly at the remains of the fire and went to find the kitchen. This was one of the cottages that had been built for lock-keepers when the canal first opened up, and although it had been extended and renovated, its rooms were still dark and poky. The shabbiness of the L-shaped kitchen was exposed under the glare of a naked light bulb. It boasted a Belfast sink, a once-white fridge, a small gas cooker layered with grease, and a few chipboard cupboards at eye level. The centre was taken up by a heavy wooden table, whose legs had been well nibbled by the various dogs kept by lock-keepers through the years. It was laden with dinner plates encrusted with stale food, bits of bacon rind, scribbles of egg yolk, and a few leftover chips that he hadn't even bothered to scrape off. On the floor in the corner were a dozen or so empty bottles, mostly whiskey. Five or six mugs ringed with coffee stains occupied the huge sink. Hardened mouse droppings adorned the draining board. This was the kind of squalor you might expect from an elderly bachelor living alone. So much for the flash car and the super-suave James Bond image he presented to the world. No wonder he'd never invited me here before.

After some rooting around, I managed to find a half-empty jar of Nescafe in one of the presses, its granules hardened and sticky. I plugged in the kettle and located a carton of milk in the tiny fridge.

'Ah, you've made yourself at home, I see.'

His frame filled most of the doorway as he stood, leaning one arm against the jamb, a bottle of Glenfiddich in hand. I tried to ignore the sarcasm of his tone.

'Yeah, I felt like a coffee. Want some?'

'Not quite my cup of tea, darling.' He snorted with laughter at his feeble wit, and waved the bottle of whiskey. 'This is my preferred beverage, as you might have noticed.'

He raised the bottle to his lips and tilted back his head. The liquid trickled down his throat. 'Aye, that's the stuff to put hairs on your chest. Sure you won't join me?'

'Thanks, but I'll just have a quick coffee and then I'll be off.'

'Off!' He let his gaze travel around the room for comic effect. 'Off where exactly? I can't drive you home. I'm "over the limit", remember?' My own words came hurtling back at me. 'The only place you're going, my dear, is the bedroom. And it's this way.'

He reached out for me and pulled, jerking me off balance. I lunged forward, straight into his arms.

'You see? You can't stop falling for me!'

His coarse laugh exploded around the kitchen while I struggled uselessly in the grip of iron that imprisoned me, a noose of fear squeezing me tighter and tighter. He kept one hand on the back of my neck while the other was travelling down, moving inside my thighs, forcing my legs apart. When I went to grab his wrist, he batted my hand away as if it was a fly, and then, for good measure, hit me a stinging blow across the cheek that left me stunned. He found the zip of my jeans, yanked, and slid his hand in roughly, clawing at me, the huge fingers probing violently. I felt a searing pain as he jabbed upwards. By now, my legs had buckled. Only those massive fingers thrusting into me, tearing mercilessly at the sensitive membrane, were holding me up. I was paralysed, lost in a fog of pain and terror.

He withdrew his hand and fumbled at his own zip, pulling it down over the bulge of his penis. With one wrench, he had my jeans down around my knees. My animal instinct kicked in at that point. I jerked my knee up in an effort to inflict whatever damage I could where it would hurt most. But he'd anticipated that and side-stepped neatly.

'Think you can get the better of me, you bitch?' His spittle landed on my lips, making me gag.

'Get on that floor. And get those fucking jeans off you. Now!' he roared.

'No.' My voice came out in a whimper.

With a deft trip, he had me sprawling on the rough tiles and had yanked the jeans over my ankles.

'No, An-drew, please, not this,' my voice quavered. In desperation, I resorted to pleading, each syllable jerking from lips as my muddled brain grasped for any tactic that might work.

In response, he plunged down on top of me, pinning me under his weight. I screamed and clawed at him. I reached for his throat with my nails, but he pinned my wrists over my head. With his other hand, he spread my legs and rammed his fully erect penis into the fragile entrance that tore like a moth's wing. There was no way back now. Stabbing pain roared through me, intensifying with each new thrust. Tears streamed down my face as I bore the pain. Worse was the humiliation of what was being inflicted on me. I was nothing. He had all the power and could do whatever he wanted to me. And I would just have to endure.

Eventually, his breathing quickened and worked its way up to a series of short gasps. A final thrust and the pumping came to an end. The now limp penis slid out, and with a grunt, the monster rolled off me. I lay there without moving a muscle, utterly broken. I was afraid to hope that the alcohol was finally taking effect and that I was free to go. He had slumped over, away from me. I heard the low drone of a first snore rise from his throat. As soon as it took on a rhythm, I rolled to one side and gingerly levered myself into a standing position, pulling my jeans back up over my hips. With one last glance to check that he wasn't watching through half-closed eyes, I limped slowly out of the kitchen, grabbed my bag from the hallway, and stumbled out into the yard. For the love of God, let Laurie answer, I prayed as I hit the speed-dial on my mobile.

No answer. I hit the number again. This time her voice mumbled a sleepy hello.

'Laurie!' I cried.

She picked up on the distraught tone immediately.

'Jesus Christ, Beth! What's happened?'

'Can you come and get me? Andrew's place. Right now.' My voice croaked with terror.

'I'm on my way. Sit tight.'

The line went dead. I staggered off down the narrow lane towards the village, shaking and sobbing, no longer able to contain the grief that was spilling out of me.

CHAPTER ELEVEN

TEN MINUTES LATER, the glare of headlights strobed through the darkness. Terrified that he might still come after me, I'd kept moving blindly on down the road trying to get as far away as I could from the cottage. Please God let that be her. Relief roared through me as the car came to a stop and Laurie jumped out.

'Beth?'

Folded in her embrace, my whole body began to shake again with uncontrollable sobs. Laurie bundled me into the passenger seat as, incoherent with grief and shock, I tried to convey the enormity of what had taken place. The ragged words that came tumbling out between sobs were enough to paint the picture. She quickly took charge of the situation.

'Listen pet, I think you should come back with me. You can't go home in that state. And we need to work out what you're going to do.'

'Do?' I repeated dumbly.

'If you're going to report it. You've been raped. The bastard could go to jail!'

The truth of her words smashed through me. Yes, I'd been raped. Yes, it was a criminal offence. Of course I should report it. But I'd been dating him for months. As far as everyone in Carrigmore was concerned, we were an item. And he was Mr Popular everywhere he went. I didn't know if anyone would believe me. Tears trickled down my cheeks, splashing onto the collar of my blouse as I tried to grasp the enormity of my situation. Her arm tightened around my shoulders.

'Right, Beth. We're going back to my place.'

'But what about the kids?' I blubbered.

'They're with their Dad this weekend. We have the house to ourselves. Okay?'

I nodded shakily. She was right. I was in no condition to go home.

Back in Laurie's kitchen, I sat cradling a mug of over-sweetened tea, staring into its swirling depths. My whole body was trembling in reaction, my mind a fog of pain and humiliation. I could feel the dampness and stickiness on my inner thighs, and the coarseness of my jeans rubbing roughly against them. I was suddenly desperate to wash his filth off of me.

'Laurie?' My voice came out in a whisper, hoarse and ragged, 'Could you run a bath for me?'

'Beth, love, I really think we should get you seen to before you wash. You've got to keep your options open. You can decide later if you want to press charges. But right now, I think we should phone the police.'

I stared at her numbly.

'They'll know what to do, where to bring you. You need medical attention. You know, just to be checked over. But that has to be done now, pet, before you clean yourself up. In case you do want to proceed.'

'I can't phone the police,' I whimpered. 'It was all my fault. I've been dating him, for God's sake. I got into the car with him.'

'Beth, listen to me. You didn't consent, at any stage. He forced himself on you. He raped you. Get it out of your head that it's your fault. It doesn't matter how well you knew him, or how long you'd been dating. HE RAPED YOU,' she emphasized, though not unkindly.

I could now taste the salty tears rolling onto my lips and

dripping off my chin.

'I'll tell you what, pet. Let me ring the Rape Crisis Centre. They'll be able to advise you on what to do.'

'Uh, okay,' I hiccoughed. 'But no police.'

She poured me another cup of tea and went out to the phone in the hall. I felt like a small child, waiting for others to make decisions for me. Right now, I was incapable of thinking for myself. I stared at the wall, my mind as blank as its painted surface.

'Okay, Beth,' Laurie was back sitting opposite me. She took both my hands in hers. 'You've got three options. One: you do nothing, in which case this could go on haunting you for the rest of your life. Two: you ring the guards, who will then bring you into the Sexual Assault Treatment Unit in Mullingar to get you checked over and gather the necessary evidence. Three: I can bring you in myself and you can decide there whether to involve the guards.'

Hospital, I thought miserably. Surely I'd been through enough without doctors poking and prodding at me. A fresh spate of tears rolled down my cheeks. All she could do was hold me while I abandoned myself to the grief that had invaded my world.

The decision I had to make seemed too large to fully comprehend. Was I going to report it or not? All of the courtroom dramas I'd seen on television where the rape victim finds herself to be the one on trial came flooding into my head. In all of them, the whole sexual history of the woman had been probed and distorted so that the rapist was made to look like the innocent party. Could I really face that? Was it worth it on the off-chance that he'd go down? I looked at Laurie helplessly.

'Listen, honey, suppose I bring you to Mullingar. You

don't have to make any decisions yet. One step at a time. But you really do need medical attention.'

She could see I was wavering. 'Come on, love. You can do this. We'll be back here in no time and you can have that bath. I'd better ring your mother and let her know you're staying here tonight.'

Oh, Lord, I must have been so traumatised that it hadn't even occurred to me Mother would be expecting me back. How on earth was I going to tell them at home? In a flash, Laurie read my thoughts.

'Don't worry. I'll just say we met up in town and ended up back here. Telling them, if you choose to, will be for another day.'

Minutes later, she was back in the kitchen. She picked up my jacket and held it out to me. I moved slowly towards her and she manoeuvred my arms into it. While I was desperate to wash all traces of him off me, I could see her point. If I didn't do this now, I was going to regret it later. Without a medical examination, there'd be no evidence if I did want to proceed. And, somewhere at the back of all my grief was a flickering anger. That bastard was going to pay for what he'd done to me. Laurie ran upstairs and came back with a tracksuit of hers and some clean underwear which she rammed into a small hold-all. She ushered me out through the door, helped me into the car and we were on our way.

AFTER AN INTERMINABLE wait and endless cups of sweet tea, at 3.55am, I was finally shown into the examination room. It was a functional, white, bare room with a hospital bed, a desk, a couple of chairs, and a hand basin. A nurse with a soft Donegal accent and prominent teeth followed me in.

'Beth, I'm Moya McDonnell and I'll be with you for the

examination.' She took my hand and gave it a sympathetic squeeze. 'I'm sorry you had to wait so long. We've had three victims in already tonight.'

Dear God! So the horror that had happened to me had been happening to other women as well. The shock must have registered in my face.

'Oh that's fairly average for a Friday night, I'm afraid. Okay, Beth. You haven't changed any of your clothes, right?'

'No.'

'Nor had a shower?'

I shook my head dumbly.

'Good girl. Now, I need you to take everything off and put your underwear into this bag, and your outer clothing into that one. Then slip this on.'

She produced two sealed plastic bags and a hospital gown.

'The doctor will be with you in a minute. She'll examine you and talk to you about your options. And try not to worry, pet. You're safe now. I'll just leave you to get undressed but I'm right outside if you need me.'

From there on, normal time slowed down. Even taking off my clothes was an ordeal, my fingers fumbling through the most everyday actions as if I was an old woman with arthritis. I put on the hospital gown with the straps that criss-crossed at the back, which left me feeling naked and vulnerable, and sat on the bed. A few minutes later, there was a knock on the door and Moya came back in with a young woman in surgical greens.

'Hello, Beth, I'm Alison Johnston, the doctor on call here.' Her voice was brisk but with a hint of kindness. 'I'll make it as easy as I can for you, but there's one thing I need to say before we start. I really would advise reporting the rape. You can decide later if you want to proceed, but for the forensic evidence to be admissible, we need to notify the guards now.'

By then I felt so weary and powerless it didn't seem to matter anymore. I was ready to give in to whatever they wanted. And if this was just another part of the formalities, then so be it. I nodded.

'Good girl. We can have them here in just a few minutes and then we can go ahead.'

She disappeared and Moya sat down beside me, making approving noises.

After what seemed like hours, Alison arrived back with a uniformed female Garda.

'Beth, this is Sergeant Cathy Quinn. She'll have a chat with you later, when you've had a chance to clean up.'

'Hi, Beth.' Another gentle voice and sympathetic smile. If there was such a thing as a 'tea and sympathy' barometer, it would be off the Richter scale by now. 'I know you're not ready to make any decisions yet, but this is just to keep your options open. Try not to worry. I'll see you whenever you're ready.'

Where had I heard that before? The most horrible thing in my life had just happened and people were telling me not to worry.

'Okay, pet.' Dr Johnston was stretching surgical gloves over her long fingers. 'Can you just lie back for me and bring your knees up. Now, let them fall apart.'

And the dreaded examination was under way. I closed my eyes in an effort to block out what was happening but the further humiliation of having to lie there with my legs open while swabs were taken was almost beyond endurance. And there was more. Once that part was finished, we were on to what precautions were necessary in terms of future consequences. The morning after pill. Blood tests which would have to be screened for STIs, including AIDS. That was something else for me to worry about, as I'd be waiting three months for the test results. God only knew what the bastard could have given me.

Eventually, I heard the words I thought would never come.

'Right, Beth. We're all done here. I'm sure you'd like to have a shower.'

Would I what! Moya gave me the clean stuff Laurie had packed for me and showed me into a bathroom complete with a pile of fresh towels, shower gel, shampoo, the lot. And gallons of hot water. The feeling of it sluicing down over me, caressing my skin, carrying with it all the filth that monster had left on me was one of the most welcome sensations I've ever known. I worked the shampoo into a creamy lather and massaged it into my scalp until I got that squeaky clean sensation they somehow manage to capture on TV. When I eventually stepped out, I felt all crinkled and soft. I towelled off, covered every centimetre of skin in layers of Johnson's Baby Powder, and put on the clothes Laurie had brought for me. Moya was outside waiting to take me through to some kind of office where Sergeant Quinn wanted to talk to me.

'Okay, Beth, I know you've been through a lot tonight.' There was genuine sympathy in her eyes. 'We'll keep this very informal. I just want you to tell me whatever you can for now. Any details that come to mind. Then we can arrange for you to come down to the station this afternoon to make a statement.'

I went through a general outline of the date that had gone horribly wrong, my ill-timed decision to dump him, the problems trying to get a taxi, and my reluctant acceptance of a lift back from him. And how, from then on, he was in control. And I was helpless. The tears began to roll down my cheeks again.

'Okay, Beth. That's enough for me to go on for now.' She scribbled something and tore the page out of her notebook. 'You should go home and get some sleep. Here's the number to ring if you decide to come in and make a statement later on. I'll just tell the doctor we're finished.'

It was over. Dr Johnston came back in with a list of numbers to call if I wanted to avail of counselling. And after she'd signed my release note, Laurie was finally allowed in.

'Okay, honey?' She reached out for me with another hug. Again, I collapsed into her arms, a torrent of distress flowing through me. We drove back to her place in silence, each caught up in our own version of the horror that had rolled into my life, dragging me into the lurid territory of nightmare.

Once back in the kitchen, she filled the kettle and took two glasses from the cupboard.

'I think a hot whiskey is in order. You must be in bits. This might help to relax you.' She set about slicing a lemon and ramming the cloves into the thick-cut wedges. She half-filled the glasses with boiling water and topped them up with huge measures of Jameson.

'Now, you get that into you and I'll just go and make up the bed.'

Left alone, I huddled up close to the range, sipping the whiskey, suddenly feeling cold from shock. The amber liquid burned its way down my throat, sending a wave of heat right through to my stomach. By now, my mind was swinging back and forth like a pendulum. Should I make a statement or not? Even if I claimed date rape, there would be no evidence of him drugging me, nothing that would fit the pattern. On the other hand, there must be witnesses who overheard the row we had in the hotel when I told him it was over, and who could testify to his behaviour at the time. But at this stage, I was too exhausted to think it out clearly. I could feel my eyelids beginning to droop. I'd leave it till later to decide.

'Feeling any better?' Laurie was back, sitting opposite me, sipping her whiskey.

'Just a bit knackered.' I smiled weakly. 'It's been a hell of a night.'

'Come on, pet. You finish that off and we'll get you into bed.'

She brought me down to Anna's bedroom, all Barbie Doll pinks and blues, with a row of teddies sitting along one wall, and dropped a spare nightie on the bed for me.

'Okay, anything you need, just call me. I'm right next door. Or if you can't sleep and just want to talk, give me a shout.'

'Oh, Laurie,' I hugged her like I'd never let go. 'Thanks for everything.' My eyes were glistening with tears once more.

'You're going to get through this, Beth, love.' She held me at arm's length. 'Whatever way you decide to tackle it, you're not going to let that bastard win. Just hold on to that.'

Then she was gone and I slid in under the duvet, hugging my knees up to my chest. My eyelids felt like they were weighted with concrete. Just then, a glint of silver caught my eye. There opposite me, on a dresser against the wall, was a ballerina doll in a glistening white tutu, legs pulled tight into a pirouette, arms in a graceful curve over her head. Probably little Anna's dream of the future. My heart lurched in terror at the thought of what could lie in store for her if life didn't go according to plan. The horrors that lurked under the surface when she moved into the world of boyfriends and dating. I prayed that she'd show better judgement when it came to men than I had.

CHAPTER TWELVE

IT WAS PROBABLY the combination of trauma, lack of sleep, and whiskey, but I completely conked out. The next thing I was aware of was the thundering of a tractor passing the window. In spite of the thick velvet curtains, streaks of broad daylight poured into the room. Anna's pink room. In Laurie's house. For a few seconds, I was baffled. Then the dreadfulness of the past 24 hours rushed in on me, dragging me back into the darkest place on earth. I peered groggily at my watch. Just after 1.30pm. Oh Christ, my mother would be up the walls. I eased myself up, conscious that any sudden movements were likely to hurt. I could hear sounds of normal life drifting up from the kitchen. I pulled on the same tracksuit Laurie had lent me last night, and made my way to the bathroom. When I emerged, she was standing outside.

'How are you, pet?'

'Uh, a bit wobbly, I suppose, but better than I was.'

'I'm glad you got a bit of sleep. That's the body's way of repairing itself after trauma. I've just put the kettle on. Come on and we'll have a late breakfast.'

'Just a cup of tea would be lovely.'

I followed her into kitchen where the smell of freshly baked soda bread convinced me that maybe I could manage something. Just a little. She cut a couple of thick slices and set them on the table with a tub of Kerrygold and a pot of raspberry jam.

'I rang your mother and told her we were making a day of it with a shopping trip. So there's no hurry back.'

I smiled gratefully at her. But the knowledge of what I had

to do this afternoon weighed heavily on me. I smeared some jam onto a piece of soda bread and took a bite. The events of last night replayed in my head over and over. The evening had started to go wrong when he ordered that second bottle of wine in the restaurant, and from there on had slid further and further downhill. My unqualified stupidity in accepting a lift from him under the circumstances. What kind of an idiot was I to fall for his palaver about being sorry, and being crazy about me, and all that guff. I should have copped on that was just to get me into his car. It was all my fault. A six-year-old child would have been more discerning.

'Beth?' Laurie's gentleness broke in on my recriminations, obviously reading my thoughts. I looked wildly at her.

'I've been such a fool. I got nothing more than I deserved.'

'Beth! Don't ever say that again. Nothing you did could be construed as you consenting to have sex with him. I'll say it again. He raped you. You have nothing to feel guilty about. So get that out of your head. You did NOTHING WRONG.'

Her passionate tone carried with it a weight of conviction that hovered in front of me and then began to settle in the outer layers of my consciousness. What if she was right? What if it really had been down to what he wanted, and had nothing to do with me? What he'd wanted was power and control. He'd wanted to humiliate me in the most obscene way. And had succeeded. I'd told him it was over between us and he wanted revenge. Nothing I did could halt the storm of anger that rolled through him and erupted in such viciousness. It was only in the hospital when they took swabs from under my fingernails for forensic evidence that I'd realised in my panic I'd fought back, clawing at him like a wildcat. Now, for the first time, fury was beginning to bubble up in my throat, like a saucepan of milk boiling over. This guy deserved everything the courts could throw at him. It was in my power to put him through hell, just like he'd done to me. I could make damn sure he'd never do it to any other woman.

'Right, Laurie. I'll ring the station and get this over with.'

'That's my girl!' She beamed at me. 'There's far too many bastards out there getting away it. We'll make sure this one pays the price.'

An hour later, we were sitting in the waiting room of the station. It was a sparsely furnished room with benches along three of the mustard-coloured walls. Peeling paintwork and a naked light bulb emphasised the dinginess of the place. The only other occupant was a lean woman with straggly hair and a worn out face, staring straight ahead of her. She looked like whatever energy had once animated her features had long ago been leached away.

'Miss Maguire?'

A ruddy-faced Garda stood at the door, looking enquiringly around the room. Laurie gave my hand a squeeze and I was on my way to the interview room. Another depressing rectangular space painted the same mustard yellow with little bubbles lifting off the surface. A square table in the centre with four plastic chairs around it. I sat down to wait for Sergeant Quinn.

'Right, Miss Maguire,' the Garda who'd brought me in seated himself opposite me. 'I'm Garda Michael Doyle and I'll be taking the statement. We just need Sergeant Evans here before we start.'

'Sergeant Evans?' The alarm must have registered in my

tone. 'It was a Sergeant Cathy Quinn I spoke to last night.'

'Ah, yes. I'm afraid Sergeant Quinn is off duty now.'

Now I was going to have to go over everything all over again. My determination to go through with it began to ebb. The door swung open and a tall, rangy man with sharp, angular features entered the room, notebook in hand.

'Miss Maguire, this is Sergeant Evans.'

I couldn't believe it. Not only was it not Cathy Quinn, it wasn't even a female Garda. They'd sent a man in to take my statement. A man who extended a limp hand and sat down with barely a glance at me. This was turning into a nightmare scenario.

'Now, Miss Maguire, you've come to report an incident that occurred on the night of April 24. Could you please tell us in your own words what led up to the situation.'

The sergeant looked at me without animation, pen poised over his notebook. My unease morphed into anxiety. While for me, this was a trauma that had upended my life, it was merely a matter of routine for him, all part of the day's work. I fiddled nervously with the strap of my wristwatch.

'Well, Andrew and I had been dating for a couple of months.'

'Ah, so he was your boyfriend?'

The word hung in the air between us. Unable to meet his eyes, I looked down. His hand, absurdly big for clerical work, splayed across the desk. Veins standing out. Fingers stretching like tentacles. Pushing towards me. Like *his*. Invading me.

'Miss Maguire?'

I looked at him blankly.

'Was Mr McKay your boyfriend?'

The interview room swung back into focus. 'Well, sort

of...' I repeated lamely.

'Could you be more specific?' The eyebrows arched quizzically.

'Well, we went out several times.' I groped helplessly for the words to describe what exactly it was that Andrew and I had together. 'But I was never sure if he saw me as his girlfriend. I mean...' I stumbled on. 'There were times it didn't seem like we were a couple.'

His sigh of exasperation was audible.

'I'm afraid we need to stick to the facts here, Miss Maguire, not what it seemed like.'

What could I tell him except what it seemed like to me?

'Perhaps you could just answer my questions.' He looked down at his notebook again. 'Did you have sexual relations with him before the night in question?'

This was an obvious assumption, so I felt almost embarrassed admitting I hadn't, and tried to convey that our 'relationship' had been floundering for a while.

'You see, I wanted to finish things between us. I told him last night it was over.'

'And?'

'He, he didn't take it very well. He became quite hostile in fact.'

Hostile; suddenly that seemed so inadequate to describe Andrew's reaction.

'Can you talk us through the events of last evening, Miss Maguire?'

I stammered my way through the meal at the Indian, and the follow-up drinks at The Jolly Fiddler and then the Longford Arms. How he'd reacted when I told him it was over. And just then, it all became real again, the fear that had gripped me as his words came hurtling towards me.

Stay where you are! His hand clamped over mine as I tried

to stand up. *No woman walks out on me.*

Once again, it took a few seconds for my present surroundings to reassert themselves.

'Did you have anything to drink, Miss Maguire?'

I stared at him.

'Well, yes. A couple of glasses of wine with the meal. And then a brandy.'

'I see.'

Disapproval seeped across the table as the pen scratched heavily in the blue-lined notebook.

'And would you say that might have affected your behaviour that night?'

'How do you mean?'

'You are aware, Miss Maguire, that alcohol impairs your ability to make decisions?'

Bastard. Now he was making out it was all my fault.

'I wasn't drunk, if that's what you mean.'

The eyebrows lifted again.

'We're not accusing you of anything, Miss Maguire. But you've made a serious allegation, and in order to proceed with the case, we have to establish its veracity. I'm sure you understand.'

Tension crackled between us. Nodding to his colleague, the sergeant put his elbows on the table and steepled his fingers under his nose.

'Now Miss Maguire, perhaps we could go on to what happened when you left the hotel.'

In my head, the scene lit up again in lurid detail. The lengthy queue for taxis, the driving rain. And the revolving door of the hotel whirring, to reveal Andrew. *Come on, sweetheart. Let me drive you home.*

With Andrew's voice ringing in my ears, I stumbled through the explanation of why I'd accepted his offer.

'So, even though you'd walked out on him and you knew he was angry, you still got into a car with him?'

It was at this point that I saw how it was going to be. I wouldn't stand a chance. So what was I putting myself through hell for? Even if the DPP decided to prosecute and we did get to court, his solicitor would tear me to shreds. My name would be tossed around Carrigmore, the one who tried to bring down a good man, the hussy who couldn't wait to get her hands on the Scot and then cried rape. A bubble of dread filled my chest No. No. No. Maybe his next victim would be brave enough to take on the system, but not me. I stood up shakily, feeling like I'd just swum through a shark-infested sea, each one of the snapping monsters reaching out to gorge themselves on my bloodied carcass.

'I won't be going ahead with the charge, Sergeant. I'm sorry to have wasted your time.'

He glanced over at his colleague and then looked at me with sympathy for the first time.

'I *am* sorry for what happened to you, Elizabeth. It's just that we have to deal with facts here, and to be honest, I don't think you would have a very strong case.'

Somewhere deep inside me, I had to acknowledge that he was probably right. Deep down, I'd known all along I'd never be able to see it through. I stumbled out of the interview room, back out to where Laurie was waiting, feeling like I had just escaped from a giant spider's web, its gluey substance still clinging to my skin.

Back in the safety of Laurie's kitchen, cradling yet another cup of tea, the impact of what I'd done was beginning to sink in. After all I'd gone through last night in the hospital, I was just going to walk away from the situation. The mix of frustration and self-pity spilled over into fresh tears, and

I blinked hard in an effort to regain control. Laurie put a hand on my arm.

'It's okay, honey. You cry all you want.'

'Oh Christ, Laurie, I feel like such a coward.'

'Come on, pet. Don't even begin to think like that. You have to do whatever is best for you, whatever feels right.' She went on. 'It might have made things a lot worse, all things considered. In a situation like this, going public might involve too many risks. For you, I mean. And then suppose in the end, he still gets off?'

I nodded dumbly. Laurie always knew the right thing to say. When I was at my lowest ebb, she found a way to nudge me back towards self belief.

'And I know involving the Guards last night wasn't easy, but at least it gave you some thinking space,' she continued. 'I think you needed that, just to be sure what you wanted to do.'

She was right, of course. And if Andrew did get nasty, I still had the option of going back to them. They had the evidence they needed.

'You know, pet, maybe you should think about seeing a counsellor. At least short term. It might help you over the next few weeks.'

'Mmm. We'll see,' I muttered. Right now, I was trying to work out how to get through the immediate future. The week ahead was going to be horrendous. And the most immediate concern was the christening tomorrow. At least the swelling had gone down on my cheek. How in the name of God was I going to handle it? I'd have to stand up there on the altar with the whole of Carrigmore looking on. And maybe Andrew down there smirking at me. No, I couldn't do it. I'd have to explain to Marie. I'd have to tell her the awful thing that happened to me. She'd understand. Of course she would.

But how would she manage to cover up for my absence? If the godmother of the child didn't show up, everyone in Carrigmore would know something was very wrong. The dilemma pressed in on me. I could do this for Marie. For Kylie. Dear little Kylie.

'Laurie, I've been thinking.'

'Yeah?' Her tone was carefully measured, giving me space.

'This christening tomorrow.'

'Mmm. I was wondering about that. But you'll be okay, won't you?'

The look in her eye was unwavering.

'I'll be okay.'

She beamed.

'You'll be grand. All you have to do is look pretty and smile. It'll be a breeze. I'd better drive you home, before your mother thinks you've been abducted by aliens.' She gave my hand a squeeze. 'It'll all seem a whole lot different tomorrow, you'll see.'

'I don't suppose things can get any worse,' I stated flatly. As the images of last night came crashing back, another wave of self-pity swept over me. 'Oh Christ, Laurie, I've really messed up this time.'

'*He's* messed up, honey. Not you. And that bastard is going to find out just how badly he's messed up. He'll be sorry he ever heard of Carrigmore before we're finished with him,' she said, a determined glint in her eye.

I nodded grimly, wondering if we could launch a campaign for the mandatory castration of rapists.

CHAPTER THIRTEEN

10.00AM THE NEXT morning and I was soaking in another bath at home. The need to wash every trace of him from me was overpowering. Submerged in the scented water, I cautiously felt for bruising. Most of it was around my inner thighs where he had forced my legs apart, with some discolouring now becoming visible on my wrists where he'd held them in a savage grip. But nothing that couldn't be disguised with quick tanning lotion. I had an almighty headache from banging my head off the wall when he spun me around, and my cheek was tender, but that didn't show. In fact, in the outfit I'd chosen, there would be no visible sign of the assault. If I could just hold it together for a few hours, it wouldn't matter if I caved in later on. Surely I could manage that much. I could at least give it a damn good try.

When Laurie had dropped me home yesterday, I'd managed to fob off my mother's enquiries with a flimsy excuse about meeting up with friends in Longford and staying on for a house party. I couldn't possibly tell her and Dad. They'd freak out. Maybe at some stage, I'd give them a watered down version of the event, but right now it was out of the question. I was still too much in shock to be able to talk about it.

I'd had an awful night, weaving in and out of a groggy sleep shot through with grotesque images of being pursued by foul smelling, scaly creatures, their hot breath on my neck. When I eventually surfaced from the nightmare, my eyelashes sticky with dried tears, the reality of what had happened came rolling back over me yet again. Being pinned to the floor under his weight, his hot, rancid breath all around me, pain splintering up through me. I would regret my decision to get into his car for the rest of my life.

'THERE YOU ARE, pet. Obviously made a weekend of it, eh?'

Good old Dad. Never one to make a fuss, he just assumed I'd had a blast with Laurie over the last two days. I managed a weak smile.

'Yeah, might have overdone things a bit. One beer too many.'

He nodded sympathetically. This was a situation he was well used to himself.

'Thought you were looking a bit off colour all right. Have something to eat and then go back to bed for an hour or two. Sure the christening's not till 3.00pm. You'll be grand by then.'

He turned his attention to the bacon and mushrooms sizzling on the pan and positioned the egg to crack open while my eyes glittered with tears at his kindness.

'There's tea in the pot, love. How about a nice fried egg with your toast? Good cure for a hangover.'

I opted for the path of least resistance and sat down to a mug of tea and a plate heaped with toast slathered in butter with two runny eggs.

By 2.00pm that afternoon, any part of me that showed was golden skinned from the tanning lotion. I slipped the sea-green dress with its soft folds over my head and stood in front of the mirror. Marie had been right. It transformed me. The full skirt swished around as I turned. The high heeled strappy sandals and waterfall style blazer I'd chosen to go with it added that special touch of glamour I needed. I was just re-doing my mascara, having smudged it all over my eyes, when the doorbell rang. Panic raced through me.

Suppose it was him. How could I face him? What the hell did he think he was doing coming to my house? Then I heard Laurie's voice on the stairs. Of course. She'd said she'd come and collect me. I erased the irrational thoughts and wiped my suddenly sweaty palms on a discarded jumper. The panic gave way to a feeling of safeness. Laurie would be with me. I'd be surrounded by my friends. I'd get through it. I took a deep breath and descended.

'You look amazing! Turn around.'

I did a little pirouette, showing off the way the full skirt swished into velvety folds, caressing my newly tanned legs.

'You're going to knock 'em all dead. Now, let's do something with your hair.'

I was going to leave my shoulder-length hair as it was, but Laurie scooped it up into a kind of French chignon that looked really elegant. We got the mascara sorted out, applied a shiny lip gloss, and lo and behold, I was transformed and ready to go.

'Okay, hon. I think we're all set. Let's hit the road.'

I shrugged the blazer on and followed Laurie out into the world.

Small knots of well-wishers had begun to gather outside the church when we arrived. It was a bright, windy day and pink cherry blossom was blowing all around the grounds. Inside, sunlight flooded in through the stained glass windows, catching dust motes in its beams. As we moved through the crowd in the porch, a wave of panic crashed over me, sending a scarlet tinge creeping from my neck upwards. Suppose Andrew had already spread the word? Boasted of his sexual prowess. I had a gut feeling he wouldn't want this out in the open. But I didn't know for sure. It was this uncertainty that panicked me. Sensing my hesitation, Laurie nudged me forward and, before I could do anything about it, we were on our way to our seats. An all-consuming sense of exposure came over me, a paranoia that everyone's eyes were scrutinizing my appearance, looking out for any sign of weakness. Would they see the wobble in my step? Hear the falter in my voice? Notice the less-than-confident demeanour? Only Laurie's hand at my elbow kept me from turning on my heel and really giving them something to talk about. She gave my arm an encouraging squeeze and guided me into our pew.

Marie and Sean hadn't arrived yet, but both sets of grandparents and other family members were already in position in the two front rows. The church clerk was busying himself with lighting candles and setting out the baptismal paraphernalia on the altar. The thrum of expectancy hung in the air, with everyone looking round each time footsteps were heard on the aisle. I froze again. What if he showed up? He knew the christening was on. He knew I'd be here. I just couldn't handle that. Laurie gave my arm another squeeze. I smiled back weakly. The next set of footsteps were definitely those of a woman. Jennifer Muldowney, looking very much the lady of the manor in a beige tweed costume and stylish court shoes. She spotted us, smiled, and slid into a pew a couple of rows behind us. The church began to fill up as those who had gathered outside made their way to their seats.

There was another flurry of activity in the porch and the hush of expectation moved up a gear. Sean's brother, Michael, who was taking on the role of godfather, had arrived. Standing at six foot four with the massive shoulders of a rugby player, he cut an imposing figure in his suit. He took his place beside me, gesturing that the main act was on its way.

Finally, the arrival of Marie and Sean was marked by the usual gasps of admiration and wonder at what the congregation was about to witness. Little Kylie was wrapped up in a silken white robe, now slightly yellowed, that Marie's mother had been christened in 70 years ago, her tiny fists clenched around the fabric. As they reached the front pew, the young curate, Fr Flannery emerged from the sacristy and moved forward to greet them. I caught the usual platitudes about introducing another little soul to God, and how Kylie was now beginning her journey towards eternal life, and my mind teemed with images of what lay ahead of her through the years. An expectant silence pulled me out of my reverie. Michael and I were being called up to the font to join Sean and Marie. The sacred ritual was under way.

THE CEREMONY COMPLETED, we all congregated outside in the grounds for the photographs, with flurries of pink blossom swirling around us. Marie and Sean took centre stage with their little bundle now wrapped in a white crocheted shawl. As godparents, Michael and I were called on to flank them for several shots. Then the photographer moved on to include grandparents, family, and finally to full group scenes, prettily arranged against the background of the cherry trees.

The formalities more or less over, people began to drift into their small groups, the buzz of numerous conversations rising in the air. I switched my phone back on to find the new message icon blinking. Moving away from the crowd, I hit the show message key to find Andrew's number flashing on the screen.

My first instinct was to delete it without even opening it, but I couldn't. I had to know what he had to say. At the flick of my thumb, the words lit up the screen:

> `'What a night! We must do it again sometime, babe.'`

A bubble of dread filled my chest as the day disintegrated around me.

'Beth, honey. How're you doing?' Laurie was suddenly at my side.

I showed her the screen.

'Bastard!' she exclaimed, disgusted.

'So, what now?'

'We'll deal with it later. Come on, let's get out of here. If we leave now, a double brandy would settle you nicely before the masses arrive.'

'You're on,' I managed a weak smile. Right now, the prospect of getting quietly sozzled in a corner seemed a pretty good option. From this distance, I could hear the babble of animated voices, a sharp reminder of the happiness of the occasion taking place all around me, from which I was as excluded as a demon from heaven. I was trapped inside a blighted universe of my own making from which there was no escape.

FAST FORWARD A couple of hours, and I was perched on a stool in the Village Inn, in the midst of the celebrations, deep in conversation with Laurie. She'd been pouring brandy into me in an attempt to anaesthetize my distress and it was beginning to take effect. The impact of that spine-chilling message had faded somewhat and I was even waxing lyrical about the miracle of babies. I caught a sudden flicker of alarm in her eyes, so fleeting as to make me think I'd imagined it. I followed her line of vision across the bar. My alcohol-fogged lens detected a familiar figure. He had his back to us, displaying those broad rugby shoulders to perfection as he inclined towards the proud mother for a congratulatory kiss. There was no mistaking Sam. And after his words of warning that had proved so prophetic, I just couldn't face him now. I wouldn't be able to pretend in front of him. He'd always been so tuned into me. He'd know something was very wrong. The ever more familiar feeling of panic grew in me.

My arm was suddenly caught in a ferocious grip. Laurie was wasting no time.

'Right, Beth. We're going to the ladies. Stop staring at him and come on.'

I found myself being propelled in the direction of the ladies toilets, away from Sam. While I knew I couldn't face him, I could feel every muscle straining to see whether he was watching me. Once inside, Laurie fussed over my make-up and hair, while I trembled in anticipation of coming face to face with him. What seemed like hours passed before Laurie judged it was safe to head back to the lounge.

'There you are. I was just wondering where you'd got to. What are you having?'

Marie had deposited Kylie with one of her sisters and was doing the rounds, stopping for a few words with each group of guests, making everyone feel welcome. By now, I'd had just enough brandy to bolster me up. Any more and I was likely to go the other way and dissolve into tears.

'I think it's time we moved on to coffee.' Laurie answered for both of us.

'Right, so. You two grab seats over there and I'll bring them over.' She gestured to a corner booth that had just been vacated. I moved gratefully in to the semi-enclosed space it offered as one of the lounge girls cleared the table. There was no sign of him in this part of the bar, and at least here I would be tucked away from the passing traffic.

'So, Beth, how's the fairy godmother?'

Marie slid the tray with a pot of coffee and three cups onto the table. The 'fairy godmother' thing was a standing joke between us, with all its connotations of my waving magic wands and showering blessings onto Kylie's life. Now, all I could think of was how badly I needed a fairy godmother of my own to get my life back on track. I tried desperately to hold back the tears that were pricking the back of my eyes.

'Sweetheart, what is it?'

Marie's expression changed to one of consternation as the first tear rolled off my chin and plopped into the coffee I was bending over. Laurie's arm was around my shoulder, drawing me in towards her.

'Ah, she's just had a bit of a rough time this week. Man trouble, you know.' The charged look of shared understanding that flashed between my two friends was enough to fill Marie in.

'Come on, honey,' she was quick to move in. 'You know there's none of them worth it. That Scotsman was never right for you. Too self-opinionated, if you ask me!'

I took the tissue Marie had fished from her bag and snuffled into it. Another warning look from Laurie stopped Marie in her tracks. With the precision of a rally driver, she veered in a new direction.

'I was talking to Sam a while ago. Nice of him to come today. I haven't seen him since…' The words died in her throat as the awareness of her faux pas sank in.

'Yes, we noticed him here all right.' Laurie was in like lightning. 'I don't suppose he stayed long. A christening wouldn't exactly be his cup of tea.'

I noticed a shadow looming over our booth. The familiar odour of aftershave mixed with linseed oil wafted over. Oh, dear God, let this not be happening. Not just now, with the state I was in, please. This was more than I could handle.

'Ahem!' Sam coughed. 'Sorry to intrude. Just wanted to take my leave and wish you and little Kylie all the best in life.'

"Sorry to intrude", "take my leave". This wasn't the Sam I knew. He must be feeling just as awkward as I was.

'Sam, how nice to see you.' I forced the words out, each one resounding in my head.

'Beth.' He gave me a cursory nod, eyes never reaching mine. My fragile mood nose-dived into a bottomless well of despair, its walls green and slimy with mould. When I looked up, he was gone.

CHAPTER FOURTEEN

THE NEXT MORNING, I woke with a blinding headache. The dread of meeting Andrew in school, of having to teach in the room next to him, caused a pit of ice in my stomach. I still hadn't worked out whether to just ignore his message, or reply with a veiled threat about involving the guards. Downstairs, the smell of frying bacon Dad had put on was enough to make me feel nauseous. I sat down to tea and toast with marmalade but had only taken a couple of bites when I felt my stomach heave. When I emerged from the bathroom, my mouth sour with the taste of vomit, Dad was outside the door, full of concern.

'Beth, love. You're not well. Is it something you've eaten?'

In spite of how bad I was feeling, I smiled. In Dad's world, everything revolved around food or drink. Even being sick.

'I'm fine, Dad. Must be a bug I've picked up.'

'Well you look terrible. You're not going into school like that, pet. You could do with a day in bed. Shake off whatever it is. Do you want to ring Jennifer?'

Relief surged through me. I'd call in sick for a day or two, just until I felt ready to face him again. After what I'd been through, a couple of days off wasn't too much to ask.

'Maybe you're right, Dad. I'll ring her now, then I'm going to head back to bed for a few hours.'

Back in the safety of my bed, I switched the electric blanket on and took two Nurofen. If I could block out the rest of the world for a short while, I might recover enough to function on autopilot. I was sinking into the chemical torpor of painkillers when there was a knock on my door; my mother, back from morning Mass.

'Elizabeth, are you all right, dear? Your father said you'd been sick.'

'I'm fine, Mam,' I mumbled into the pillow. 'Just need some rest.'

'You look terrible. Should I call Dr Moran?'

'No, Mam. I'll be fine. I just want to sleep for a bit.'

'How about a nice cup of tea, dear? I'll make a fresh pot.'

'For Christ sake, Mam, I don't want tea.' I turned away from her towards the wall, by now wide awake again with a headache pulsing across my temples.

'Well really, Elizabeth. I was only trying to help. Maybe I shouldn't have bothered.'

Right now, I had more than enough to worry about than my mother's injured sniffs as she left the room.

Some hours later, I woke with a dull sense of being in the wrong place. The time display read 2.34pm. As the fog in my head lifted, the events of the weekend once again came drifting back and clarified into a handful of grotesque images. Andrew making a scene at the Indian restaurant; Andrew lurching towards me in his kitchen; the ordeal of having to act normal in public yesterday, wondering if he'd already spread the word of his 'conquest'. And, looking ahead over the next few months, the unthinkable nightmare of working alongside him. Misery lapped around me, floating me along a river of self-pity. This was not something that would be resolved by taking a couple of days off work. It was something I was going to have to take one step at a time with. I still had the numbers of counsellors the doctor had given me if I needed help. For now, I just wanted to get through today.

In the kitchen, Mother was ironing a pile of shirts, the steam hissing between us. She looked up at me, a vague look on her face.

'Oh, Elizabeth. I'd forgotten you were upstairs. How are you, dear?'

I had a mother so self-absorbed she wasn't even aware of my presence in the house. I filled the kettle and snapped down the switch.

'I'm all right, Mam. Just some bug I must have picked up.'

'You'd want to look after yourself, dear. Once your defences are down, those bugs can really get a grip.'

Just the words of comfort I needed to hear, I thought sarcastically. The 'bug' I was suffering from couldn't possibly get any more of a grip than it already had. I spooned coffee and sugar into a mug and put two slices of bread into the toaster.

'Maybe you should think about taking a supplement. And perhaps get more exercise, dear. You're looking a bit peaky.'

That woman seemed to have perfected the knack of saying precisely the wrong thing at the wrong time. Her concern was appreciated, but the delivery left something to be desired. If there was a national award for the Mother from Hell, she'd scoop it every time. I spread strawberry jam onto my toast, stirred milk into the coffee, and, with a curt nod in her direction, took the lot into the sitting room where I could sink into my misery, uninterrupted by her nagging. Amber followed me in and settled herself at my feet, head resting on her paws. The familiar drone of an afternoon TV chat show, where nothing more traumatic than cookery or gardening was under discussion, engulfed my brain like cotton wool.

I must have nodded off on the couch. The next thing I knew, the ascending wail of an infant was breaking into the fringes of my subconscious. I opened my eyes to see Marie sitting opposite me with Kylie in a little carry-cot beside her.

'Well, sleepyhead! Feeling any better? Your mother said you've been poorly.' Concern was etched in the lines around her eyes.

'All the better for seeing you two.' I struggled to the surface, through the fog of oblivion. 'And how's my favourite god-daughter? In fine voice, I see.'

'As always. I can't remember the luxury of a decent night's sleep. You know, there are times I'd give her away to anyone who'd take her.'

'Ah, the poor little Kylie,' I sat up, offering her a finger which she immediately closed her fist on. 'Is she a hungry little girl, then?'

'Hungry,' Marie snorted. 'Aren't I feeding her round the clock? Sure she's nearly doubled in weight since birth. Here, feel how heavy she is.'

The little creature nestled into my arms, looking up at me as she studied my face intently. Out of nowhere, a smile lit up her face and she gripped my finger again. In spite of all that had transpired in the last few days, the world suddenly became a better place filled with teddy bears and cuddly toys. My god-daughter and I were sharing a special moment. I looked at Marie in incredulous delight.

'Looks like you've won her over. Guess that's my babysitting problems sorted for a while,' she grinned wickedly. 'How'd you like to start your godmother duties right now and join us for a walk?'

Minutes later, we were strolling down a lane between hedgerows that shimmered with wildflowers. Amber was tagging along by my side, tail thumping. A warm April sun dappled the meadows to either side as the ragged clouds scudded by. Kylie had nodded off again, her mind probably flitting through a landscape of teddy bears. But in the middle of all this, the weight of last night's episode hung between us, forcing its way to the surface.

'Want to talk about it?'

The concern in her eyes melted down whatever resistance I had left. Marie had been the first teacher I'd met in the school all those years ago, and she'd always looked out for me. There were few secrets between us. I filled her in on the gist of what had happened.

'Oh, Jesus, Beth. I'm so sorry. What class of an eejit was I to encourage you?' she chided herself.

'No more of an eejit than I was. I should have seen through him long ago. I just chose to ignore all the warning signs.'

'And you didn't go to the guards?'

'Well, yes. I did, and they were really great when I was in the hospital after it happened, but then I had to go down to the station to make a statement, and that's when I realised just how difficult it would be.'

'How do you mean?'

I tried to convey how sceptical the sergeant had been, and how it felt like I was the one facing trial.

'But, Beth, darling, they have to establish all the facts. It's their job.'

'Yes, but if it was that bad just making a statement, how do you think it'd be in court? "And you'd been in a relationship with the accused for how long, Miss Maguire?" I'd be laughed out of the witness box.'

'Oh, come on, date-rape is so common these days. Even within marriage, nonconsensual sex is seen as rape. And there's the fact that you'd just split up with him. Anyone could see that he was just taking revenge on you.'

For a brief second, an image of Andrew McKay in the dock being given a life sentence flashed across my brain.

But it was immediately replaced by me in the witness stand, shaking and terrified, being bullied by the defence counsel into admitting that yes, I had led the defendant on, yes I had gone willingly to his house, and yes it was all my fault.

'No, Marie. I can't go through with it. No. I've decided not to press charges.'

'And what about work? Are you going to tell Jennifer?'

'I don't know.' I hadn't quite figured out how I was going to handle the situation in school; whether I'd be able to face him every day, work alongside him. I supposed the longer I put it off, the more difficult it would be. Right now, I felt like a rabbit living amongst wolves. I hadn't received any more messages from him, but neither had I done anything about the one I got in the church grounds. I suppose I just hoped if I ignored it, I could pretend I'd never got it. But facing him at work was something else. I decided I'd ring Jennifer later and take one more day off. By then, I'd have regained a little more composure. Anyway, he'd be as anxious to avoid me as I was to avoid him. I'd just make damn sure I was never alone with him.

THE FOLLOWING DAY, I stayed in bed until 11.00am, playing the part of a patient stricken with an unnamed bug. By midday, the rain had cleared off so I decided to go for a drive to try and untangle the seething mass of confusion in my head. I loaded Amber into the back of my car and headed south east through Mullingar and on out to Lough Ennell. In typical postcard fashion, wispy cirrus clouds were strewn across a cornflower-blue sky. I pulled into a viewing point near Belvedere House and set off on the boggy track around the lake. After the recent rainfall, the foliage glistened dark green. Sunlight slanted through the fretwork of branches overhead, creating dappled patterns on the forest floor. A crow sailed slowly across the sky, leaning into the wind. There was a plopping sound as a fish broke the surface of the lake and ripples widened out in concentric circles. In a flash of metallic blue a dragonfly landed on a bulrush nearby. Amber nosed happily in the undergrowth, scenting endless possibilities to delight her hunting instinct. Gusts of wind sent wavelets slapping against the reeds, while further out, the lakewater shimmered in the sunlight.

I drank in the scene before me as the claw of fear that had held me in its grip since Friday night began to loosen ever so slightly. There was a whole universe out here untainted by the viciousness of Andrew McKay, and I had come a little closer to finding the key to unlock it. I was never going to forget the awful thing that had happened, but the emotional scars he'd left on my soul would fade with time. He, on the other hand, would always be trapped inside a violent compulsion to exercise power and control over those weaker than himself. In a flash of insight, I realised that holding on to this thought would free me from the tyranny of fear he had imposed on me. As if on cue, from the fringes of the lake, a scatter of starlings rose skywards in a frenzy of birdsong, their music filling the air. It was like a tiny measure of healing had found its way through the horror.

CHAPTER FIFTEEN

THE KNOT IN my stomach tightened as I swung my car into the school parking area. There was just one other car there, Sheila's little Punto. No sign of the BMW. Was it possible he had upped sticks and gone back to Scotland? The very idea of us continuing to work side by side was ludicrous. After what he'd done to me, there could be no question of pretending things were normal. Jennifer would be advertising for a new substitute. And please God, it would be a woman this time. My clammy hands loosened their grip on the steering wheel and I switched off the ignition.

In the staff room, Sheila was spooning instant coffee into a mug. I must have looked like I needed one because she immediately reached for another, a sympathetic grin crinkling her face.

'Jesus, Beth, you look a bit rough, girl. Are you sure you've shaken off that bug?'

I'd thrown on a layer of make-up to disguise the evidence of another night of fitful sleep, but it obviously wasn't working.

'I'm grand, thanks Sheila.' I forced a weak smile. 'Just a bit drained.'

'What was it you had? Food poisoning?'

'Yeah, some kind of stomach bug. Throwing up all round me.'

I'd decided this was the safest card to play. Something I could shake off in a couple of days, no questions asked.

'You poor pet. Sure let us know if you don't feel up to a full day. We'll cover for you.'

I nodded gratefully, and took the proffered mug of

coffee.

Jennifer was next to arrive in, as always a flurry of activity.

'Ah, Beth,' she deposited her load of copybooks on the table. 'Feeling better?'

'I'm grand, thanks Jennifer,' I lied.

'You look a bit peaky. Was it a bad dose?'

So much worse than any of you could imagine, I thought to myself, coming perilously close to tears at their kindness. I trotted out the lie about the stomach bug again and reassured Jennifer that I was fine. I just sat down with my coffee, and waited. And waited. Was he going to show up? Surely they would have mentioned it if a teacher had gone AWOL. He must have just come in on Monday as if nothing had happened. The thumping pulse of dread filled my chest.

Two minutes later, my worst fears were confirmed. The sound of a car door slamming outside announced his arrival. My mind went spinning towards panic.

'Morning, all!' His abrupt tone cut a swathe through the female camaraderie as he made straight for the recently-boiled kettle and snapped down the switch, brushing past me on his way across the room. I was paralysed by his presence. I had to get away from him. I muttered some excuse about having to set up the classroom for drama practice and, coffee in hand, fled the tiny staffroom.

A few minutes later, as I was trying to gather my scrambled wits, the thud of heavy footsteps coming down the corridor grew louder. I held my breath willing them to continue on to the next room, but of course, they didn't. The door swung open, and his huge bulk filled the doorway. I shrank back against the cupboard where I'd been fiddling with pencils.

'Ah, the lovely Beth.'

His malevolence seemed to expand and fill the space between us, the words of his text dancing in front of my eyes. My voice came out as a squeak, not unlike that of a cornered mouse.

'Don't you dare come near me, you bastard!'

'Now that's not quite what one expects to hear from a lady, is it?' He was moving menacingly close to me. 'Just because you didn't appreciate my charms, there's no need to make a scene about it.'

My panic escalated.

'You lay a finger on me and I'll scream the place down. See if you can smooth talk your way out of that.'

'Oh dear, oh dear.' He held his hands up in a mock backing-off gesture. 'So all the staff will see you having a nervous breakdown. That's not really what you want, is it Beth? Even if you are a frigid, dried up old prune. We don't want you branded as a loony as well, do we now?'

'Just keep away from me,' I hissed with all the venom I could muster.

'Oh, I'll do that all right.' He grinned. 'Don't worry. You really think I'm interested in a pathetic little bitch like you when I can have whoever I like? Dream on, baby.'

He crossed to the far side of the room and stopped at the door leading to the first and second class.

'Just one thing, Beth. I like to be discreet about my romantic escapades. And I expect the same from my lady friends. You wouldn't want it getting out how useless you are in the sack, would you?'

Fury surged up in me, but he was gone. Back to his side of the glass partition. I took a couple of deep breaths and tried to focus on the homework I would be giving back in a few minutes. I couldn't. All the veiled hints and warnings of my friends swam around in my head, each one raising the question that now hammered through me. What kind of an imbecile was I not to have listened to them? With so much evidence to condemn him? The dogs on the street would have been more discerning. I sank into my misery for the few minutes left before the kids piled in from the playground.

The thousands of minutes in that day crawled around the clock face, each hour stretching out longer than the last. I went out of my way to avoid eye contact through the glass panel, but any time I did glance in his direction, I was caught like a rabbit in headlights, pinned down by the force of his glare. When 2.30pm finally arrived and my charges were released to their waiting guardians and buses, I gathered my stuff and made straight for the car park. My fingers fumbled with the key in the ignition in a desperate attempt to get away before he caught up with me. The engine fired up, I slammed down on the accelerator and shot out through the gates, leaving behind me a sea of indignant faces waiting to collect their children.

'ELIZABETH! YOU'VE GOT a visitor.'

My mother's pronouncement once again set the panic bells jangling in my head. Ensconced in my room, I'd felt that little bit safer, removed from the misery of the last few days. Now here was all the uncertainty of the outside world barging in on me. What if it was him? While I was still frozen with fear, the soft tones of Laurie's voice exchanging small talk with my mother came floating up the stairs. I felt like singing with relief. I threw open the bedroom door and stood waiting for her.

'Hi, hon.' Her arms reached out for me. 'How are you

doing?'

I shrugged. 'Well, I got through today anyway. Although maybe not quite with flying colours.'

She looked at me sharply. 'Go on.'

'Yeah, well, he was there all right. And he kind of threatened me. No, not exactly. Nothing like the text message. But he warned me to say nothing. Laurie, he scares the hell out of me!'

An overwhelming sense of bleakness closed in on me. He still had a hold over me. Every day going in to work, I would be afraid, and Marie's maternity leave would last through to the summer break. Two more months of seeing him every day through the glass panel, leering at me, being terrified of meeting him on my own in the staff room. I couldn't live like this. I'd have to quit my job. I have to get away from him somehow.

'But you have told Jennifer, haven't you?'

'Well, I…' I began lamely. 'I was kind of hoping he'd just disappear. Go back to Scotland. I mean it's impossible for us to go on working together now, isn't it?'

'Beth, listen to me, sweetheart. You can't just leave things as they are. You've got to do something. Otherwise, he *will* make your life a misery. The fucker knows you're scared of him. Even if you're not going ahead with the charges, you need to show him you're prepared to take him on. To expose him.'

Had she any idea what she was asking me to do? How he was likely to react if I did tackle him? I'd just have to avoid him as best I could. Make sure I wasn't left alone with him. Laurie's searching gaze read my thoughts.

'Beth, I know what you're thinking, but you can do this. Bastards like him are always cowards underneath it all. He won't be expecting you to put up a fight, and when you do, it'll knock him sideways.'

Of course what she was saying made perfect sense. But that didn't change the terror that set in my heart at the thought of having to confront him.

'Of course, Plan B would be to tell Jennifer and let her deal with him.' Laurie went on. 'That way, he'll be out the door before you can blink. She'll find a way to get rid of him. Hasn't his erratic behaviour in class drawn attention already?'

Laurie was right. His tendency to lose it in front of the kids had become an issue of late. Leaving it with Jennifer was certainly an option, but it brought with it the risk that he might stay on in Carrigmore anyway. He'd know I'd spoken out. I could bump into him around any corner.

'I need to think about it for a bit,' I muttered.

'Don't wait too long.' Laurie's concern was audible. 'If he thinks he has you in a corner, he may not leave it at that. Especially as you two were seen as an item around here. He could be saying anything about you.'

I thought back to what he'd said that morning, threatening to reveal that I was useless in the sack. He probably would try to discredit me. But two could play at that game. All I had to do was drop hints about his deficiencies in that area and his Casanova image would be blown to smithereens. And then a few well-chosen words about his drinking habits and temper. I could hang him without ever going near a court. I had a lot more artillery to threaten him with than he could possibly have against me. And when I was ready, I'd let him know exactly where he stood.

THE NEXT FEW days passed without incident. Apart from the odd poisonous glance he shot in my direction, there was no communication between us. But even that venom was beginning to recede. I was starting to see my way through the terrors that had crowded around me. Starting to regain some measure of control. Starting to believe that my life would eventually get back on track.

I'd just worked through the final revisions on a short story I was entering for a competition. The deadline was the following day, so I'd gone straight into Ballymartin after school to post it. I was feeling quite chuffed with myself at having managed to complete it after all that had happened, and even a little bit excited that I was in with a chance when I walked out of the post office and straight into Andrew.

'Well, well, well. If it's not the lovely Beth, the ice-queen.'

I tried to ignore the cold stone of fear in my stomach and pasted a chilly smile onto my face.

'Andrew.'

'Keeping well, are you?'

The smirk on his face was impossible to miss. I could feel outrage gathering force inside me. This was it. I was ready.

'We have one or two things to talk about, you and I.'

A look of amusement spread across his face. I steamrolled on.

'I think you may not fully understand the situation.'

'Oh, I think I understand it very well, my dear. You rejected my advances. End of story. I move on to new pastures, and all that. On to someone more appreciative of my charms.' His upper lip curled in a sneer.

'No, that's not quite it.' I paused for effect. 'You see, there are people around here who might take a different view. People who might even consider a rapist fair game for dragging down a dark alley. Know what I mean?'

'Well now, let's not get carried away.' The glint of panic that briefly flickered in his eyes was already under control. 'After all, you've had the hots for me from the day we first met. Who do you think is going to believe some fairy story you concoct about being raped? You practically pulled the trousers off me. I mean, what's a man supposed to do?' He spread his hands out in a gesture of mock helplessness.

I pasted that ice-cold smile on my lips again. 'Too bad the hospital documented the bruises that prove it. And then of course, there's all my friends who'd be horrified to hear about what really happened. They might be a little less welcoming to you than before. If I were you, I'd be very careful what I say or do from now on, Mr McKay'

'Get out of my way,' he hissed, pushing past me into the post office. 'Pathetic little bitch!'

'Everything okay, Beth?'

I whirled around to find Sam behind me, alarm written all over his face. How long had he been there? How much had he heard?'

'Sam,' I stuttered. 'I— I— yes, I'm fine. Everything's fine.' My voice came out in a shrill squeak.

'Are you sure? You look like you've seen a ghost. Maybe you should sit down for a bit.'

I looked at him, numb with misery. I wanted nothing more than to feel his arms around me. Comforting me. But all that belonged to the past. I could never get it back.

'I really don't want to intrude, but was he harassing you? Did he upset you? Beth?' he asked urgently.

I felt a heave of grief fill my throat, robbing me of the power of speech.

'Come on, let's go into the hotel. I'll get you a coffee.' I felt his hand on my arm, and panicked. I automatically flinched away. He let go at once and stepped back.

'I— I'm sorry.' His tone stiffened as embarrassment spread across his face. 'I shouldn't have bothered you. Do excuse me.'

It was like all the colour was draining out of my life. He was gone.

CHAPTER SIXTEEN

SINCE OUR CONFRONTATION at the post office, Andrew and I'd had no communication, only barely acknowledging each other's presence in front of the other staff. But I was always aware of exactly where he was. I could feel his eyes on me all of the time, boring into my back. It was as if I had developed a special Andrew McKay antenna.

This morning, as we were all heading into class, he had stumbled into the staffroom, eyes bloodshot and accusing, muttering something about the traffic. Jennifer had given him a pointed look, but said nothing. He was obviously in the grip of a merciless hangover and better left alone.

We were just getting to the high point of today's storytime when my attention was arrested by raised voices from the other side of the glass panel. I looked across, my stomach churning with anxiety, to see Andrew towering over a little girl, his face and neck suffused with rage. One of the other kids had come to his sister's defence, and was standing, hands on hips, mouth pursed in mutiny, taking on the teacher. Even through the double glazing, his words rang out.

'You leave her alone.'

Andrew spun around to face this unexpected opposition, incredulity written all over his features. I had to do something. I knew what he was capable of. My feet somehow carried me over to the glass doors separating the two classrooms, and, with no idea of how I was going to handle it, I marched in.

As he saw his second opponent advancing, some warning device must have clicked in Andrew's brain. By the time I reached the little group, his thunderous expression had been wrenched under control, and the beginnings of a thin smile were curling his lips.

'Ah, Miss Maguire. Was there something you wanted?'

I looked at the two children, who regarded me warily. The little girl was on the brink of tears, but much as I wanted to comfort her, I needed to try and defuse the situation. Satisfied that Andrew's temper was now under control, I said the first thing that came to mind.

'I seem to have lost my board marker, Mr McKay. Would you have a spare?'

The tension pulsated in the air between us, and then, for a fraction of a second, I thought I saw a glimmer of relief cross his face. Without a word, he went to his desk drawer, took out a blue marker, and handed it to me. My fingers trembled as I took it from him.

'Thank you, Mr McKay. You're very kind.'

It was only then I noticed Jennifer outside my room, staring openly at us. She'd obviously been passing and was alerted by the teacher-less class. I waved the marker at her to explain and she nodded and kept going. How much had she seen? And was it enough?

'So, YOU THINK she's aware of how dangerous he is to have in charge of children?'

Laurie held the cream doughnut an inch from her lips.

'Not sure yet,' I mumbled, through a mouthful of Danish pastry. It was our Saturday morning treat in a café in Longford town, a ritual we'd established earlier in the year, and tried to keep to as often as possible.

'She'd want to be blind not to realise the risks involved. I mean, he's already losing his temper with the kids. The next thing you know he's going to hit one of them, and then she's really in trouble.'

There had been another couple of minor episodes during the week when Andrew's conduct in class had certainly deviated from the standards advocated in the Manual of Good Teaching Practice. In fact I was surprised we hadn't yet had any parents in complaining. The children, a combined group of first and second class, at first so captivated by him, were by now beginning to view him with distrust and suspicion. He'd also had a run-in with the Diocesan Advisor who'd been in to provide extra support with the preparation for First Holy Communion. When she'd made a couple of suggestions to him, he'd taken exception to what he called an outsider 'meddling' with his pupils, and told her in no uncertain terms to mind her own business. Even so, I knew it would take a lot for the School Board to terminate his contract.

'Yeah, I know that,' I agreed. 'But she can't sack him without having serious grounds for dismissal.'

'Well, the sooner he supplies her with them, the better. It must be hell on earth for you.'

I shrugged. 'Only six weeks to go, Laurie. I'll survive.'

'Hey,' her face lit up like a beacon. 'What are you doing tomorrow?'

This kind of enthusiasm meant she was hatching out a plan for me.

'Why don't you come to the show in Moate with us? Little Keith is jumping in the 128cm pony class. Making his debut, no less. Come on, you'd enjoy it.'

A horse show. Now that'd be different. And it'd fill in my Sunday.

'Ah, sure go on. Why not?'

'Yee-haa!' she yelped. 'I'll bring the picnic, you bring the wine, and we'll make a day of it.'

It was only later that night that I remembered the last

time I was at a horse show. Ten years ago. With him.

12.00PM NEXT DAY, and I was driving into the showgrounds in Moate. It was one of these horse and pony shows, without all the paraphernalia of cattle, sheep, pigs, ducks and the fairground attractions that the bigger agricultural events attract. Even so, there were several rings with competitions already under way, and children on ponies cantering around a practice ring with a little cross pole in the centre. The odour of horse sweat and dung was everywhere, and the air was full of high-pitched whinnying, the excitement of ponies out for the day. I spotted Laurie's jeep and trailer and made my way over towards the pony rings to find them.

'Beth, Beth!' Little Anna was the first to see me, arms waving frantically over her head. 'Come and see Keith's pony.'

Excitement ran through her childish voice. She worshipped her big brother, and was clearly in raptures to see him competing in his first show.

'Hi, hon,' Laurie grinned as she unclasped the lunge line from the bit. She obviously wasn't taking any chances. This pony was going to be well settled before it went into the ring. It was a golden palomino mare with a cream-coloured mane and tail, and dainty hooves, well oiled up for the occasion. They'd called her Honey, after the great mare of Paul Darragh, Heather Honey. Laurie had bought her last year for Keith's birthday, and the little boy spent hours every day grooming her, riding her, cleaning her tack, and even checking up on her every night before bed.

'Well, look at you.' I smiled up at Keith astride the pony, all spruced up in jacket, jodhpurs and boots. 'You sure do clean up well.'

'Let's hope he's going to clean up in the ring too,' Laurie

winked at me. 'Or at least leave the fences up.'

'Sure he will, won't you Keith? He'll be bringing home a rosette. You wait and see.'

'Mam's going to let me start riding soon,' piped up eight-year-old Eoin, not to be outdone. 'Then I'll be bringing home rosettes too, won't I, Mam?'

'Course you will, pet. But today, it's Keith's turn, so let's cheer him on.'

'Watch me do the cross pole, Beth.' Keith, eager to show us what he could do, pushed Honey into a trot and joined the others in the practice ring. He cantered once around and then approached the 60cm fence, allowing the mare to stretch out in the last three strides so she sailed over. Anna, Eoin and I applauded wildly, while Laurie nodded in approval.

'That's good, Keith. Make sure you keep that rhythm in between fences. Well done!'

Before we knew it, it was Keith's turn to go in, and we all took up position at the best vantage point we could find, just in front of the double. He trotted up to the judges' box, saluted them, and he was on his way. He was clear over the first fence, an inviting rustic, and then back around in a U turn to an upright. There was a collective intake of breath from our corner as Honey was fighting for her head on the approach to the spread at the halfway mark, but then she stood off and soared upwards, Keith crouched over her, his hands up around her ears, giving her free rein. Then, as he cantered up to the final line, concentration etched into his face, a toddler, having wriggled free from its mother, ducked in under the rope cordoning off the jumping ring and into the path of Keith's pony. Honey took fright, shied and veered off to the left of the fence. Seeing the reason for the run-out, the judges rang the bell to signal they were giving Keith another chance. With the toddler safely back in the grip of its mother's hand, Keith cantered a circle and approached for a second time, but by now, the pony was unsettled and the back bar came crashing down. Four faults. Of all the rotten luck when he so deserved a clear round. My heart went out to him. I looked at Laurie, making a throat-slitting movement in the direction of the mother who'd allowed her kid to wander off.

'Oh, well,' she sighed. 'That's the way it goes. He might as well learn now that he needs to be a good loser if he's ever going to be a future champion.'

An hour later, after Club Orange and chicken sandwiches for the kids, and a bottle of Rioja with smoked salmon on brown soda bread for Laurie and I, Keith's disappointment was almost forgotten. We were all nicely chilled out, and Honey was munching on a hay net in her trailer. While the others wanted to keep an eye on the higher pony classes, I decided to explore what else was going on. I set off towards the adult rings where the 1.3m class was just getting underway. As this was a qualifier for the Dublin Horse Show, there was a lot of interest in it. A number of well known sponsors were standing around the ring, watching closely how their promising young horses were being handled by the semi-professional riders they had engaged. First to take up the challenge was a fractious silver-grey mare who tried to dive at her fences once she saw them coming, in spite of her rider's attempts to calm her down. Halfway round, she began to knock back poles on spreads, and then got really upset, hitting pretty much everything and ending up with a cricket score.

Five or six horses later, and we still hadn't seen a clear round.

'And now we have a chestnut gelding, Golden Sunrise,

owned and ridden by Samuel Butler,' the P.A. announced.

Of all the emotions that rushed through me as I watched Sam riding the course, I think it was the sense of loss that dominated. The churning confusion in my head was fuelled by the pain of our last meeting, when he'd seen how upset I was and reached out to me but I'd pulled away from him; and the infinite regret that I'd made the mistake of walking away from him ten years ago. I felt an overwhelming desire to have him back in my life. Standing there at the ringside, I couldn't take my eyes off him. With hands of velvet, he eased Golden Sunrise up to each fence with minimal interference, always allowing the horse its head in the last three strides to ensure fluid jumping. The rich smell of sweaty horseflesh released a surge of memories that pulled me back to our early days together, to the world of happiness I'd lost. As Sam turned back for the final fence, an oxer at full spread, I willed him on. The thudding of hooves came closer, and the whole crowd held its breath. In a surge of power, the gelding stretched out its head and neck, soared up, and flicked its heels out over the back bar. A roar of applause erupted around the ring like thunder.

The desperate need to talk to him again had grown into a physical ache, so much that the embarrassment of our last meeting was beginning to fade. This time would be different. This time, if he initiated any physical contact, I wouldn't pull away. All I had to do was walk over to the collecting ring and let him see me. Surely he'd want to talk to me? With the wall of applause still ringing in my ears, and my heart hammering, I started to walk in his direction, my longing to see him a painful tug inside my chest.

Ten paces away from the collecting ring, I stopped dead. He had just dismounted. Among those who had gathered around him were his sister Miranda and a couple of staff members from the local riding stables, and there offering the horse a mouthful of grass in her extended palm, was his mother. The woman who had been so cruel to me in the past, who had considered me to be way beneath her only son. The woman about whom Sam and I'd had so many rows when he didn't defend me in the face of her hostility.

'Beth?'

I'd dithered a fraction of a second too long. He'd spotted me. He'd handed the reins to his mother and was striding over to where I stood.

'Beth, it's good to see you.' His tone radiated warmth.

'Well done, Sam. That was a great round.'

'You saw it?' Pleasure glowed on his face.

'Sure did. Very impressive.'

'Thanks, Beth,' he smiled and my heart flooded with insane happiness.

'I didn't know you were a follower of the show circuit.'

'Oh, I'm here with Laurie,' I rushed into an explanation. 'Her little Keith had his first pony class today. Did well too. Just the last fence down.'

'Excellent!' Sam looked really pleased. 'It's great to get kids started early. Haven't a nerve in their body at that age.'

'Yeah,' I grinned ruefully, 'Unlike me when I started. Remember how terrified I was?'

'I remember,' his voice became more ragged, as the sheet of tension that the years had strung between us began to billow.

I had managed to drag us back to the embarrassment of our failed past. The offending sentence stayed in the air between us.

'Actually, Beth?' He looked at me, his voiced laced with apprehension.

'Yes?'

'I wondered if we might have a talk?' With that, he put a hand on my arm. And I jumped back, terror crowding my mind. I tried immediately to move back into his reach, but it was too late.

'I'm so sorry,' he stepped backwards as if away from a nest of vipers. 'I'd better get back, you know?' He gestured over towards his circle of friends. He walked away, and a gaping, black hole opened up in my heart.

CHAPTER SEVENTEEN

THE MONTH OF May passed in a haze of unhappiness. In school I lived in a state of constant anxiety, always trying to sense exactly where Andrew was. Break-times had become an ordeal where I would crouch into a corner of the staffroom with my coffee, nose buried in a textbook. He in turn had changed from being outgoing and jovial to surly and withdrawn, and gave me as wide a berth as the confines of a village primary school would allow. By now, everyone had noticed the difference, but no-one made any comment on it.

Having Sam back in my life was the one thing I wanted more than anything else, and now, just when he was starting to show some interest in me again, I froze every time he tried to touch me. Laurie suggested I think again about the option of counselling but I didn't feel ready to take that step. I was terrified at the thought of having to relive the whole nightmare again. So I dragged on from day to day, desperately hoping that the next casual encounter with Sam was just around the corner. But it wasn't. The days rolled into weeks as the hedges whitened with mayflower.

The weather kept fine with light breezes and azure skies. Laurie, bless her soul, was really looking out for me, and had persuaded me to go with her to Strokestown House. Little Keith had started Irish history at school and was mad to see the Famine Museum so we were making a day of it.

We'd done the tour of the house, gardens and museum, and had just demolished a feed of scampi and chips in the carvery lounge of the Percy French Hotel. On our way through the foyer, Laurie's gaze was drawn to a new arrival stepping out of the revolving doors. She was a tall slender woman, hair pulled back into a French plait accompanied by a stocky middle-aged man dressed in tweeds. There was something about the way the woman moved that looked familiar. I grimaced to myself as I realized that it was Miranda, Sam's sister. She'd spotted us, so there was no escape route.

'Oh, hello there.'

The lukewarm tone spoke volumes. My stomach turned over.

'Hi, Miranda.' Laurie was quick to react, pasting a smile on her face. 'So, what has you in these parts?'

'Oh, just a little business trip.' Now on her favourite subject, Miranda motored on. 'I came to look at a showjumper. Only a two-year-old filly but with serious potential. Clearing 1.20m in loose schooling already.'

'How impressive.' Laurie's sarcasm fell on deaf ears. 'We're just here for a bit of culture. The Famine Museum and all that. Right, Beth?'

She was deliberately trying to involve me in the conversation. Now Miranda had no choice but to acknowledge my presence.

'Nice to see you again, Beth. How've you been?' Her eyes were as dead as those of a fish.

'Oh, you know. Keeping busy enough with work and stuff.' I sounded croaky, as if I had to force each word out through a parched throat.

'Of course, you know Sam's back, don't you? We needed him to take over the yard after Father's stroke.'

'Yes, yes.' I stammered. 'I was sorry to hear about that. Your father's stroke, I mean.' Oh, God, now I sounded like a total moron. Again, Laurie came to the rescue.

'So, how is Sam? I expect he's kept going with the livery stuff?'

'Well, there are only five horses there now but he's been

asked to do some instructing at Castle Edmond.'

That was our local equestrian centre where they taught riding, ran competitions, pony club games, all that sort of thing.

'Oh, yeah?'

'Yes, he's getting on quite well, I believe. He tells us he's really enjoying it. He's also teaching the trainee instructor class, and apparently, there's one girl in particular that's taken his fancy. It seems he's been giving her a bit of extra coaching, if you know what I mean,' she said with a smirk.

Her words roared in my ears like distant gunfire. The restaurant buckled around me as if its foundations had shifted. This was something I hadn't anticipated. Looking up, I could see her prickling with curiosity to see how I was taking the news.

'Well, isn't that nice.' Laurie's tone bore only the slightest trace of sarcasm. Taking this as encouragement, Miranda carried on, her eyes glittering with spite.

'Yes, it would be great to see him happy with someone. Hasn't had a lot of luck with women, has he?'

Was I imagining it or was she looking pointedly at me? What a bitch.

'Well, do give him our best regards.' Laurie sensed this conversation had gone far enough into dangerous territory. 'And enjoy the rest of your visit here.' She'd taken my elbow and was guiding me towards the exit.

'You too. Nice to see you again.' The honeyed voice trailed off. I tottered out onto the street.

The thought of him with someone else was sickening. I thought he'd seemed to be trying to get closer to me. But of course each time I met him I'd flinched when he tried to touch me. No wonder he'd moved on. Sooner or later, I was bound to meet them together. My heart shrivelled up at the prospect.

THE NEXT DAY, I arrived home from school to find a letter propped on the hall table with a Zambian postmark.

St. Gabriel's Mission
Kawambwa
Luapula
Zambia
22 May 2009

Dearest Sis,

I wanted you to be the first to know I've come to a decision. I know it's probably not the one you wanted to hear, and that it's going to rock a whole flotilla of boats at home, but I'm afraid it's the only way forward for me. I'll be travelling back home the weekend of June 13/14 and will be going to our mother house to request what they call a period of reflection. In other words some time out to reassess my situation. Of course, I'm still not a hundred per cent certain, but I need this space to make a final decision. I'll probably be involved in some form of community work back in Ireland. Or possibly part-time teaching. With English at degree level, I might be able to get some hours, even temporary, just to tide me over for a bit.

You know me, Beth, and you know I haven't

done this lightly. I've been turning it over in my mind for almost a year now. Sometimes, I think if it wasn't for Mother, I'd never have ended up here in the first place. But it was always about what ***she*** wanted, wasn't it? I know she's going to hit the roof, but that's her problem. I now have to do what's best for me, and she's just going to have to live with her disappointment. I don't want to sound harsh, but she's brought a lot of this upon herself. If she hadn't pushed me so hard, I'd have been in a better position to make up my own mind as to what I wanted to do with my life.

I'll be met at the airport by someone from the order so it'll probably be the Sunday when I get to Carrigmore to break the news. It might be better if you said nothing until then. No point in starting the war just yet!

I'll be looking forward to catching up on all the news, especially about this Scotsman I'm hearing so much about. Mother's letters have been full of him. I gather there's romance in the air? If that's the case, I'm really delighted for you. You deserve the best.

See you soon. Hugs and kisses.

Your favourite brother,
Brian

My mouth hung open in shock. Just when I thought things couldn't get much worse. This was going to send the Maguire family rocketing into the biggest galactic war imaginable. There was no doubt about it, Mother would see this as the scandal of the century. She'd be the laughing stock of the parish, no, of the whole county. She'd never accept that she might have been just a tiny bit responsible for pushing him in the wrong direction. Well, now she was going to reap her reward. For now, I had my own problems to deal with. And she wasn't exactly blameless there either. If she hadn't kept on at me about Andrew being my last chance, maybe I wouldn't be in this mess. By now, I was on a roller coaster of self pity that kept going down, down, down, dipping into the deep regions of misery. Once I got started on the recriminations road, there was no stopping me. Ten years ago, when I was truly happy with the man who meant more to me than anyone else in the world, she had to wreck that too. God, that woman had so much to answer for. I was almost looking forward to the weekend, to see all her dreams come crashing down around her, lying in dust at her feet. She deserved no less.

Apt. 28E,
Learmouth Terrace,
Edinburgh EH4 1PQ
May 26, 2009

Dear Ms. Muldowney,

My name is Monica McKay. From information recently received, I have reason to believe that my ex-husband, Andrew McKay is currently employed in your school. I am writing to alert you to the potential risk attached to this situation.

My husband and I separated in May 2007. In September of that year, in breach of the barring order against him, he broke into the apartment I had moved into, and sexually assaulted me. I pressed criminal charges, and the case came to trial in August 2008. In spite of the evidence, Andrew was acquitted by a jury.

I only heard last week that my ex-husband had gone to Ireland to take up a teaching post. Naturally, I was perturbed that someone of his volatile temperament should be entrusted with young children. I would strongly urge you to reconsider his position.

For your information, I enclose the newspaper report of the trial.

Yours sincerely,
Monica McKay

Jennifer reread the letter three times. Then glanced at the enclosed clipping. Her hands shook slightly. This was the man she'd taken on the recommendation of a colleague in Lanesborough, the principal of a school there who had been friendly with his mother. And of course he had supplied a written reference from his previous employer, an Evelyn Denniston, Principal of Queen Anne Middle School, Edinburgh. She opened the filing cabinet and located the application.

> Mr. Andrew McKay taught at Queen Anne School from September 2006 to June 2008. During that time, he worked with junior and senior infants and always carried out his duties efficiently. He was punctual and attentive to the needs of his pupils.

There was more of the same to follow. But nothing that really revealed his character. With a sinking heart, Jennifer picked up the phone and dialled the number on the headed paper.

'Good morning, Queen Anne School. How may I help you?'

'Evelyn Denniston, please.'

Ten minutes later, Jennifer hung up. Andrew McKay had left the Queen Anne voluntarily after he'd been acquitted in a high profile court case in which he had been accused of the rape of his ex-wife. Her head reeled with what-could-have-happened scenarios. A man capable of that level of violence in close contact with seven-year-old children, how could he possibly have escaped screening? But of course he hadn't been convicted. So there was no record.

Various incidents from the past few weeks swam into her field of vision. Minor aberrations that had seemed insignificant at the time, but that now took on a more sinister aspect. The scene with Sr Breda, the Diocesan Advisor came sliding back.

'Of course I don't want to make an issue of it, but he was out of line. And to be honest, it seems to me he could do with all the help he can get. He's not too well versed in the way we do things here.'

'I am sorry, Sr, I'll have a word with him.'

With their First Holy Communion only weeks away, Sr Breda had been in to check that preparations were on course. This was mainly the responsibility of the second class teacher, but Andrew had neglected to follow the guidelines and the children had fallen behind in their religious education. When Breda had pointed out to him that he had some catching up to do and that she'd be glad to help, he'd reacted badly, telling her to stop interfering in his class management. Then when Jennifer had taken him aside, he'd mumbled an apology, but was still resistant to the idea of anyone checking up on him.

There had also been a letter of complaint from Dolores Conway's mother. Jennifer hadn't given it much thought at the time as the woman had overreacted in the past, but now she saw again the spindly words on the Basildon Bond writing paper. She stated that Mr McKay had shouted at Dolores and 'nearly scared the wits out of her' and that her brother, Jimmy, had to stand up to the teacher in her defence. This had come just after the incident when she'd seen Beth coming from Andrew's class with a board marker. With the speed of a shark scenting blood, Jennifer's mind began making connections. Suddenly, a number of episodes were illuminated by this awful new understanding. Unexplained mood swings. An occasional smell of drink in the mornings. A certain hostility of late towards other staff members, especially Beth. Jennifer had, of course, noticed the attraction sizzling between the two several months back. And had also noted its absence of late. More than that, they seemed at pains to avoid each other. She'd have to talk to Beth. Without delay.

CHAPTER EIGHTEEN

I WAS IN the middle of an information gathering session on the Land of Lilliput where we were taking the kids for their school tour when Jennifer came in.

'Sorry to interrupt, Miss Maguire, but I need to see you for a minute. Can you give the class something to do?'

This was unprecedented. Normally if Jennifer wanted to speak to one of us, it was done outside teaching hours. We simply didn't have enough staff to supervise extra classes. I quickly outlined a reading task for my class, got them started, and hurried to Jennifer's alcove. I found her looking over a handwritten letter, adjusting her varifocals to see better. She motioned me towards the visitor's chair.

'Sit down, Beth' She hesitated. 'Something alarming has just come to my attention. I'm afraid I need to ask you a couple of questions.'

Whatever the letter contained, it had her worried. She looked down again at the letter in her hand.

'Please forgive me, Beth, for the personal nature of these questions, but I have reasons for asking them.'

Now I was really uncomfortable, aware of the skin at the back of my neck damp with sweat.

'I've noticed you and Andrew seem to be avoiding each other lately.' She looked directly at me. 'Is there a particular reason?'

What exactly did she know? While I looked at the floor, scrabbling desperately for an answer, she carried on.

'Believe me, Beth, I'm not trying to pry. It's just that I've got some information about him that I find very disturbing. I need to establish if it's true, and I thought you might be able to throw some light on it.'

'Well,' I stammered, 'as you probably know, we were going out together for a while, well, sort of. And then we stopped. So we don't really get on too well now,' I finished lamely.

'When you were going out, Beth,' she went on gently, 'was Andrew ever aggressive towards you in any way? I mean, did you ever see him lose his temper?'

The knot of dread expanded. My voice came out in a hoarse whisper.

'Yes.'

'Is there anything else, Beth?' Her eyes were full of concern. 'You see, I have a letter here from Andrew's ex-wife. She claims that after their marriage ended, he broke into her apartment and sexually assaulted her. The case went to trial but he was acquitted by the court. She's just discovered he's here.'

So this was the piece of the jigsaw that was missing. I hadn't been the first. The guy the whole of Carrigmore had seen as a Casanova was a serial rapist.

'Beth.' Jennifer's voice seemed to come from a distance. 'Beth, I need to know. Did anything happen to you? Did he hurt you in any way?'

The first tear rolled down my cheek onto my upper lip. I felt it rest there for a moment, before falling to the floor. I recounted the events of that night to a startled Jennifer.

'Oh, Beth, I'm so sorry.' Her hand reached out for mine. 'You must have gone through hell, trying to work alongside him.' I nodded dumbly. 'Obviously, you didn't press charges.'

'How could I?' The words tumbled out. 'After I'd been dating him for months? Who'd have believed me? They'd have torn me to pieces in court!'

'Does anyone else know about this?'

I told her about Laurie coming to rescue me, and then what had happened at the christening and how I'd had to fill Marie in.

'Listen, Beth. You go on home now. I'll look after the class. And don't worry about Andrew. I can't dismiss him on the grounds of this,' she waved the letter in her hand, 'but I will find a way to get rid of him. I've already had to warn him about his unacceptable behaviour in class. I'll just give him a little more rope and then bam! He won't know what's hit him.'

She folded the letter, put it in her bag and stood up. 'I know you're not going to take this any further, Beth, but maybe you should see a counsellor. Anything that'll help you through it.' The compassion in her eyes was beyond professional concern. 'And perhaps some time off now might be appropriate. I can get someone to fill in. Take a few days while I work out what to do with Andrew. If you feel up to it, we'll see you again on Monday.'

The kindness in her eyes had me on the edge of tears again. I thanked her and went to the staff room to collect my things. The bleakness of my situation hit me. Jennifer, bless her soul, was acting in my best interests, but that wasn't going to protect me from Andrew McKay's fury if he suspected I'd told her. And no matter what pretext he was dismissed on, he'd probably blame me anyway and track me down. For as long as he stayed around Carrigmore, I'd be watching my back.

GOING HOME AT this hour of the day to face a barrage of

questions from my mother wasn't an option. What I needed right now was some space. Somewhere no-one would bother me. I drove on through Longford and, on sheer impulse, headed out on the N4 towards Sligo. Maybe a walk on the beach and the feel of sand squelching through my toes would help. When I came to the base of Knocknarea, I followed the road out to Strandhill. Although we were now into the month of June, the beach was almost deserted with only a handful of surfers gathered at the far end and a middle-aged woman walking her dog over the sand dunes. The day was bright and cool, with an Atlantic wind whipping the waves up into rivulets of lacy white froth. A scatter of seagulls tore through the air, their raucous screeches rising above the sibilant whispering of the incoming tide. The constant ebb and flow of the ocean always had a soothing effect on me, just what I needed now to sort out the mess in my head. I kept imagining the scene when Jennifer confronted Andrew, and tried to guess at his reaction to news of his dismissal. From what I knew of him, he'd hit the roof.

When I thought of Sam, it was those recent meetings that came floating back to me. Outside the Post Office in Ballymartin. The horse show in Moate. His reaching out to touch me and my pulling back. When the thing I wanted most in the world was to get close to him, a deep-seated terror came roaring into life at the first sign of any kind of physical contact. What was it Sam had said? "Be careful, Beth. There's something about him… Be careful." I had paid no attention. Just walked straight into the trap. Any distant hopes I had of drawing closer to Sam had faded into ashes. Miranda's words grinded around in my head. *One girl in particular that's taken his fancy. Seems he's been giving her a bit of extra coaching.* I had to stop thinking about him or I'd just disintegrate into a million pieces of misery.

And then the images of Brian surfaced, when he'd looked so distant and ill at ease. It should have been so obvious how resistant he was to all Mother's exhortations to go visiting half the parish. Then there was that ludicrous House Mass. I could still feel embarrassment creeping up my cheeks when I remembered my mother's absurd behaviour. How must Brian have felt? All hell was going to break loose next Sunday.

I walked barefoot along the seashore for miles, the waves slapping up against my legs, breaking in dirty-white froth on the hard-packed sand. The sharp tang of the sea blew into my face, tasting of salt. Far out, a lone gull drifted on the heaving swell. There, on the edge of the vast expanse of ocean, all the stuff dashing around in my head began to slow just a little.

DAD SPOONED A knob of Dairygold into the mountain of mashed potato on his plate, while Mother tut-tutted.

'School holidays must be just round the corner then, eh Beth?'

'Yeah, just another few weeks, Dad.'

Of course I'd said nothing about Jennifer's news or my whereabouts earlier that day. I just wanted to get through this dinner and retire to the privacy of my room. Unfortunately, Dad was in one of his garrulous moods.

'Isn't it well for you teachers, free as a bird for two whole months. Any plans for the summer?'

I was used to hearing the same comment every year at this time but it still niggled me.

'Well, I thought I might take in a world cruise. Maybe stop off in Hollywood, see if they have any vacancies for superstars. Or go on one of those tours into space, you know the one with the moon landing?'

Mother gave one of her sniffs of disapproval.

'You know, Elizabeth, it's really time you took life a bit more seriously. Nearly 35 years of age, and what do you have to show for it?'

It must have been my failure in the marriage stakes that she was referring to. This time, after the day I'd just had, it was more than I could take.

'And what exactly would you like me to have to show for it?'

'You know what I mean, Beth.' Her expression hardened, eyes narrowing. 'The one opportunity you had just now, and you've let it slip through your fingers.'

Fury spurted through me, erupting in strangled words full of razor sharp edges.

'The one opportunity I had, as you call him, is a self-obsessed arsehole with an inflated sense of his own importance and a serious anger management problem. Oh, yes, and he could be facing trial now if I'd pressed charges against him for raping me.' I spat the words out at her, impervious to whatever effect they were having. 'Yes, Mam, the man you decided was Mr Right for me. He's a control freak, a bully, and a RAPIST. But of course that wouldn't matter to you as long as you get your daughter married off so you can hold your head up in Carrigmore.'

Both of them had gone ashen. A shocked silence filled the room, reaching its tentacles into every corner. With outrage leaping through me, I thundered on.

'And if it wasn't for you and your interference in the past, the real love of my life wouldn't have "slipped through my fingers" would he? But because you were so bigoted and so narrow-minded, you decided he wasn't good enough for me. Only that wasn't your decision to make, was it?'

The accusation hung in the air. Both of them were staring

at me as if I was a creature from another planet. They were speechless. They'd never seen me lose it to this extent before. This was not the Beth they knew. And there was no going back from a revelation like that. They were just going to have to live with it. Although it would probably be overshadowed by Brian's homecoming. I teetered on the brink of telling them, but stopped myself just in time. After all, it was his news.

'And now, if you'll excuse me.' I stood up, leaving a heaped plate of steak and onions behind me on the table, 'I need some fresh air.'

'Beth, wait.' Dad stumbled to his feet. 'Please, sweetheart. Tell us what happened.'

'Some other time, Dad.' I kept walking not looking back until I reached the door. Behind me, the silence echoed in the vastness of the room.

'OH JESUS, BETH. I never liked the guy, but to think he's done it before? And that he could have slipped though the net like that. What happens now?'

I filled Laurie in on Jennifer's plans.

'Do you think he'll bugger off now that the game is up?'

'I suppose that'd be the best possible outcome. The idea of him hanging around Carrigmore is really scary.' I shuddered involuntarily.

'Oh, come on pet. What on earth is there to keep him here now? He'll probably be gone by the weekend.'

'Please God.' I automatically crossed my fingers. 'Um, the other thing. I've just told them at home. Well, I sort of flung it at them. My mother was doing my head in and I let her have it.'

'Ah. So now they know it all.' Laurie took a deep breath. 'But that's good, isn't it? I mean you'd have had to tell them sometime.'

'Yeah,' I smiled ruefully. 'And at least it's out now.'

We were sitting in her old, farmhouse-style kitchen, ensconced in the cosy chairs on either side of the Stanley range and cradling large mugs of well-laced coffee. By now, my anger had deflated, giving way to a sense of dread. This was going to change everything at home. They'd see me now as a rape victim, or worse still, one who'd brought it on herself. I could see Mother pursing her lips grimly as she told Dad that she'd never approved of the way I 'tarted myself up.' At least I wouldn't have to worry about them spreading it round. This was one thing my mother would definitely not want the parish to know about.

'Yeah, well anyway, it's done now. I told her in no uncertain terms just how lethal the consequences of her interfering have been. I laid into her about Sam too. Her and her effin' prejudices.' I took another sip from the mug, feeling my anger mounting again. I nodded grimly to myself. 'Oh and just for good measure, she's about to get another shock.' I filled Laurie in on the bombshell that was set to rip the Maguire family apart.

'Oh, dear Jesus. Wouldn't you nearly feel sorry for the poor woman?' Laurie's words were somewhat belied by the glee in her voice. 'But seriously, poor old Brian, he must really have been through the mill in the last few months, trying to come to terms with something that big.'

We chatted on and the conversation meandered back full circle to Andrew, and to Jennifer's intention to find a way to terminate his contract. That too was going to set off its own ripples. The term was nearly over, but such an event would still be more than adequate to feed the appetite for scandal that abounded in Carrigmore. Questions would be asked the length and breadth of the parish, and no doubt, the story that emerged would grow with the telling, nourished by the prevailing winds of malice as they whispered in glee.

CHAPTER NINETEEN

THE REMAINDER OF that week passed without further incident. I returned home to find both my parents tiptoeing around me, neither really wanting to bring up The Subject. I suppose in their day, it would have simply been brushed under the carpet, rather than have attention drawn to the family of the victim, so they just didn't know how to handle it. Dad showed his concern by plying me with mugs of coffee, and even inviting me out for a drink with him. I think Mother was torn between feeling sorry for me, maybe even tinged with shades of guilt, and her more customary niggling rancour for the way I'd spoken to her. She did make some effort to be pleasant, but we were both so wary of each other it never went beyond small talk. I split my time between going for long, rambling walks with Amber and pouring out what I was feeling into my diary.

Meanwhile, Sunday 14 was inexorably drawing closer, and with it the upheaval of the century. I felt like an actor waiting in the wings for the battle scene of Armageddon.

'DID I TELL you I've got an appointment with Richard next week?'

Having spent an hour or so trawling through the shops, Laurie and I were now sitting in front of frothing mugs of Cappuccino and buns squelching with whipped cream.

'That's great, Laurie. So, what do you expect from it?'

Richard was her solicitor. Obviously, things were moving on with her legal separation.

'I think basically, he's looking for my instructions in response to the correspondence from 'the other party' And do you know, I'm not sorry we've reached this point. After what he's done to me, I'd never take him back.' She tore a chunk out of the cream bun on her plate. 'So the sooner we get things properly sorted, the better, and I feel safer going through our legal teams than I would dealing directly with Keith. Kind of like I've got someone fighting my corner. Does that sound stupid?'

She looked at me forlornly.

'Oh, Laurie, of course not.' I reached out for her hand. 'The more big guns you have on your side, the better you're going to come out of it. Do you know yet what he's looking for?'

'As I understand it, regular access to the kids.'

'No mention of dividing property or any other assets?'

'No, at least not yet. Though that'll probably come later, knowing him.'

'Well anyway, best of luck with Richard next week. I'm sure it'll work out fine.'

'Thanks, Beth,' she smiled weakly. 'So all ready for the big showdown?'

'Don't remind me. Another week and she'll know.'

She licked the remaining froth off her spoon. 'Just remember if you need a place to crash for a bit...'

'I'll bear that in mind.' I sighed heavily. 'Anyway, bad and all as that's going to be, it's not the only black cloud on my horizon.'

'Beth, that cow could have totally misread the situation. At the very least, I'll bet she blew the whole thing out of proportion, just for your benefit.'

Laurie'd read my mind. I couldn't get Miranda's words about Sam out of my head. It was only now the realisation was sinking in of how deep my feelings for him still were.

MONDAY MORNING, I arrived back at work after the few days break, heart hammering with anxiety. Would I have another three weeks to get through with him glowering at me on the far side of the glass? Alone in the staffroom, I filled the kettle to pass the time. The next car to pull into the parking space was Sheila's. Now at least I might hear something.

'Heard the news, Beth?'

I suddenly felt *déjà vu*. The last time someone had asked me that, it was Marie, all agog about the Scotsman who'd been appointed to cover her maternity leave. I looked blankly at Sheila while the hammering in my chest became almost audible.

'Andrew's been fired. Well, put on Administrative Leave. Which amounts to pretty much the same thing.'

A gigantic wave of relief rolled over me.

'Really? Tell me more.'

'Ye know how he's been a bit unpredictable lately, losing it with the kids? It seems he really went over the top the other day, and the sub covering your class got worried and told Jennifer.'

'And?'

'Jennifer hauled him into the office there and then and told him she couldn't have children in his care. Apparently, she'd already issued a couple of verbal warnings, and notified the Board, so he was on his last chance.'

There was a God in heaven. The menace that had lurked in every corner of the little staffroom was blown away. I was free again. He surely wouldn't stay in Carrigmore with this disgrace hanging over him. I could finally break out of the jagged nightmare that had taken over my life.

'You don't look all that surprised.' Sheila unscrewed

the instant Nescafe and spooned granules into two mugs. 'Although, I suppose working right next to him, you'd have seen more than the rest of us.'

The enquiry in her tone was clear.

'Let's just say he seemed to have quite a few off days.' I stirred milk into the coffee. 'He wasn't always the most pleasant person to be around.'

'Ah, sure maybe it's just as well. Doesn't do to have someone like that around kids.' She settled herself into the armchair. 'Funny the way things turn out. Didn't we all think he was Mr Nice Guy when he first arrived?'

Yeah, I thought bitterly. We'd all thought he was bloody terrific.

Andrew's replacement was an old friend of Jennifer's, a middle-aged lady who'd taken early retirement from teaching and had agreed to step in for the remaining weeks of term. A Mrs Devine, with a frizz of grey hair, gentle eyes, and a slightly flustered, but motherly manner. The children had warmed to her already, finding they didn't have to be wary of unexpected outbursts of temper. As for me, there would be no more looking over my shoulder, dreading the sound of his voice. As the week rolled on, I was visibly more relaxed and beginning to enjoy again the varied challenges thrown up in the course of the teaching day. In spite of this, the storm that was about to hit the Maguire family was always at the back of my mind. And each day brought it closer. All I could do was hope that, in time, Mother would reconcile herself to the inevitable, but for the next few weeks at least, our home was going to resemble a war zone.

JUST BEFORE LUNCHTIME on Sunday, Brian called me to say he was on his way. He'd been met at the airport and supplied with the same slightly battered Ford Escort he'd had at Christmas; the one they kept on standby for visiting priests. He was going to spend a couple of days with us before reporting to the mother house. At his request, I had said nothing, leaving it to him to make the announcement.

When he arrived, Dad had just meandered off for a round of golf. I was in the garden, attacking the weeds that were threatening to choke the roses. And Mother was sitting in the bay window of the living room, leafing through the latest *Home and Garden*, no doubt gleaning ideas for the next makeover for our house. Hearing the car on the gravel driveway, she glanced up, her face registering first bewilderment, then delight. She sprang up with an agility belying her 65 years to greet the returning hero.

'Fr Brian!' The hug was enough to almost suffocate him. 'Of all the wonderful surprises. Why didn't you let us know you were coming? I'd have had everything ready.'

He flashed me a sideways grin while trying to extricate himself from her embrace.

'Whoa, steady on, Mother, sure what's to get ready. I'm not the Crowned Prince.'

Of course, in her eyes, that's exactly what he was, and she'd been caught out without having the house scrubbed from top to bottom. I could see annoyance competing with her delight at having him home again. She was so predictable. Her brain went into overdrive searching for possible reasons for his return after only a six-month spell back in Zambia. Anxiety showed in her eyes.

'You're not ill, are you? I mean with all that malaria and stuff out there. You haven't contracted any of those awful tropical diseases, I hope.'

Brian propelled her into the living room and over towards

the sofa.

'Relax, Mother. I'm just fine. Don't I look the picture of health?'

While she had to accept that he did indeed appear to be in good health, she still hadn't found the answer she was looking for.

'So, what is it then? A bonus holiday for all your hard work out there?'

The gnawing sense of unease must have shown in my face. She was in like a light.

'Beth, what do you know about this?'

The question took me by surprise. I faltered.

'I eh, I think you'd better ask Brian, Mam.'

Her gaze swung back in his direction, eyes narrowing in sudden trepidation. 'Well, son?'

Brian moved over to the window and turned to face her.

'You know the last thing in the world I'd want is to disappoint you, Mother. I've always tried to do what you thought right for me.' He paused and then plunged on. 'But maybe I should have been more honest with myself.'

'What exactly are you saying?' Her face was alive with panic, the words coming out tight and forced.

'There's no easy way for me to tell you, Mother. I can't continue with the life I've chosen. Deep inside me, there's another person desperate to get out. I'm sorry. I can't go on pretending to be something I'm not anymore.'

Her knuckles tightened on the fabric of the sofa. This was a calamity so far outside the contours of her world that she had no way of dealing with it. No words with which she could combat the enormity of what she was hearing. For a moment, I thought she was going to faint. Perhaps mistaking her silence for a more favourable reception than he had expected, Brian carried on.

'I know that for years now, I've been coasting along, doing what was expected of me. But there was always something missing. The best way I can describe it is like I've been going along with the flow. It was easier that way than to face the truth.'

'The truth?' The two words were articulated with icy distinction.

'You know what I'm saying, Mother. At the very least, I need some time out to think things through. I'm sorry.'

The silence stretched to breaking point. Then, like a series of small explosions, her words detonated around the room.

'Sorry, is it? Sorry. Sorry for what exactly? Sorry you've brought humiliation on this family? Sorry you've betrayed your sacred calling? Sorry you've made me a laughing stock?'

Her anger hissed and spat like a sackful of cobras. Brian winced.

'Have you given any thought to what people are going to say? To what your father and I are going to have to face? To the disgrace of having a failed priest in the family?'

An expression I'd never seen before hardened Brian's face. He was seeing a side of Mother he never knew existed.

'Do you honestly think that's what's important here? What other people think? What the repercussions will be for you and Dad?' He sighed. 'This is not about you, Mother. This is *my* life we're talking about. And I can't go on living a lie.'

'Living a lie? You took solemn vows in the presence of God. How can that be a lie?' Her voice had risen to the level of hysteria as she stood to face him.

'And what about your part in those solemn vows?' He took a couple of paces towards her, fists beginning to clench, his own fury gathering pace. 'Have you ever thought about that Mother? Was this ever really my choice? Or was it not wanting to let you down, hah? Way back, when I was only a kid, it was always "Oh little Brian is going to serve Mass. Isn't that great?" and then "Have you heard my Brian is thinking of the missionary life — yes, it looks like we'll have a priest in the family. How wonderful."'

I almost felt sorry for her as she flinched under the mockery of his mincing tones. The realisation that it was her vision of him that had shaped his adult life and propelled him forward into a superficial existence that had constricted his thinking dawned on her. They had entered barbed-wire territory, and there was no going back. With trembling hands, Brian picked up his jacket and walked out of the house. Trapped inside the ruins of her dream, Mother collapsed back onto the sofa, shaking. Outside the window, the sycamore trees rustled in a fit of restlessness as a cloud of sparrows broke from the branches, and rose brawling into the distance.

June 6, 09

To: angelamckay@yahoo.co.uk
From: andrewmckay@gmail.com
Subject: Update on plans

Dear Mother,

Hope all is well with you and Dad. Is he getting out for a few rounds of golf these fine summer days? Or still as much as ever a slave to the practice?
I've decided to finish up a bit early in school. The weather's too good here to be wasting time stuck in a classroom with a pack of seven-year-olds, half of them retarded, or what they call "Special Needs" nowadays. Some of these little country schools can be so backward, can't they? I think I need something with more of a challenge. Maybe a masters could be the way forward for me. So if you could have a word in Dad's ear about a wee loan. Tell him how much it would improve my chances in

clinical psychology. Just think, you could have another Sigmund Freud in the family!

Anyway, I'm going to stay on here for a few weeks, do some sightseeing around the West. It's supposed to be quite spectacular, from what I hear. Lots of mountains and castles. And after spending six months stuck in this dump, I could do with a change of scenery.

Anyway, that's all the news from here, Ma. All the best to you and Dad. Don't forget to ask him about that loan. I'll send you a card from Connemara.

Yours, Andrew

CHAPTER TWENTY

ROSEMARY LINED UP the knife and fork on her plate and wiped her lips delicately, leaving streaks of pale pink lipstick on her serviette. Obviously a mannerism she'd picked up from Dublin 4. Summoned home for the council of war, she'd spent the last hour making pointed references to the fact that she was 'late', and that perhaps she should be thinking of doing a pregnancy test. She was always one to put herself first, our Rosemary, even at a time like this with Mother toppling towards a nervous breakdown. When Dad and I had adamantly refused to hassle Brian into changing his mind, Mother resorted to enlisting the support of her younger daughter. And while Rosemary tut-tutted and dear-oh-deared about the whole sad business, she didn't actually seem all that concerned. The situation was hardly likely to impact on her and her genteel life in semi-detached suburbia.

Brian had spent most of the day with an old school friend of his, just turning up in time for dinner, which he took to his room to eat off a tray. Solitude was preferable to the hostility that permeated the dining room, with Mother eyeing him across the dinner table. The Maguire household was not what you might describe as a barrel of laughs.

'Well, I think he's being very selfish,' sniffed Rosemary. 'Has he thought at all of what people are going to say around here?'

'My point exactly!' Mother rowed in triumphantly. 'It's all very well saying he's having a crisis of faith. These things pass. But the shame we're all going to face when news of this gets out. Oh, I can't bear to think about it.'

'Oh, come on, Mary.' Dad was losing patience. 'It is his life, after all. He should be the one to decide how he wants to live it. Give the poor lad a break.'

'But didn't he decide that years ago, when he joined up?' Rosemary's petulant tone underlined her failure to grasp that it never had been Brian's decision.

'You mark my words,' Mother waved her fork ominously in Dad's direction. 'This is a sad day for the whole family, a day we'll all live to regret.'

Dad sighed and put down his knife and fork. Several pieces of chicken casserole remained on his plate. Obviously worth the sacrifice if it meant he could make his escape.

'I just want my son to be happy. And it looks to me like he's taken the first step in that direction.' Pushing back his chair, he heaved himself up. 'Maybe it's time you stopped trying to run his life for him.'

His retreating footsteps sounded the death knell to any hopes she might have harboured of getting him on her side.

'Well, I never!' Her indignation escalated. 'Anyone would think he didn't care about the family.'

By now, I too had had enough and decided to leave herself and Rosemary to their woes. It was a fine June evening with a mackerel sky, just perfect for a stroll down the canal bank with Amber. While she mooched around happily, nose to the ground, busily living her life at knee-level, my mind drifted once again to Brian, Andrew and Sam. Mostly Sam. My 35th birthday was just around the corner, and, as my mother so kindly reminded me, I had nothing to show for it but a litany of failed relationships. It seemed whoever had handed out the pieces of the jigsaw that made up my life was having a good laugh at my expense. What was it Shakespeare said about the sport of the gods? All the important bits seemed to be missing.

'I DON'T SUPPOSE you'd fancy a pint, Beth?'

Never was an invitation to the pub more welcome. I'd just arrived back with Amber. Mother and Rosemary were ensconced in the living room, no doubt planning their next strategy. Brian, not surprisingly, wanted to get out for a bit, and the Village Inn seemed the obvious choice.

Ten minutes later, we were sitting in one of the corner nooks, in fact the one I'd been in with Andrew on our first night together. It was funny how things could change in the space of a few months. Although it was now a week since he'd been relieved of his teaching duties and I hadn't seen a trace of him around the village, I still worried about running into him. Not knowing his whereabouts was the worst part. He could turn up at any time, around any corner.

'Ah, that's good stuff.' Brian was savouring his first mouthful of Guinness. 'Not one of their specialties in Zambia.'

'No, I don't suppose it is,' I grinned. 'But you must have tried the local hoosh?'

'Paint stripper,' he grimaced. 'They use it for rubbing on cows with milk fever. Does the job, apparently.'

I took a deep swallow, enjoying the sharp bite of Heineken on my palate. It was good to get away from the crackle of tension at home.

'So? What's all this I hear about a handsome Scot?'

My face darkened. His eyes narrowed with concern.

'Things didn't exactly work out, as they say.' My lip wobbled.

Now seriously worried, he gripped my arm. 'What's been

going on?'

There was no point in fudging the issue. I gave him a brief outline of the last few months, culminating with what I now termed The Episode.

'Oh, Beth. God love you.' The tremor in his voice said it all as his hand closed over mine. 'Is he still around?'

'He was suspended about a week ago, but I think he's still in Carrigmore.'

'How are you coping?'

'Just getting on with things, I suppose,' I muttered, 'But there's more.' I stared into the pint of Heineken in front of me. 'Guess who's back from the States?'

'No way!' It must have been clear from my tone that this was not entirely good news. Brian was aware of the terms on which Sam and I had parted. Although in the seminary at the time, he'd been following my romance with interest, and was dismayed to hear of its sorry end.

'Yeah, his father had a stroke and he was needed to manage the yard here.'

'And?'

I outlined the couple of disastrous encounters we'd had and then crowned it with the news we'd heard from Miranda about the trainee instructor. Just saying the words out loud brought on another gush of despair.

'Listen to me, Beth.' He put his hands on my shoulders, turning me to face him. 'I may not be the best qualified to say this to you. I sure as hell haven't been a shining example of getting things right. But I do know this.' The urgency in his tone gathered strength. 'You and Sam belong together. Forget about what went wrong in the past. It's obvious you're still besotted with him. And after all this time, that's not something to just throw away. No matter what it costs you, I think you should go after him.'

The conviction in his words sent hope surging through me. I was beginning to feel like Maria in *The Sound of Music* being exhorted to climb every mountain. And my Reverend Mother was in full flight.

'Leave him in no doubt that you're still there for him.' His fingers were now shredding a beer mat on the table, screwing up each sliver he peeled off. 'You've got to fight for him. Besides, you only have his sister's word that he's involved with anyone. And even if it's true, it's probably only a passing fancy. He might even be trying to make you jealous.' The beer mat was now in tatters on the table. 'Come on, Beth, you owe it to yourself to make this happen.'

His sense of urgency was infectious but I knew it wasn't going to be that easy. How could I go after him when I didn't know if he still felt the same about me? And that was looking pretty doubtful with this latest development. It was like there was a vast space in between us in which a thick fog of silence had gathered and any attempt at communication was smothered before it took shape. Like I was stumbling around in the dark, without any markers to guide me.

THE FOLLOWING DAY, Brian was heading off to Navan to see his Provincial, so Mother was like an antichrist. I think she'd still believed there was some hope that he'd change his mind, but now that he was officially setting things in motion, she had little left to cling to. It was now a question of steeling herself for when the news broke in Carrigmore, leaving her 'the laughing stock of the parish.' The atmosphere over breakfast was way beyond North Pole cold. Rosemary had already packed her stuff to return to her insulated life in suburbia, so as far as Mother was concerned, she was being abandoned by her two most cherished offspring. Her only contribution to the somewhat strained discourse was to make pointed references to the base ingratitude parents could expect from their children, and other barbed comments along similar lines.

In school, things were winding down towards the summer break, so the kids were looking for any excuse to run riot. They'd just finished their end-of-year assessments, and keeping them focused on anything was a full-time chore, so by hometime every day, I was knackered. That Thursday, rather than go home and face my mother's ire, I decided a little retail therapy might help. I could go to the new Town Centre in Athlone and while away a couple of hours. Anything would be better than the Maguire household right now.

HALF AN HOUR later, and I was working my way through the sales rail in one of the fashion boutiques. Much of the stuff was obviously intended for the younger crowd, only available in sizes eight to ten, designed with the teenage body in mind. It was yet another reminder of my advancing years. Once you were over 30, you were into a completely different clothes market. The middle-aged market. I'd soon be shuffling along in a tweed coat with a walking stick.

Just to emphasise how out of place I was here, the handful of other shoppers browsing through the glitzy party dresses looked about 16. And here came yet another one in low-slung designer jeans with a studded belt low on her hips, showing off her tanned midriff, strappy high heels and french-polished toenails. She looked behind her impatiently, as if expecting to be followed in, but her companion had obviously gotten waylaid. She stationed herself at the rail by the door, and began looking cursorily through the accessories on display there. Her frequent glances out towards the shopping mall suggested her attention was more focused on the whereabouts of her friend than on the bits and pieces she picked up and as quickly discarded.

'There you are.' The pitch of her voice carried a hint of accusation as the object of her expectation appeared in the doorway. To my horror, I caught the familiar whiff of linseed oil. A lightning glance confirmed it. The little madam most definitely did exist. And there was no escape route. With them standing right at the door, I would have to pass directly in front of them to leave the store. I swiftly edged my way further towards the back, trying to bury myself in among the rails of designer dresses. But the gods were not on my side. Once satisfied she had her man in tow, the girl moved down through the various rails, now so close that I could smell her perfume, with Sam following on her heels. I decided rather than wait to be found skulking in the inner recesses of the store, the preferred option would be to brave it out. I took a deep breath.

'Hello, Sam. Good to see you again.'

'Beth!' His astonishment quickly turned to acute embarrassment as the girl put a protective arm through his and gave me a frosty smile. 'Yes, em, you too.'

'Hi. I'm Gillian, Sam's girlfriend.' Unmistakably a Welsh accent, with that upward inflection at the end of the sentence. The smile she'd pasted on had settled into a rictus-like mask and froze even further as she stuck out a hand, limp as a dead fish.

'Sorry, Beth, this is Gillian. Gillian, Beth.' The words came out sounding forced. Panic flared in me, prompting an automated response.

'Nice to meet you, Gillian.'

'You too,' she purred, clearly more secure now that she had staked her territory.

'Well, we'd better, you know…' Sam tailed off, not even trying to hide his discomfort as he nudged Gillian away from the rail, in the direction of the door. 'Take care, Beth.'

'Yeah, see you around, Sam. Bye for now.'

I exhaled very slowly and blinked back unwelcome tears.

'SHE COULDN'T BE more than 18, Laurie. And she was making very sure everyone in the store knew he was *her* man.'

Brian's words about Sam and I belonging together rolled around in my head, converted into a vicious parody. I'd lost him ten years ago and in my world, there were no second chances.

'And the way she was hanging off of him!' The unbearable flashed into my head. 'Laurie, do you think she's sleeping with him?'

'Listen, Beth.' Laurie put her hands on my shoulders. 'Whether she is or not, it won't last. Can you really see Sam settling with some chit of a girl half his age? She's just a distraction for him.' She took the empty glass from my hand and refilled it. 'Didn't Miranda say she was his student? It's a teenage crush, nothing more. He's probably just flattered by her attentions.'

'Yeah. So flattered that he follows her around like a lost puppy. And look at all they have in common.' I was starting to blubber. 'Horses and that. The next thing, he'll be taking her to shows with him.'

The thought of them doing the show circuit together nearly killed me. We used to do that. It was how I came to associate the pungent smells of straw and well-oiled leather with the heady excitement of physical proximity to him. It was the aroma that would fill the air when I used to help him with the warm bran mash liberally flavoured with treacle and Guinness the horses got every Sunday. And when I was taking my first steps on the end of a lunge line, how lavish he was in his praise any time I got something right, or even half-right. He was a born instructor.

After my preliminary lessons when I was able to walk, trot, and stop on my own, he would let me potter around in the sand manège while he was schooling the young horses destined for the show jumping circuit. These training sessions were always followed by a hack around the woodlands on the Butler estate, winding our way through a sea of brown and green foliage, with Sheba, Sam's golden Labrador padding along behind us. In my memory, there was always sunlight shining through the overhanging branches, throwing clear-cut patterns onto the boggy track. I loved the feel of the placid mare rolling beneath me, her head bobbing in rhythm with the stride. As I grew more confident, Sam would increase the pace to a canter on the long stretches between clearings, and we'd lose ourselves in a world of whirling leaves and interlacing branches with sycamore and beech trees swaying overhead. We would always finish by walking the horses into the shallow reaches of the River Inny that bordered the estate, the swift-flowing water bubbling up around their fetlocks.

That was ten long years ago. The nothingness between us had grown like a cancer through those empty years. Now Sam was home again, but there was an 18-year-old kid who had probably been born on a horse laying claim to him. I didn't stand a chance.

Andrew rammed the gear lever into first and the BMW surged forward. Despite the cushioning effect of the half dozen pints he'd drunk, along with the couple of chasers, his father's words continued to hammer out a drumbeat of mockery, the sloping letters dancing in his brain. Tight-fisted bastard. It wasn't as if he didn't have the money. He was fucking loaded. Just didn't want to see his son make a success of his life. In spite of all the Ma's pleading, he'd refused to even consider the loan. *No intention of throwing good money after bad. About time you started to fend for yourself.* The fucking nerve of him. But he'd regret it. Oh, yes, that was one thing Andrew would make damn sure of.

Turning onto the straight stretch of road towards Oughterard, he accelerated, sending the needle quivering up over 150km, 160km, 170km. As for that prissy schoolteacher, that was another loose end that needed tying up. She sure as hell wasn't going to get away with messing him around. With her come on looks and her low-cut blouses. He'd find a way to throw a spanner in her works. If it was the last thing he fucking did before leaving this godforsaken country, he'd fix her good and proper. After this time out in Connemara, he'd go back to Carrigmore and let her see exactly what happened to prissy little madams who messed him around.

As if in sympathy with his mounting rage, the BMW responded to his touch, the growl of the engine increasing in volume. The glare of its headlights stabbed the blackness of the night, eating up the road ahead of him. Then, out of nowhere, the hard shoulder was gone and the road narrowed and curved off to the left. God damn it, why couldn't they have decent roads in this country? His foot slammed down on the brake. The car veered to the right and hurtled towards an oak tree. There was a sickening crunch of metal and the world went black. When he came to, Andrew became aware of a crushing pain in his chest, and the flow of viscous, sticky blood from his temple. The front end of the BMW had crumpled and the steering wheel and dashboard compacted into one mangled mess. He struggled to prise the door open but it had buckled inwards, the twisted metal angled sharply against his hip, trapping him in his seat. Black smoke began to billow from the shattered bonnet.

His throat was already clogging up. His mind raced, grappling for a way out. Small flickers of yellow flame curled up from the twisted metal of the engine. A fit of coughing shuddered through his chest as the noxious fumes invaded his lungs. In a rush of hot air, the fire spread to the roof of the car. A cushion of heat enveloped him and his vision began to blur. Now wouldn't his Da be sorry. And that tight-arsed bitch that had messed him around. She'd regret the chance she'd thrown away. Terror rushed through him as the bluish flames dripped from the roof onto the padded shoulders of his Armani jacket, cooking the flesh beneath. The screams of pain grew weaker as he slipped towards unconsciousness and slumped forward.

By the time the emergency services arrived, Andrew McKay was a charred, blackened lump, to be positively identified only through dental records.

CHAPTER TWENTY-ONE

At last Friday, June 26 had arrived, and with it two months of freedom. In keeping with tradition, Jennifer had designated it a half-day and treated all the staff to lunch in the hotel in Ballymartin. With the holiday mood running high, Laurie and had I decided to head back into town for an Italian that evening, followed by a few drinks in Molloys. The conversation had meandered round to Brian and his plans. He was still under the jurisdiction of the order, but was free to choose whichever type of work appealed to him for the period of his 'time out', and had decided to focus on the area of adult education.

'So, things are going well for him then. I'm really pleased.'

'Yeah,' I agreed. 'It's great to see him free from the worries and doubts he was carrying around with him last time he was here.'

Laurie tipped back the last of her wine and signalled to the barman. 'You think he's going to stick around here for a bit?'

'It looks to me like he's got every reason to. I suppose it depends on how things turn out.'

'Yeah, I suppose,' she assented. 'But so far, it's looking good, yeah?'

'Very good, I really can't see him going back in. Ever!'

Our conversation was interrupted by the sudden increase in volume of the television in the corner. The 9.00pm *News* always attracted the attention of the regulars, constantly on the look-out for an item of local interest.

'A single-car collision early this morning in the

Oughterard area of Co. Galway has claimed the life of one man. The deceased is said to have been a Scottish national in his late 30s, who had been working in Co. Longford. He was pronounced dead at the scene of the crash.' All around us, there was a sudden, collective intake of breath.

I looked at Laurie in horror. Could it be him? What other Scottish national had been working in Co. Longford, and probably driving like a lunatic. She reached for my hand.

'Gardaí are appealing for witnesses. Anyone driving in the area between the hours of 12.00am and 2.00am who saw a red BMW registration C401 WLA is asked to contact Oughterard Garda Station.'

Red BMW? It was him. The sense of horror grew, swelling in the pit of my stomach. Laurie's hand tightened over mine.

'Listen, Beth. It may not be a very charitable thing to say right now, but he only got what was coming to him. Come on, honey, you know that. He was probably out of his head with drink.'

'Laurie.' My voice was hoarse with shock. 'No-one deserves to go like that. What was he thinking of?'

All around us, the stunned silence had given way to tut-tutting and mutters of disapproval. All of the locals would have had some passing acquaintance with Andrew, and most would be familiar with his drinking habits and erratic mood swings, especially of late. Laurie's words about getting his come-uppance were being echoed among the little groups all around the pub. They all knew that Andrew had been my colleague, with some guessing that our relationship had gone further than that. This was, after all, the venue of our first date, when we had come to the trad session on that Monday night so long ago. I was fast becoming the focus of sympathetic glances and whispered conversations.

'Come on, let's get out of here.' Laurie was on her feet. 'Come back with me for a bit. No-one's going to bother you there.'

Anxious to get away from the expressions of sympathy coming my direction, I followed her out. As we drove away from the town, the initial shock started to dissipate into something else. Something tinged with relief. This was finally the end of the nightmare I'd been living for months. I felt guilty that someone's death could make me feel that way, but still couldn't shake off the sense of freedom that was rising through the guilt. Of course, I regretted Andrew's death, but I couldn't help agreeing with Laurie that he had it coming. Anyone who drove like he did with too much alcohol in his system was going to come to grief some time or other. His luck had just run out.

NEWS OF THE fatal accident swept through Carrigmore like a forest fire. Reactions tended towards the charitable, "Ah, he wasn't such a bad soul. Maybe a bit too fond o' the gargle," with just a few more honest comments about how it was a mercy he hadn't killed anyone else with the way he'd drove.

The following day, his parents arrived, numb with shock. His mother Angela, originally from Lanesborough, was a tiny frail figure dressed in black. She had retreated into a cave of silence, wordlessly accepting the formal condolences that were offered. His father, a medical doctor, remained aloof and guarded. They were met by Frank Moran and Fr Flannery, who took them to the hospital mortuary where the remains of their son had been brought from Galway. After a brief service there, the cortège made its way to Carrigmore Church, where a small crowd of locals had turned out to pay their respects. The body would repose there overnight before being brought home to Scotland for burial. Laurie, Brian and I took up a position at the back of the church and listened to Fr Flannery's empty words about the tragedy of a young life being lost in such circumstances, the appalling waste of great talent etc. When the traditional queue of sympathizers began to form, we took the opportunity to make our escape. There was only so far I was prepared to go out of respect for the man who'd done me so much damage. As his former colleague, I had little choice but to attend the service, but enough was enough.

We emerged from the gloom of the church, blinking into the bright June evening.

The next few days were dominated by the shock of a rural community being hit by a tragedy, and their attempts to come to terms with it. Although Andrew had not been one of our own, and had antagonised quite a few locals in the recent past, his premature death ensured a certain measure of sympathy about a young man being cut down in his prime etc. As for me, while I would have preferred to see him go down for rape and serve a lingering prison sentence, it was pretty clear that scenario would never have happened, and given his history, he would very likely have gone on to assault other women. I would have been happier to have extracted justice from him and seen him publicly shamed, but at least I now knew that he would never hassle me again. As the days passed, the news that had been shocking gave way to whose husband was running round with whom, and who'd just been caught for unpaid tax. And so, the everyday routine of village life returned.

I'D JUST ARRIVED back home from the library where I'd spent half an hour browsing the Irish fiction shelves, immersing myself in some of my favourite works. I'd been highly commended in the short story competition I'd entered a couple of months ago, and was so chuffed that I'd decided to start fleshing out an idea I had for a novel. I was anxious to learn as much as I could from a close reading of what was being published now and I'd found a selection of contemporary women's fiction that would fit the bill nicely. I already had the rough outline of a story in my head, and was now eager to get a shape on it. As I turned the key in the lock, voices from the kitchen cut short my musings.

'We can't push her into doing something she's not ready for.'

'Maybe she is now. She's not getting through this on her own. She needs help.'

'Beth, hi.' Laurie had spotted me at the kitchen door and tried to overcompensate, her cheeks flaming.

'Oh, hi Sis.' Brian wasn't often caught off-guard but right now, he was floundering desperately, grappling for something to say.

'Well?' I glared from one to the other, waiting for an explanation.

'We're just really concerned about you, Beth.' Laurie was in first. 'And we thought that maybe it would help if you could see someone.'

'A counsellor, you mean?'

The word hung in the air, immense in its implications. Was I messed up? Damaged? In need of professional help? Was I really that bad?

'At least think about it, Beth.' Brian was quick to spot the advantage they'd gained. 'You've been through the most dreadful trauma. The kind that could have a long-term effect on future relationships.'

There was a theatrical pause while they let that sink in.

'So?' Laurie looked expectantly at me, while the air

crackled with tension.

'I dunno.' Visions of drab, clinical consultation rooms complete with couch and regulation box of tissues crowded into my mind. Then all the misery of recent meetings with Sam came back to me. All the times I'd been aching to get close to him and couldn't. Maybe the co-conspirators had a point. Anything that might help with that part of my life was worth considering. Brian was the first to recognise that I was wavering and zoned in immediately.

'Come on, Sis. You know we only want the best for you.'

I looked from him to Laurie. There was no getting away from the delighted anticipation in their faces. Maybe there'd be no harm in going for one session, just to keep them happy.

ONCE I'D MADE the phone call, the system had cranked into gear, offering me an appointment within days. Since then, several times a day, I'd been tempted to cancel; the whole idea of reliving the horror hovered over me like a black cloud. But some tiny voice inside my head kept needling me, insisting that this was the only way out of the morass I'd been sinking into. With my finger hovering over the doorbell, the urge to turn and run almost overpowered me, until I remembered Sam's face that last time I'd pulled away from him. Minutes later, I was sitting opposite Deirdre Donoghue in a thickly carpeted room with two leather armchairs, a filing cabinet, and a coffee table, on which was a jug of water and, of course, a box of tissues. In one corner was a mini-kitchen from which a half-sized fridge hummed. The scent of sandalwood rose from three lighted candles on the worktop. A hand-carved clock on the wall ticked the seconds by.

'Okay, Beth.' Deirdre's voice was gentle, like the rustling of leaves. 'Would you like to tell me why you're here?'

She was waiting for me to put it into words. The awful thing he'd done to me. I had to come out and say it. Like drawing the poison out from a festering wound. Into a silence that had stretched to encompass the world, I whispered the words, 'I was raped.'

She waited for me to go on. And waited.

'And I've been such a mess ever since.' My voice was beginning to wobble.

'But of course you have, Beth. That's not something you just walk away from.'

'I feel like I'm afraid all the time.' I swallowed desperately, trying to gulp back the tears that were building up. 'Even though he's not around anymore. You see, there was an accident and he was killed. But what he did to me is still with me.'

'Take your time, Beth. And just tell me whatever you want to.'

And so, the sequence of events that had unfolded came spilling out in an incoherent jumble; I went through our dating history, and then how he'd seemed to be getting more possessive about me; how his drinking had gotten out of hand, and finally the night we'd had the row when I'd finally lost it and told him we were finished. And how after that, in a moment of madness, I'd accepted a lift home from him. The worst mistake I could have made. I went on to describe the squalor of the lock-keeper's cottage, and how Andrew had mocked my helplessness, pinning me to the floor under his weight, humiliating me in every possible way.

Now I was starting to blubber. Deirdre held out the box of tissues. And waited.

'The worst of it is how it has affected me since.' The

words jerked from my throat while I tried to control the fit of crying that was threatening to overwhelm me.

'Can you tell me about that?' The gentleness in her tone was an open invitation.

'You see, there's someone really important to me. My ex-boyfriend. And he warned me about this guy. But I didn't listen. It's all my own fault. I was asking for trouble.'

'Listen to me, Beth.' She paused, waiting for my full attention. 'No matter what you think you did to contribute to what happened, what he subjected you to is not your fault.'

I looked at her blankly. I'd been telling myself for so long that at least some part of the blame was mine that her words weren't making any sense to me.

'You have to believe me here, Beth. Before you can move on, you've got to accept that nothing you did or said made him rape you. He wanted to humiliate you and he used his superior strength to do just that. It doesn't matter that you'd been dating him. Even within marriage, rape is still a criminal offence. And you'd just dumped him. So he was looking for revenge. It wasn't your fault. Okay?'

I smiled weakly. 'Okay.'

'And this other guy you mentioned? Your ex-boyfriend? That's obviously an area that's troubling you.'

She paused again, leaving space for me to arrange my thoughts, to try to articulate the mess I now found myself in with regard to Sam. The reasons we broke up; the roles played not only by both our mothers but the hide-bound prejudice of the entire community; all the heartbreak of seeing him heading off to the States to a new life, without me. And the ten lonely years on my own until last January when Andrew McKay had breezed into my life, and had almost destroyed me.

'And now, Beth?' she asked quietly. 'He's back on the scene?'

'Yes, but...' My throat had gone as dry as grains of desert sand. 'But every time we meet, it's a disaster. I so much want to get close to him but...' The tears I'd been trying to choke back were now spilling from my eyes. I reached for a tissue.

'But the terror you've been through is coming between you?'

'Yes, that's it,' I gasped. 'Whenever he tries to touch me, I...'

'You can't handle it?'

'No.' The tissue was now a sodden ball in my fist. 'And of course he doesn't know why. He must think I'm such a... freak,' I sobbed. Thick tears continued to roll towards my upper lip and down onto my chin.

'I think you already know what you need to do, Beth.'

I looked up at her in horror.

'I can't tell him, Deirdre.' I shook my head for emphasis. 'I can't.'

'Beth, you've been through the most dreadful ordeal. And it sounds like this man really cares about you. Don't you think he'd want to know? If only to understand where you're coming from?'

Her words danced around me, a flash lamp wavering at the end of a black tunnel, illuminating a possibility that hadn't even occurred to me. My mind went skidding across a number of scenarios in a frantic search for the right one. Sam being utterly repulsed by my having anything to do with Andrew and by what I had allowed to happen; Sam reminding me of his words of warning; Sam feeling sorry for me but wanting nothing further to do with me; Sam putting his arms around me, telling me what I most wanted to hear, that he'd always be there to protect me, that he still loved me. I sighed. This was the only way forward for us.

'You could be right.'

My voice still heaved with uncertainty as the niggling doubts crept out of the shadowy corners of my brain. But this was something I had to do. It could be the only lifeline I'd be given out of the darkness that was threatening to engulf me.

'Thanks, Deirdre.' I stood up to leave.

'Just give me a call whenever you want to come back. And don't lose heart. Remember, Sam needs to know what's going on with you. Okay?'

'Okay,' I smiled.

I walked out feeling drained, but also, in a strange way, less burdened than before. It was as if the ball of wound-up worry and fear that had taken up residence inside me was beginning to unravel. Maybe this really was my first step towards finding the way forward.

I was making my way towards the café where Laurie and I had agreed to meet when I realised that Brian and her had been right. I'd only consented to go for one session, partly to get them off my back, but had somehow come round to thinking another couple of chats with Deirdre might do no harm. No harm at all.

'So?' Laurie's face was clouded with apprehension.

'Well, I got through it.' I sat down with a frothing mug of Cappuccino. 'Not exactly a barrel of laughs, but that was hardly on the cards, was it?'

'But, you're okay, yeah?'

Her tone was almost pleading, like she was willing me with all her strength to have moved just a little bit forward from the awful place I'd inhabited for months.

'I'm okay, yeah.' I smiled. 'In fact, it wasn't all that bad.'

'Beth, that's great! So will you be, you know?'

'Going back for more?'

She nodded.

'Well, I said I'd give her a call. Maybe in a couple of weeks. We'll see.'

Her eyes lit up with relief. 'You're going to be fine, Beth. I know you are. This time next year, we'll be looking back on this as just a minor blip in your life. You'll see.'

I couldn't quite see that far ahead, but I had to smile at her optimism. There was something very comforting about having my friends rallying round me, knowing they really cared. Now all I had to do was make sure Sam knew how I felt.

THURSDAY, JULY 2. My 35th birthday. If I reached average life expectancy of around 70, I was already halfway there. And what exactly had I achieved? I was a single woman still living with my parents in the village where I grew up; teaching in the school I went to as a child; recent victim of a sexual assault that had left me emotionally scarred; and oh yes, the love of my life was back in Carrigmore but seeing someone else. I was well on my way towards a pointless existence. I had known what it was to be loved, and to have lost that love. And I knew that, for all his fine words, Tennyson hadn't a bull's notion what he was talking about. However awful my experience with Andrew had been, the heartbreak of losing Sam and the subsequent emptiness that had invaded my life was infinitely worse. I still remember the desolation I felt when it became clear that we no longer had a future together. It was like a giant fist had tightened around my heart and started squeezing. When I finally told him I thought we should break off our engagement, hearing him agree that perhaps it was for the best was the saddest moment of my life.

So, where did that leave me now? After such a dreadful year, what did life have in store for me next? Where would I be in ten years? 45 years old and still living with my parents? Still teaching in Carrigmore Primary School? Perhaps the object of pity and scorn among the locals as a middle-aged, single, childless woman? It was time for a new direction. I needed to find my way.

'Close your eyes.'

I'd just blown out all 35 candles on the squelchy coffee cake brought out by a smiling waiter with all of the restaurant staff in a semi-circle behind him, their inharmonious voices raised in a chorus of *Happy Birthday*. Laurie had whisked me off for dinner to a rustic style eating house just north of Longford, on the banks of the River Shannon. Keith had taken the kids for the night, so we were planning a real bender, even splashing out on a taxi. I'd started out with a Caesar salad, followed by crispy roast pork, and finished off with my obligatory birthday cake and the now empty bottle of Shiraz. And now it was birthday-present time. I shut my eyes, anticipating the feel of a book-shaped parcel, but felt instead the flimsy contours of an envelope. Maybe a gift token? I turned the envelope over by its edges, trying to gauge the weight it contained. There was something more than a single card inside. By now my curiosity had ignited and my fingers were ripping at the sides of the glued foldover. I extracted the contents, a card with a scene reminiscent of Constable's *Hay Wain* on the front. I flipped it open, revealing another smaller envelope, also sealed.

'What have we here?' I smiled at Laurie, intrigued by the package within the package.

'Just thought you might like to get a little more active this summer.' Her eyes crinkled in amusement. 'Now that you've got two months holidays stretching ahead of you, you'll need something fun to do.'

I tore open the second envelope and pulled out a sheet of headed paper.

Oakwood Equestrian Centre
Moyglass,
Co. Longford
Phone 043 3372943
info@oec.ie

This voucher entitles the bearer to a ten-week course of riding lessons at any level. Booking must be made in advance.

Signed: R. McKenna

Valid until 2nd January 2010.

It was an open door leading back into the landscape contoured by the familiar smells of sweaty horseflesh and well-oiled leather. This was exactly what I needed to take my mind off of all the bad things that had happened lately. Good old Laurie.

'Like it?' she looked at me with something approaching trepidation.

'Of course I like it.' I reached across the table to hug her. 'I can't wait to get started. You know how much I enjoyed it in the past.'

Her face lightened into a broad grin of relief. 'And you never know who the instructor might be.'

'Ah.' Now I understood. I should have known Laurie better. Of course she had an ulterior motive. But the initial apprehension that rolled over me became tinged with a quiver of anticipation. Hopeful anticipation. At least it would throw me back into contact with him. And I could certainly live with that.

My reveries were interrupted by the twittering of my mobile phone. It was some birdsong ringtone I'd downloaded but which was now starting to annoy me. I looked at the display.

'It's home. I'd better take it.'

As soon as I hit the green button, my mother's panic spilled down the line.

'Elizabeth!' Her voice was. 'It's your father. He's had some kind of a turn.'

'Hold on a minute, Mam. What kind of a turn? What happened?'

'He was watching *Prime Time*, having his tea and his ham sandwich. And then the cup slipped from his hand and his head just lolled back. He's unconscious. The ambulance is on the way. Elizabeth, I don't know what it is, and your brother's staying in Dublin tonight. Gone off to visit some friend of his. Can you come back right now?'

For a woman who always insisted on being in control, hearing her sound so helpless was what frightened me the most.

'I'm on my way, Mam. And please don't worry. The ambulance crew'll know what to do. They deal with this all of the time. Just sit tight and I'll be right with you.'

I was filling up with panic, aware that I was just talking gibberish. By now, Laurie had grasped what was happening, ordered a taxi, and called for the bill. Minutes later, we were pulling out of the car park and back onto the broad stretches of the N4.

CHAPTER TWENTY-TWO

We sped off the bypass and onto the Ardagh road. By now aware of the situation, the taxi driver had cut out the small talk and was focused on getting us to our destination as quickly as possible. We continued in silence, each sucked into our own imagining of the scene ahead.

The still whirling neon rooflights of the parked ambulance bisected the darkness as we raced up the driveway. Before the car had stopped, I was out of it and in through the open front door. In the living room, Dad was stretched out on the floor, his face the colour of peeled potatoes. A paramedic was kneeling over him, sticking the adhesive pads of the defibrillator onto his bare chest. Amber lay crouched in a corner, whimpering quietly. Mother was standing ashen-faced at the table, her fingers clasping and unclasping the bevelled edge behind her. When she spoke, her words came tumbling out in broken gasps.

'It's a heart attack, Elizabeth. Your father's had a heart attack.'

The room went into a spin. I sank down onto the sofa, and Laurie was suddenly there, her arm around my shoulder.

'Dr Moran is on his way.' Mother's voice teetered on the edge of hysteria. 'But maybe it's a priest he needs right now. And this is the night that brother of yours picks to stay in Dublin!' Vehemence gathered in her eyes as her awareness of Brian's perceived betrayal and its impact on Dad deepened. Our other options raced through my mind.

'What about Fr Flannery? Should I call him?'

'Yes, dear. Do that. Just in case.'

She was doing everything she could to convince herself that Dad was going to be okay.

'Try not to worry, Mrs Maguire. He's in good hands.' The second paramedic was clearly in charge of handling distressed relatives. Meanwhile, his colleague had pressed the shock button. It was the nightmare scenario you hope you'll only see in a TV drama. Dad's body convulsed, but when it settled, there was still no movement in his chest. Large beads of sweat glistened on his forehead. Amber slunk even further into her corner, head down on her paws.

The only sound in the room was the computer generated voice of the defibrillator issuing instructions to continue CPR for a further two minutes, and then a further two. While the paramedic was working on him, a stain spread slowly down the inner legs of Dad's tweed trousers. The faint tang of urine rose on the air. The rhythmic pressure to the chest continued, and continued. By now, a solid bar of fear had formed in my gut. I dialled the priest's number and relayed the news.

'I'll be right with you, Beth. Please God he'll pull through.'

The empty words of the priest reverberated in my head as I watched the drama of CPR being played out in front of my eyes, exactly like what you'd see on *Casualty* or *ER* except that this was happening in our living room. To us. To my Dad. Please God, I thought, please don't do this to us. Not now. Not tonight. The rhythmic thumping went on and on.

Through the bay window, we saw the headlights of a car sweeping into the yard, lighting up the porch. The corpulent figure of Frank Moran with his ruddy face and hooked nose scurried in, medical bag in hand. He was a man who always took his time, so the urgency of his movement was terrifying. As he felt for a pulse, the paramedic rattled off the technicalities of Dad's condition.

The silence in the room became palpable as Frank took over the compressions and all of us strained to hear even a whisper of breath lift Dad's chest, but the minutes ticked by and still the only thing we heard was the strengthening pulse of our despair. Amber got to her feet and lumbered over towards Dad, flopping down at his side. Suddenly, her whimpering rose to a sustained howl. With a look of defeat at the paramedic, Frank got to his feet heavily, placing the stethoscope into his bag. Laurie's hand closed over mine in a tight squeeze.

'I'm so sorry, Mary. There's nothing more we can do. He went very quickly.'

A thin wail rose from my mother's throat, similar to that of a wild animal in distress. Inarticulate with grief, she came tottering towards me. She had the look of a bewildered child. In my arms, her body seemed fragile, a mere huddle of bones, as we clung to each other, united in our incomprehension of how abruptly and with so little ceremony death had stolen into our home. It must have been the first time we'd been physically close since I was a child. Now, after everything that had happened, all I saw was the distance between us, between what she was capable of giving and what I needed from her. In recent years, that gap had widened to the point where we seemed to speak different languages, growing ever more unintelligible to each other. So in spite of being brought together by sudden tragedy, we were both alone in our grief. A black lake of sorrow lapped around me. I felt my chest constricting sharply as the reality began to bear down on me. Our little universe had been thrown off kilter, and was now spinning in a foreign orbit. My Dad was gone.

'Maybe you could put the kettle on, Beth. Hot sweet tea is what you both need right now.' Frank bustled around. 'I'll ring the undertaker. They'll bring him into St Joseph's and tidy him up for you.'

In the kitchen with Laurie, putting the milk and sugar on a tray, waiting for the kettle to boil, it seemed everywhere I looked, I could see Dad. Having a peek into the fridge, checking out the goodies tin, slathering butter onto mounds of toast. This had been his domain. Grief surged over me. In a household soured by my mother's constant nagging, he was the one who always came to my defence. And now I'd never see him again. I blundered my way through the tea-making routine, hands automatically finding mugs, spoons, milk and sugar, caught in the grip of unbearable sorrow.

When I got back in, Mother was kneeling over Dad's body, stroking his hands over and over, locked into her own world of grief. Amber had still not relinquished her place beside him, but the howling had dropped back to a whimper. Frank was just finishing his notes for the death certificate. He looked at Mother.

'Is there anyone you'd like me to ring, Mary?'

She looked at him wildly. In the state of shock that had paralysed her thinking, it hadn't occurred to her that Brian and Rosemary had yet to be contacted, as well as Dad's two brothers.

'Oh dear Lord! We've no way of reaching Fr Brian.' Even in the circumstances, she couldn't drop the title. I felt a dart of irritation.

'He's due back in the morning, Mam. And maybe Rosemary knows where he is. I'll ring her now.'

As expected, my sister collapsed in a frenzied hysteria at the other end of the line. As far as I could make out, her overriding concern was that Dad had gone so suddenly that there were to be no deathbed scenes with his family gathered round him, like you'd see in weepy films. And no, she had no idea where Brian was staying. Yes, of course she would be down first thing tomorrow morning.

The next to arrive, as expected, was Fr Flannery. An

officious little man with a bald head, he seemed to me to relish the additional stature to be gained from his powers to speed the souls of the dead towards heaven. One look at the scene before him was enough to confirm that the worst had happened. Puffed up with a sense of his own importance, he kissed his stole and placed it around his neck. Mother stood back to allow him precedence. Kneeling over Dad, he touched his forehead with anointing oils, and began to murmur the words reserved for the dying.

'Proficiscere, anima Christiana, de hoc mundo!

Saints of God, come to his aid!

Come to meet him angels of the Lord.

Go forth upon thy journey, O faithful Christian soul,

Go forth from this world; from your family, your friends, your home.

In the name of God the Father who created you and gave you life,

In the name of Jesus the Son of Mary who gave his life for you,

In the name of the Holy Spirit of God who was poured into your heart.

May your home this day be in paradise with the angels and saints,

And with your own people who have gone before you on the great journey.

May you see the face of the living God.

May you have the fullness of life and peace forever.

May Jesus the gentle shepherd number you among the faithful ones,

And bring you to the waters of peace.

May you have eternal rest. Amen.'

'I'm so very sorry.' Standing up, he proffered a hand to each of us in turn. 'He's with God now. May he rest in peace.' The worn-out platitudes dropped from his lips. The obligatory decade of the Rosary was said. And then the silence hung between us.

'Maybe you'd have a good suit you'd like to bury him in, Mrs Maguire?' The undertaker's voice was gentle, discreet.

'Elizabeth?' Her stricken voice sounded like it came from an immense distance. 'Would you find something?'

I went upstairs to their bedroom and opened his wardrobe, overpowered by the middle-aged male odour that I would always associate with Dad; the musty smell of tweed jackets and Chrombie overcoats mixed with hand-knitted sweaters. My heart lurched as more memories crowded in on me. I found the suit he usually wore on Sundays and brought it downstairs.

The rest of that night rolled into a blur for me. It was like being set adrift from normality, with no control over the direction that I was being floated towards. Dad was laid on a stretcher, covered up, and brought out to the ambulance. The back doors closed and the tail lights disappeared off into the night. He was gone. After several cups of tea, Laurie and I set about hoovering, dusting, and polishing. The following day would see a deluge of friends and neighbours calling to pay their respects. We'd need to stock up with food and drink. There would be the funeral arrangements to be made, a notice put into the newspaper, Dad's brothers to be contacted, all the paraphernalia that accompanied the ritual of death. The to-do list began to take shape in my head. But right now, all I wanted was to collapse in a heap and give in to the immense grief that was swirling around inside me.

AFTER ABOUT THREE hours of fitful, broken sleep, I surfaced into the fog of semi-consciousness, my dulled senses struggling to focus. The events of last night closed in on me, filling my world. The digital display read 7.35am. I could hear movement downstairs. I pulled on a dressing gown and made for the kitchen. Mother was hunched over the sink, scrubbing at the draining board with limescale remover. God love her, she wasn't going to let the neighbours catch her with anything less than a gleaming kitchen.

'Oh, Elizabeth. I didn't wake you, did I? I just wanted to, you know...'

'Don't worry, Mam. I was awake anyway. You've the place looking great,' I moved towards her, but her attention was fixed on another imaginary stain. I picked up the kettle instead.

'Cup of tea?'

'No, I've just had some, dear. I think I'll go and have a bath.'

There it was again. That distance between us. She pulled the loose folds of the housecoat around her and shuffled aimlessly out of the room; an ageing woman who'd just had the bottom knocked out of her world. In spite of everything, my heart went out to her.

By 9.00am, the word had got around, and Annafrid was on our doorstep. Her plump arms encircled me in a hug. There was no need for words. This was what finally broke open the floodgates. The tears came, hard and fast. I gulped convulsively, while Annafrid held me, murmuring words of solace in German. I felt as vulnerable as an abandoned child. Immense sorrow clogged my chest, threatening to choke me. But within a few hours, Dad would be arriving back in a hearse, and the house would be overrun with people. And there was so much to be done.

'Of course, you know Dad was never one to look after himself.'

Rosemary was on one of her favourite hobby horses, launching into her theory that a healthier lifestyle would have seen Dad live into old age, while at the same time pointing the finger at those of us who'd kept ladling fried breakfasts into him. Since she'd arrived an hour earlier, she'd sat in the kitchen with the air of a visiting dignitary, graciously receiving the condolences that poured in from the neighbours who came and went. David was planning to follow her down when he'd gotten his work appointments rearranged. I'd finally tracked down Brian through an old school friend and he was on his way. Laurie had arranged with Keith to keep the children for the rest of the day, and she and I had done some emergency shopping and were still busy making up sandwiches, although nearly everyone who'd dropped in so far had brought something; an apple tart, a quiche, a cold chicken. Annafrid, bless her heart, had made up a huge pot of goulash and left it simmering on the range, "in case the peoples are hungry." Everyone wanted to do their bit in seeing that there was enough to feed the mourners. The hearse carrying Dad's remains had arrived and the open coffin was positioned in the front room. The poor man was now the focus of more attention than he had been at any stage during his life. Mother was knocked for six by the whole drama into which our lives had been pitched. Given time, I reckoned she would probably settle into the role of the grieving widow quite comfortably, but right now, she was cut off from everything she knew by the tragedy that had rolled into her world.

Just after 11.00am, Brian's Ford Escort swung into the yard. Mother's lips tightened. She wasn't going to let him away with not being there last night to perform the Last Rites for Dad. In her eyes, once a priest, always a priest and no second thoughts he might be having about his vocation were going to change that. Whatever plans were going through that confused head of his would have to be put on hold. The implication of his homecoming hadn't yet registered in Carrigmore, and she was going to make damn sure it didn't until after his father was safely buried. She went to the door to meet him, and undoubtedly, to dictate to him what his role would be over the next few days.

'Fr Brian's going to lead a decade of the Rosary for Paddy.' There was a glint of triumph in her tone as she preceded her son into the kitchen. Obviously, she'd laid on the guilt trip with a trowel, so he had very little option but to go along with her wishes. By the time she finished with him, he was probably going to feel like Judas Iscariot.

'Isn't that grand. Ah, sure isn't it a great blessing to have him home with you at a time like this.' Miss Maloney was one of those who made a point of turning up at the house of the deceased no matter how slight the acquaintance. She was a self-appointed official consoler who relished all things to do with death. Had she known how sensitive a nerve she'd hit unawares, she would have jumped for joy at the prospect of such news to pass on. Mother didn't bat an eyelid. Brian looked over at me helplessly, the fire of defiance that raged through him last week nowhere to be seen. Dad's death had presented Mother with her trump card.

The next few hours slid into one another; callers passed through the front room to say their goodbyes and then sat with us in the kitchen, having endless cups of tea, eating endless sandwiches, and drinking endless supplies of whiskey. Volunteers came forward to man a 24 hour vigil over the remains, and floral tributes started to pile up in the hallway. Dad's brothers, Seamus and Danny, arrived from Roscommon, two bewildered old men peering through round spectacles, the eyes behind them clouded with shock and puzzlement, unable to grasp that their Paddy, their youngest brother, had been taken from them with so little warning. All through this, the sense of unreality deepened. It was like acting out a part in a play, waiting for the curtain to come down so that we could resume our normal lives and go back to the comfort of the familiar, where Dad would amble in from the office looking for his dinner, or in from the pub at night and head straight for the fridge to check out its snack potential. It was impossible to believe that only this time yesterday, normality was still in place. Sudden death was always something that happened to other families, not to us. At this stage, I was numb with shock and just going through the motions required. That would have to be enough for now.

CHAPTER TWENTY-THREE

'IN THE NAME of the Father and of the Son and of the Holy Spirit'

Brian's voice barely reached down the length of the parish church. It was raw and strained. He and Fr Flannery were concelebrating the Requiem Mass. Mother had arranged it. A high July sun filtered in through the stained glass windows, throwing varicoloured light onto the sombre scene. The heavy scent of flowers and candle wax drifted down from the altar. In the front pew, Mother, Rosemary and I were flanked by the uncles, Seamus and Danny, looking anything but comfortable in their starched Sunday suits and hair they had Brylcreemed flat for the occasion. Marie, Jennifer, and the rest of the teaching staff had gathered just across the aisle. Behind us stretched endless rows of those who had come to mourn with us. Dad had been well-known in Carrigmore. The church was packed to capacity.

'My brothers and sisters, we are gathered here to pray for the soul of Patrick Maguire. Let us begin...'

The familiar words rolled towards me like stones. Three days after the event, I was still acting the role of bereaved daughter, but somewhere inside my head, I was just waiting for normality to reassert itself whenever this hideous charade came to an end. The removal yesterday had passed by in a haze of countless hands extended in sympathy, the occasional hug, and the stock phrase "I'm sorry for your troubles" muttered a million times over. I was drained. And there was still today to get through. The ancient ritual continued, its jumble of words running on and on.

'Grant onto him eternal rest, oh Lord, and may perpetual

light shine upon him.'

Brian was now walking around the coffin shaking the sprinkler over it, sending droplets of water flying. Fr. Flannery stood back at a respectful distance, allowing him precedence. What it was costing my brother to go through with this pretence, I could only guess. Finding himself locked again into the role he had abandoned must be a bit like walking back into an iron-jawed trap he thought he had escaped from. His expression was inscrutable as he came down to take his place with us as a family member. The interminable queue of sympathisers began to snake its way up the centre aisle to file past us. The same words of condolence were mumbled over and over, eyes half averted, embarrassed to encounter such raw grief head-on. The procession crawled by, faces passing us in a blur of sameness, each one needing to be thanked for their kindness.

'Beth, I'm so very sorry.' Jerked out of my trance-like state by the familiar, clipped accent, I looked up into Sam's eyes, which were filled with concern. He reached for my hand and enclosed it in both of his. I nodded dumbly.

He gave my hand a squeeze and swiftly moved on. In the midst of one of the most dreadful days of my life, a tiny bit of hope stirred. In spite of so many odds being stacked so high against me, every time he showed concern for me, my world lurched alarmingly. And right now, although he was just expressing his condolences along with hundreds of others, I couldn't help reading more into his words than was probably intended.

'SOME MORE, BETH?' Annafrid was making sure no-one went hungry, doing the rounds with plates of sandwiches and vol-au-vents. Mother and I had decided last night we just couldn't face prolonging the public part of the funeral with a hotel meal, and had opted instead for a family gathering with some close friends and neighbours back at the house. All around us, a muted babble of conversation filled the air. The worst of the collective grief had been spent and everyone was reaching for a way back to normality, except that, for us, normality wouldn't ever return. As I looked around our living room, every ornament, photo, or item of furniture seemed to have a link with Dad, and the raw heartbreak of loss opened up in me like a fresh wound. Thick tears lodged in my eyes. I sobbed uncontrollably onto Annafrid's shoulder.

'It's all right, liebschen, you cry all you want, it's all right.' Murmuring her own words of comfort in German, she manoeuvred me towards the kitchen. 'Maybe it's time for a little whiskey, Ja?' She poured a measure that would have done Dad proud into a tumbler and handed it to me neat. I tossed back the first mouthful and felt it burn its way down my throat. Another couple of gulps and the sobbing had turned into something more like hiccoughs. Annafrid topped up my glass.

By now, the humming voices in the living room had loudened considerably. There must have been about 20 people sitting around in small groups, all reminiscing and swopping memories of Paddy Maguire. The whiskey had blunted the razor-sharp edges of heartbreak and I was managing to contain myself. I had just gone into the kitchen with Laurie to make up more sandwiches when the chimes of the doorbell rang out. I heard my mother's footsteps tapping down the hallway.

'Oh, Samuel.' The coldness in her voice sent mortification shuddering through me. 'Would you like to come in?'

'I don't wish to intrude, Mrs Maguire. I just wondered

how Beth is doing.'

'Thank you, Samuel. She's fine. That's very kind of you.' The icy tone belied her words.

'Perhaps I could see her for a minute?'

The question hung, unanswered in the air. For a microsecond I hesitated, then strode decisively into the hallway. This was one occasion she was not going to sabotage.

'Sam, how good of you to come.' I brushed past my mother and took his hand.

'Beth, I... I just wanted to see if you were okay. See if there's anything I can do... anything that might help.'

His words were like a soothing balm to me. But Mother was still standing behind us, disapproval etched into the lines of her face.

'Thank you, Sam.' His hand was still in mine. 'Please come in and have some tea or something.'

He hesitated, glancing in my mother's direction. 'Well, perhaps just for a few minutes.'

She stood back to allow him past, naked aversion in her eyes. At that moment, I hated her. I led Sam towards the kitchen and poured him a whiskey. He sat by the range, staring straight ahead, clearly affected by her hostility. I could think of nothing to say. As well as my mother's behaviour, the whole ugliness of what had happened with Andrew was in the way. Every attempt I made at conversation faltered and died. Ten minutes later, he was gone.

THE FOLLOWING DAY, Brian and I were sorting through the Mass cards, making a list for acknowledgements when a jeep swung into the yard. Sam again. This time, I got to the door before my mother had the chance to slight him.

'Beth, hi.' He shifted awkwardly.

'Sam.' Seeing him standing on the doorstep, open-necked shirt showing golden hair, was like a summer breeze blowing into the rank air of a tomb.

'I hope I'm not disturbing you?'

'Not at all, not at all.' I was desperate to make him feel more welcome than had been the case yesterday. 'Won't you come in?'

'Actually, I wondered if you might like to come out for a coffee? Get away from the house for an hour or so? We could go to the hotel, maybe?'

My heart lifted. To get away for an hour from all the trappings of death that surrounded me here was just what I needed.

Ten minutes later we were in the hotel lounge in Ballymartin with two frothing cappuccinos in front of us. Now that I was actually here with him, all the words in my head had dried up again. I waited for him to start.

'Beth, I'm so very sorry about your Dad. I know how close to him you were.'

'Thanks, Sam.' The pain came crashing back, the image of Dad stretched out on the floor while the paramedics pummelled his chest crowded into my mind.

'And I just wanted you to know I'm here for you if you need someone to talk to. I mean, after what happened to Andrew so recently, losing your father now must be dreadful.'

I looked at him blankly, trying to make sense of his words. Why should he be attaching so much importance to what had happened to Andrew? Then, it dawned on me. As far as he was concerned, Andrew had been my boyfriend. How could he have known otherwise? He probably thought I was mourning Andrew's death.

'Sam, there's something I need to tell you.' I faltered. How much did I need to tell him? Just that we'd split up? Or everything? He was the one person who knew me better than anyone in the world, could always read me like a book. He'd know if I was holding back. Already the edge in my voice had alerted him to the importance of whatever I had to say. Anxiety flared in his eyes.

'What is it, Beth?'

'Andrew and I. We weren't, well we weren't seeing each other when he died. In fact we hadn't been together for a long time.'

'Oh?'

'No. Things had been kind of going downhill between us for a while.' I stared into my coffee. Just talking about Andrew was enough to unnerve me. 'And then, the night after we met you in the theatre, everything sort of came to a head.'

Understatement of the year, I thought bitterly.

'So I told him it was over.'

'Oh, Beth, I'm sorry.' He reached for my hand. 'But I have to say I didn't think very highly of him. He was nowhere near your league.'

The first tear splashed into my coffee.

'Beth! It's okay. It's over.' He gave my hand a squeeze.

'No, it's not.' My voice came out high-pitched and strained. 'It'll never be over. You don't know what he's done to me.'

His face filled with horror as realisation began to dawn. Now there was no going back. In stammering phrases, I relayed how I'd accepted the lift back with Andrew, how he'd forced me into his cottage, the nightmare scene in his kitchen, his foul breath all around me, and the callous way he'd humiliated me, pumping his filth into me.

'Beth!' His face drained of colour, shock and distress etched across it. 'Oh, dear God. For him to do that. To you. What kind of animal was he?'

His disjointed words sent my mind leaping with hope.

'I'd have killed him if I'd known. I'm only sorry it's too late. I hope the bastard died in agony in that car.'

The anguish in his voice spoke volumes. And the tormented look in his eyes.

'Why didn't you come to me earlier? And why the hell didn't you listen to me? Couldn't you see what an asshole he was?' He reached for my hand again, but stopped short. 'I knew he was bad news. I tried to warn you. Remember?'

I nodded dumbly. How could I forget?

'I'm sorry Beth, I just mean, oh Christ, I don't know what I mean. I just can't bear the thought of him hurting you. Especially that way.'

He gulped down a mouthful of coffee and jumped to his feet.

'Just give me a few minutes, Beth. I need some air.'

Before I could say reply, he was gone. I was left with a storm of impressions whirling in my head: Sam incoherent with rage at what Andrew had done to me. Sam wanting Andrew alive again so he could kill him in retaliation. Sam not able to bear the thought of me being hurt. All of them pointed in one direction. Could he still have feelings for me?

The seconds continued to tick by and fifteen minutes later, there was still no sign of him. A deepening sense of unease gathered inside me. Maybe I'd misinterpreted his reaction. I might have been over-optimistic. Or completely wrong. Suppose he thought I was now damaged goods? Tainted by association with Andrew McKay? He might even think I'd been asking for it. After all, he had warned me, just the day before it happened.

'Sorry about that, Beth.' He came back in, face rigid with pent-up emotion. 'I just needed a few minutes. Are we all done here?'

I was right. Now he didn't even want to be seen with me. What I'd told him had unleashed a wave of disgust that would carry him as far away from me as he could get. Heartbroken, I stood up and blundered out onto the street after him. On the way home, we both stared straight ahead, each in our own particular hell. When we pulled into the drive, he laid a hand on mine before shutting down the engine.

'Beth, I'm truly sorry for what happened to you. I don't know what else to say.'

'Yes, well. Thanks for the coffee.' I couldn't get out of the jeep fast enough. 'See you around.'

Without looking back, I hurried up the steps and twisted my key in the door. When I got to the kitchen window, the jeep had gone. Sam was now out of my life, for good. After all the effort I'd made to overcome the emotional scars Andrew had left on me, all the counselling, all the deluding myself that Sam still wanted me, this was how it was going to be. And nothing I could do would ever change that.

For the next couple of days, I stumbled around in a fog of sadness, unable to focus on anything for more than five minutes. Images of Dad shuffling around in the kitchen in his slippers, his fawn cardigan pulled over his ample belly, went around in my head. Rosemary and I went through his clothes, setting aside what could be given to charity. Mother sat in the kitchen, drinking endless cups of tea, repeating the same things about him to whoever dropped in, listening to the same platitudes assuring her that time heals everything and that he'd never be forgotten, and so on. And Brian became more withdrawn, spending long periods of time in his room. After his very public role in celebrating the requiem Mass, his plans to make his decision known were thrown somewhat off course. Apart from Annafrid, no-one outside the family suspected anything, and that was the way Mother intended to keep it. For as long as possible.

Then there was Sam. Whenever I thought of him, I'd get this sickening sensation in my stomach like an overloaded tumble drier in constant motion. All the times he'd shown concern for me and all the efforts he'd made to get closer to me, came hurtling back to torment me. Perhaps I should have thought through the consequences of carrying out Deirdre's advice. I should have anticipated how he'd react.

On Wednesday, Rosemary and David took their leave and disappeared back to their insulated world of leafy suburbs and cabbage-patch gardens. Life was going to carry on, regardless of the devastation that had knocked us sideways. Laurie called in at least once a day, which provided a link with the outside world, but once our front door closed at night, it was like we'd been lifted out of our normal routine and set down in a foreign country where we found ourselves tiptoeing around each other's depression, alone with the immensity of what had happened. A huge, aching gap yawned open every time we went into a room and saw the chair he used to sit in, now empty.

THE FOLLOWING WEEK, it was time to discuss practicalities. Decisions needed to be made about Dad's business, now being run by Joey, his manager, and Tina, the part-timer. In the last couple of years, Dad had been delegating quite a bit, just putting in a few hours a day, easing his way into retirement, so they were quite capable of keeping it going, at least in the short term. But with none of our family directly involved, the question of whether to sell it outright, or to lease it for a given period, was on all of our minds. True to form, Mother had strong views on the matter.

'Your father would turn in his grave to see it pass from the family.'

'But, Mam, look at the nest egg we'd have if we sell it.' Rosemary, back home for the family conference, had her sights set on a share of the proceeds. 'And you wouldn't have to worry about maintenance and leases and all that.'

'What do you think, Brian?' I was trying to involve my brother, who so far had made no contribution to the discussion. He shrugged.

'Will it make any difference what I think? It's going to be Mother's decision anyway.' He looked balefully at her. 'Dad has left everything to you after all, hasn't he?'

For once, she seemed a little nonplussed. She wasn't used to such naked hostility from her beloved son and didn't know how to handle it. She stumbled on further into the danger zone.

'Well, yes of course, dear. But it's still a family matter. Something we need to discuss together.'

'Family, huh?' he snorted. 'Since when were we ever a family in the real sense of the word? Answer me that. And now with Dad gone, there's even less chance of it.'

His face was like granite.

'Remind me again what you said I'd done to the *family*. Something about bringing nothing but shame on it? Oh yes, the disgrace of having a failed priest in the *family*. And you not ever again being able to hold your head up in Carrigmore. Wasn't that it? And now you want me to be part of this *family* again? No thanks!'

These last words were flung over his shoulder as Brian got to his feet and walked out of the living room, leaving Mother trembling in the wake of his anger. I'd never known him to harbour such resentment. Her words had obviously been festering like maggots in his head. Whatever threads of attachment had once bound him to her had finally snapped. It must have been a whole series of events that had driven him to this. Mother's extreme reaction to the circumstances of his return home, the uncertainty of his future, and the shock of Dad's death had all combined to turn his world into a desert of shifting sands with no clear path ahead. A dark forest where the tangles of duty and obligation reached out to trip him up and bar his way forward.

CHAPTER TWENTY-FOUR

'A LITTLE TIPPLE, Beth?'

Laurie was pouring a Shiraz into long-stemmed glasses. She'd gotten part-time hours in a bookshop, and was enjoying the opportunities it afforded her to meet new people and chat about books, so she'd decided to celebrate by having myself and Brian around to dinner. I'd had the call I'd been waiting for from the hospital: the results of the AIDS tests were in and I was clear. So double celebrations were in order. A huge platter of spaghetti carbonara sat on the range and the aroma of garlic filled the kitchen. As she set the bottle back on the table, little Keith popped his head around the door from the television lounge.

'Right, Keith, that's it. Bedtime.'

'Oh, Mam, come on. Just another ten minutes.'

Little Keith shot a surreptitious glance in Brian's direction. All three of Laurie's kids had taken to Brian like flowers to sunlight, but Keith in particular hero-worshipped him for his "travels in Africa", always asking him for more gory details on "life in the bush" and "the tigers and elephants". This time, however, it was no dice.

'Hey, buddy. What about football tomorrow? You don't want to be too knackered to win the game.'

My brother had a gut instinct for the right way to handle any situation. Keith's little face furrowed in thought before capitulating.

'I suppose. Okay so. Night, everyone.' And without further protest, the little boy gave his mother a quick hug and was off down the corridor to the bathroom.

'Be with you in ten minutes,' Laurie called after him, with a grateful glance in Brian's direction. 'Don't forget to floss your teeth.'

I caught a flash of envy in Brian's eyes. He'd said to me on a couple of occasions how much it would have meant to him to have a child of his own. Every time he was standing at the altar holding an infant to be christened, it broke his heart, knowing he could never be a father himself. He continued slicing the garlic bread, staring into space.

'So, Brian.' Laurie's voice broke into his reveries. 'What's the latest?'

'Oh, just starting to immerse myself in the real world,' he grinned impishly. 'Got a lot of catching up to do.'

He'd gone into the adult learning centre in Longford the day before to check out opportunities there, and was hopeful of securing some hours with them once he'd completed the tutor-training course.

'And no better man to do it.' Laurie filled another glass and handed it to him. 'Great to see things starting to fall into place for you.' There was a glimmer of excitement in her eye.

'Well, anyway. Here's to second chances. For all of us!' She raised her glass in a sweeping gesture to include me in the toast. 'May we all find what we're looking for.'

'To second chances!' Brian and I both chorused, clinking glasses with Laurie. A definite frisson trembled in the air between them. There was no mistaking it.

I'D JUST GOT back from another counselling session to find Marie had dropped in with Kylie. They were installed in our kitchen, chatting to Mother over a coffee. At six months old, Kylie was sitting up in her buggy and taking stock of everything. Mother had given her some spoons to play with and she was banging them merrily off one another, eyes narrowed in concentration.

'Just thought we'd look in for a bit. You and I have some catching up to do.' Marie was on her feet to greet me with a warm hug.

'And how's my favourite godchild?' I knelt down and held out a finger for her to grab. After a few seconds of staring at me in wonder, her little face crinkled up in a huge smile. We chatted in baby talk while Marie looked on indulgently.

'Fancy a stroll, Beth? We're just heading off around the bog road.'

Five minutes later, we were soaking up the late afternoon sunshine, the sound of bees droning from the hedgerows around us.

'So?' Marie's query was tentative. 'How're things?'

'Oh, you know, a bit all over the place.' I hesitated. 'Just back from a session with my counsellor.'

'And?'

'Well, I suppose it's going to take time. Right now, I feel I'm still caught up in a vortex of after-effects. It's like once the stone is dropped into the water, the ripples go on forever.'

'I guess when something that traumatic happens, it's going to impact on you in all sorts of ways. What does your counsellor say?'

I told her about Deirdre's advice on telling Sam and how he'd been avoiding me ever since.

'Oh, but hon, that's only to be expected. He's still in shock. He needs time, just like you did, to come to terms with it.'

'Anyway, I'm pretty sure he's going out with this stable girl. Gill something. 18 years old! So what's the point in dwelling on it?'

'An 18-year-old stable girl? That doesn't sound like Sam's style. Are you sure?'

'Pretty sure,' I cringed inwardly. 'I've seen them together, and boy was she staking her claim.'

'Ah, one of those,' she grinned. 'Somehow, I just can't see Sam lasting with a tart like that, can you?'

No matter how awful I was feeling about the whole Sam thing, deep down, I had to agree with her.

'So, HOW ABOUT it then?'

Laurie drove the brush through the pony's coat one last time and looked up at me. As little Keith was tucked up in bed with a vomiting bug, she was on stable duty and had roped me in to help. I'm sure her real agenda was to give me a yearning to be with horses again and make me think about starting that course of riding lessons she'd bought me.

'I don't know, Laurie. You know Sam's been avoiding me like the plague since I told him what happened. If he is the instructor, it could be really embarrassing.'

'All the more reason to go for it. You're going to run into him sometime. At least this way, you'll get to see him on a regular basis, *and* see how he behaves with that Welsh moron.'

And there lay the crux of the matter. Not only would I have to endure the more distant instructor/student relationship with Sam when we had once meant the world to each other, but to see him flirting with a girl half my age was just more than I could stomach.

'Come on, Beth. Has it occurred to you that he just doesn't know what to say or how to behave towards you? That it's taking him a little time to absorb what you told him?'

That was exactly what Marie had said. His words resounded in my head again, *I just can't bear the thought of him hurting you. Especially in that way.* Surely that had meant something?

'Yeah, well maybe I'll give it a go. Just for one night, okay? If it's too excruciating, I'm not going back.'

'That's my girl.' Laurie handed me an empty water bucket with a handful of soggy hay floating around in the bottom. 'You never know, you might even enjoy it.'

The sound of tyres crunching on the gravel yard interrupted our chores. It was Brian. By now there was no mistaking the soft glow in my brother's eyes whenever Laurie was around. And she in turn lit up like a Catherine Wheel in his presence.

'Well, well, well. Women at work.' He leaned over the stable door, eyes full of mirth.

'Hi there,' Laurie grinned as she pushed a loose strand of hair back off her face. 'Just giving your sister some lessons in stable management. You know she's going to take up riding again?'

'Oh, yeah? Good on you, Beth.' His smile broadened into delight. 'When do you start?'

'Whoa. I said I'd think about it.'

'What's wrong with next week?' Laurie was quick to spot the advantage. 'They have evening lessons on Wednesdays.'

'That's settled so.' Brian was obviously in on the ploy. 'I'll give them a ring and book you in.'

I couldn't miss the look of delighted complicity that passed between them. It had 'mission accomplished' written all over it.

THE FOLLOWING WEDNESDAY, I swung left through the stone

piers and continued along the tree-lined passage that led to Oakwood Equestrian Centre. At some points, the tangle of branches interlaced overhead, and rays of evening sunlight were filtering through, creating a real fairytale landscape, although I was feeling far removed from a fairy princess. In my denim jeans and welly boots, I felt more like a hillbilly trying to gatecrash an exclusive gathering of the super-rich. I was going to be totally outclassed here. Although riding was considered within the reach of the farming community in Ireland, for others it remained one of the more expensive hobbies with a certain status attached to it. This was my first formal lesson in an indoor school, where all the others would probably be togged out in tailored jodhpurs and leather boots, and of course be way ahead of me in their equestrian skills. A ripple of apprehension travelled down my spine.

All this was minor compared to the real issue that was tying my stomach up in knots as we drove in. Would it be Sam? Would he be cold and aloof, and try to put as much distance as he could between us?

'So, all raring to go then, are we?'

Laurie's high spirits broke into my preoccupations. Since it was all her fault I was here in the first place, I'd dragged her with me for moral support.

'Oh, yeah,' I growled. 'Remind me, just whose bright idea was this?'

'Come on, Beth. You'll be grand. Sure there's nothing to it.' She grinned wickedly. 'You just throw your leg over, sit back, and away you go.'

'You know that's not what I mean.'

'Will ye relax, Beth. If it is Sam, he'll be only delighted to see you.'

'Yeah, right...'

There were about eight or nine cars in the yard lined up along the side wall of the indoor school. There was a sand manège to the left where a girl was lunging a pony, sending it forward in a steady trot with verbal encouragement and an occasional flick of the whip. In a paddock beyond, lit by a peach-coloured sky tinged with gold, nine or ten horses grazed sporadically, reefing tufts of grass as they shifted from spot to spot. From the sounds we could make out coming from inside the school, there was an earlier lesson still going on. Laurie led the way around to the side door that led into the viewing area.

'That's good. Keep that pace. Allow the forward movement. And keep your leg on.'

Instinctively, I drew back. But Laurie was too quick for me. She nudged me in through the door from which I had a full view of Sam centre stage, calling out instructions to the rider now approaching the spread fence in the middle of the arena. At the far end was a row of stalls where the horses for the next lesson were being tacked up. Their soft snuffling sounds and occasional whickering rose in counterpoint to the muffled hoof beats thudding on the sawdust of the arena. The girl who was fussily making adjustments to the bridle she was fitting; even with her back to me, I recognised her. She was the youngster who'd had Sam in tow that day in Athlone. I quailed. I wanted to see him again to try and put right what kept going wrong every time we met, but not with a jealous girlfriend watching his every move.

'Well done. Just give him a little more headroom next time. He needs to stretch out more over the spread.'

In spite of my misgivings, even though they were addressed to someone else, his words dropped like honey into my parched soul. As the stream of his advice and encouragement rolled on, I found myself longing to be on the receiving end. I couldn't get his words out of my head. *I just can't bear the thought of him hurting you. Especially in that way.* Surely that meant his past feelings for me hadn't been totally extinguished. His evenly modulated voice with its clipped tones brought those early days of our romance hurtling back to me. Excitement brushed like feathers across my skin. I couldn't wait to get on a horse and into the arena. The prospect of hearing that voice addressing me, and maybe praising my efforts gave me a rare feeling of delight.

BECAUSE I'D ALREADY covered the basics, I'd been put into an intermediate level class, and it was my turn to trot on from the front to the rear of the ride. I'd been given a piebald mare called Gypsy with a back the width of Africa. I squeezed my lower leg against her sides and she ambled forward into a sort of shunting pace, bouncing me around in the saddle like the proverbial sack of potatoes. I'd put on a little weight since my last time on a horse and every ounce of extra flab was now screaming in protest. I tried desperately to remember the technique of pushing myself up and down with the trotting motion, but felt like a piece of flotsam being tossed from wave to wave. It had been so long since I'd done this that I was like a beginner all over again. I grabbed hold of the neck strap and hung on grimly.

'Let the weight sink into your heel, Beth. That's it. Now, shoulders back. Try to relax. A bit softer when you come down on her back. Yes, that's the idea. That's good. Keep that up.'

His voice flowed over me like silk. Although I was still bouncing around like a jack in the box, I felt like I'd just been awarded first prize for Horsewoman of the Year. Sam was pleased with me. I finally made it around to the rear of the ride, red-faced, out of breath, and burning with pride. Gypsy heaved a sigh as she fell back into a leisurely shuffle and resumed her place in the line. I glanced in Sam's direction, hoping for more approbation, but he was already focusing on the next rider.

After another half hour of trotting in circles and some canter work, Sam and Gillian put up a little cross pole, about six inches off the ground. My mind went back to our days of riding through the woodlands, negotiating the odd fallen log in our path, with the sycamore trees swaying overhead. Surely I'd be able for this. One by one, each rider trotted up to it and somehow scrambled over. I pointed Gypsy at it, clamped my legs around her enormous girth, and hoped for the best. She shuffled on in the general direction of the fence, then slowed down, and finally ground to a halt just in front of it. Gillian's face split in two with an amused grin. Bitch. Mortification seeped through me, flooding up into my cheeks. It would have to be me, wouldn't it?

'Okay, Beth. Just bring her round again and this time, keep your leg on.' He motioned to Gillian to be ready with the lunge whip. I turned Gypsy back onto the track and rammed my heels into her sides. I was going to make damn sure she went over it on wings this time. 'Go on,' I yelled, arms flapping and legs flailing. She quickened her pace and, seeing Gillian with the whip on one side and Sam on the other, stretched out her head and neck and cleared the cross pole by a foot, with me clinging on for dear life to the neck strap.

'Well done, Beth. That's more like it. Make much of her.'

I was ready to kiss Gypsy for her part in making me look good. I thumped her neck in gratitude and told her what a superstar she was. Better than Shergar and Arkle rolled into one. From her vantage point in the viewing area, Laurie beamed at me, giving me an exaggerated thumbs up gesture. Insane happiness flooded over me, as tiny shreds of hope began to tingle again in my veins. I glanced over at Sam but of course he was concentrating on the next rider approaching the fence. Gillian was standing beside him, a grin of complicity on her stupid Welsh face, ever ready to help with idiots like me who just couldn't get it right. Jealousy flared up in me, tightening its hold like a vice grip. My ebullience of a moment before evaporated.

'Okay everyone, we'll leave it at that.'

Although I'd known we were coming to the end of the lesson, I felt a surge of disappointment. Now I'd have to wait another week before I could see him again. The thrill of his praise ringing in my ears faded into nothing. We all turned into the centre and dismounted. The horses were going out to the field for the night so we unsaddled them and led them outside. I was waiting at the gate with the others when Sam came to take Gypsy from me.

'You did well tonight, Beth. Really well. You should keep it up this time.'

The glow spread up all the way from my toes.

'Thanks, Sam. I really enjoyed it.'

'So, how are you doing?' His tone had softened, his eyes almost meeting mine.

'Oh, you know. Still missing Dad a lot.' I opted for the obvious, not wanting to venture into more hazardous waters.

'Of course, of course.' He hesitated. 'Beth, I am sorry I haven't been around for you. It's just that...'

His unspoken words spoke volumes. Embarrassment roared between us. He blundered on.

'I mean, I should have come over. I wanted to. I just

didn't know what I could do, I mean how I could help...' Again he trailed off miserably, his eyes sliding away from me. I had to say something.

'It's okay, Sam. I understand. And I don't blame you.'

'Sam!' Gillian's strident voice pierced the moment. 'I need help here.'

The connection between us was instantly broken.

'Well, anyway. Thanks a lot, Sam.' I handed him Gypsy's reins. 'So, see you next week, I guess.'

I held my breath in anticipation. Surely he'd pick up on the door I'd left open. He must have sensed my eagerness to be with him.

'Take care, Beth.'

With that, he was gone, leaving me deflated.

'So?' enquired Laurie.

'So much for your matchmaking,' I snorted, ramming the gearstick into reverse. Now I'd been reminded just how much Sam meant to me and how desperately I wanted him. It was a bit like dangling a carrot in front of a donkey and keeping it always just out of reach, like some perverse system of Chinese torture. And now, of course, there was that simpering Gillian to contend with.

'Ah, come on, Beth. At least you'll be seeing him on a regular basis now. Give it a chance.'

With my mood darkening by the minute, I couldn't share Laurie's optimism. The knotted rope of my past with Sam still reached out to choke whatever future we might have. Driving back down the tree-lined avenue, with the shades of an autumn evening closing in, all the hope that had been swilling around deep in my subconscious drifted away.

CHAPTER TWENTY-FIVE

The following weekend, incredibly, saw us four weeks on from Dad's death. Friday, July 31. The Month's Mind Mass. Brian would attend as a member of the congregation, but no force on earth would persuade him to officiate. This time, he was adamant. By now, word of his 'taking time out' had scattered to every highway and byway of the Irish midlands, and of course had taken wings on the journey. All of Mother's worst nightmares had become reality. Instead of indulging in the part of the grieving widow, she would, as she saw it, be an object of ridicule and have to endure the commiserations of her neighbours, not on her loss, but on her only son's defection from the Church. This perceived stain on the family honour clung to her like a shadow.

The Mass was well attended and passed without incident, in spite of Mother's fears. This time, we'd opted for refreshments in the Village Inn afterwards; the usual tea and sandwiches with a selection of wraps, quiches and salads. Although I'd been dreading the occasion, I found it strangely comforting to be surrounded by people who knew and loved Dad, and who wanted to remember the good times they'd had with him. Even the likes of Miss Maloney, usually crabby and pinched with bitterness, shared with us a memory of how he'd changed a wheel for her when she'd been stranded on the side of the road one rainy night. The passing of four weeks had stirred up so many reminiscences, softened by time and recast in a glow of fondness. I really hoped Dad was looking down from wherever he was now on what had become a celebration of his life. What a pity Mother was so wrapped up in her humiliation over Brian she couldn't really be a part of it.

'Lovely occasion, Beth, lovely. Great to see such a turnout.'

Fr Flannery, glass of whiskey in hand, was munching through a slice of smoked salmon quiche, working his way around the lounge, exchanging a few words with everyone who had come along. I agreed politely that it had indeed gone well and that Dad would have been thrilled to hear so many speaking so well of him. Just then, I caught sight of a familiar figure in the crowd.

'If you'll excuse me, Fr.' I edged to one side, trying to make eye contact with Sam.

'Of course, of course, Beth. You need to move around. Have a few words with everyone. No more than myself. Eh?' He gave me a wink of complicity before heading back towards the bar for a refill. Sam was still hovering just beyond the immediate gathering. As I caught his eye, he eased out from the crowd and began moving in my direction.

'Ah, Beth. Everything okay?' Uncle Danny materialised at my side at the worst possible moment. He and Seamus had arrived to stay with us the night before and, perhaps to insulate themselves from the grief of losing their brother, had proceeded to get pissed. Danny was now milky-eyed and slightly unfocused, looking for someone he could drift about with on the seas of the past.

'Grand, Danny,' I shifted slightly in an effort not to lose Sam from my view. 'Wouldn't Dad have loved to see all this?'

To my horror, his eyes filled with tears. Instead of making him feel better, I'd only served to remind him that his baby brother, the little fella he'd taught how to fish for pinkeens in rock pools, was no more.

'Oh, Beth,' he reached out a frail hand and with surprising strength gripped my arm. 'Who'd ever have thought he'd be taken from us like that?'

My heart went out to him. Okay, he might be a bit under the weather right now, but he'd grown up with Dad, probably stood up for him to school bullies, and gone with him to his first dance. I rested my arm on his shoulder.

'He's in a good place now, Danny. Probably eating to his heart's content at that great banquet in the sky.'

His eyes lifted to mine, brightening. 'Sure he wouldn't be our Paddy if he wasn't stuffing himself. At least now he can do it in comfort, without that wife of his nagging him about his weight.' His hand flew to his mouth. 'Oh, Jesus, sorry Beth. No offence to your mother.'

'None taken,' I smiled. 'Sure we all know what Mam can be like.'

I moved sideways again, risking a glance across to where Sam had been standing. The spot was now empty.

'Ah well, here's to our Paddy.' He raised his pint glass to shoulder level, eyes swimming in reminiscence. 'May he find eternal happiness at that big banquet in the sky.'

I clinked glasses with his and moved away towards the knot of people around the door, hoping Sam might have joined them. He hadn't. I'd drawn a blank once again.

AND SO THE days rolled by with constant reminders of Dad's absence. Just getting up in the morning knowing there would be no telltale smells in the kitchen of the fried breakfasts he loved so much, triggered a renewed rush of grief. Each visit to the cemetery brought home the finality of his death. As did the Mass cards that still dropped through the letter box. Through all this, the one constant, no matter how much I tried to suppress it, was the longing to see Sam again. By now, I was counting down the hours to Wednesday evening and my next riding lesson. I was trying to work out a plan to get talking to him afterwards. I couldn't shake off the feeling that he'd wanted to come over to me that night in the pub, but there were just too many others in the way.

THE FOLLOWING MONDAY, Annafrid found an orange crate covered in polythene dumped at her gate with a litter of mewling pups inside, some kind of sheepdog cross-breed. They were just about four weeks old and still in need of their mother, or someone to bottle-feed all eight of them until they could be weaned. So the SOS call went out.

'Christ, I could slit the throats of whoever did this!' Annafrid's rage at the perpetrators sizzled. 'In Germany, thugs like these would be punished. Such cruelty is seen as a crime.'

She ranted on while I heated some watered-down milk to mix with the preparation the vet had given her. I picked up one of the little creatures and stroked it rhythmically. It nestled into the crook of my elbow, its heartbeat thrumming under my fingers. I couldn't comprehend how someone could have just left them to their fate.

'You will help me with the advertising, Beth, Ja?' Annafrid, practical as ever, was thinking ahead. She drew some of the warmed milk mix into a syringe and handed it to me.

'Of course I will. And don't worry.' I could see the lines of anxiety gathering around her eyes. 'We'll find homes for them.' A thought began to take shape in my mind as I began to syringe fluid into the mouth of the pup I was cradling.

'I bet Laurie'd love one. You know her kids have been at her to get a dog for ages now.'

Annafrid beamed. 'Ja, of course. And Brian would be pleased too.'

'What's Brian got to do with it?' The words were only

just out when I caught her meaning. 'Ah now listen. It's early days yet.'

'No such thing as early days when two people are in love.' Her whole face creased with pleasure. 'I see them together, the way they look at each other, the tenderness between them.'

'And I thought I might have been imagining it.'

'No imagining. This is love.' Annafrid nodded emphatically. 'Isn't it great for them both? Ja?'

I couldn't hold back the smile as I thought of how Mother would react to this latest development. It was one thing Brian having doubts about his vocation and needing time for reflection, but Brian turning his back on the religious life to marry a woman would really send her into apoplectic frenzies.

'And how about you, Beth?' Her eyes twinkled with mirth. She knew Sam was back and, with her typical rose-coloured world view, clearly had visions of us getting together again. She'd been one of the very few in Carrigmore who hadn't seen our engagement as a problem, and was genuinely upset when we broke up.

'Oh, nothing to get excited about, Annafrid.' I was still nurturing a tiny seed of hope that refused to go away, but didn't want to tempt fate. There was nothing to go on, no concrete evidence that he still had feelings for me.

'Tell me, Beth.' Her face softened. 'You still have a thing for Sam, no? How you say, a candle flame?'

I had to smile at her attempt at direct translation. 'That's all in the past, Annafrid. It's over.'

'I think not.' She draped an arm on my shoulder. 'I know you, Beth. I know you're unhappy. And I know you and Sam should be together. Ja, this is what should be.' She nodded again. 'And you know this also.'

And there was the problem. Yes, of course I knew it, but there was a world of difference between knowing what should be and being able to bring it about.

'OKAY, BETH. ON you come. Canter this time.'

Wednesday evening had finally arrived. I was like a newly-strung violin, every nerve quivering with anticipation. Every word Sam addressed to me I imbued with special significance, even the monosyllabic commands that told me to get my heels down or my hips back. We'd just moved on to the jumping phase. What had been a little cross pole had gone up to 80cm with a spread. The highest I'd ever attempted. My God, he must have some confidence in me to let me have a go at this. I pushed Gypsy on into a trot, rammed my outside heel into her, and she struck off at a canter. We came around the corner and lined up for the jump. Blood roared in my veins, pumping exhilaration through me. I was going to fly over this and really impress him. Gill was in attendance as usual, a simpering grin on her face.

With every stride, the fence loomed closer, and looked bigger and bigger. By now my heart was hammering like a piston. We were only about four strides away from it. Now three. Now two. This was it. I gave Gypsy an encouraging kick and launched myself forward, crouching down over her neck like I'd been taught.

The next thing I knew, I was lying in a heap on the sawdust floor on the other side of the jump from Gypsy, who was standing placidly looking at me. The bloody cow had slammed on the brakes at the last minute when I was already committed to going over, which had resulted in us parting company.

The first thing I registered was the grin of amusement

on Gill's face as she walked over to collect Gypsy. Bitch. Then I became aware of a sharp pain in my ankle. In an instant, Sam was at my side, bending over me, eyes filled with concern.

'Okay, Beth. Just sit where you are. Don't try to move anything. I'm going to ease the boot off to have a look.'

The pain receded into the background while I enjoyed his attentions. He loosened the laces of the ankle boot I was wearing and gently drew it down over my instep. I was suddenly aware of the fluff of golden hair on the back of his arms. He peeled off my sock and ran his hands over the joint, checking for any sign of a fracture. I almost hoped there might be just so he could go on taking care of me like this.

'I think you've been lucky, Beth. It's a nasty sprain but I don't think it's broken. But just in case, I'm bringing you in to Casualty. Gill, can you take over here?'

That wiped the smirk off her ugly Welsh face. The attention Sam was giving me was probably only in his professional capacity, but how could she be sure? She had no option but to comply with good grace. My ankle felt like it had been crushed by a roller, but I was in paradise.

'Right, Beth. Can you put your arms around my neck? I'll carry you out to the car.'

Without waiting for an answer, he reached down and scooped me up in the manner of Willoughby coming to the rescue of young Marianne Dashwood. My last view of the indoor school was Gill staring after us, suspicion clouding her face.

CASUALTY IN MULLINGAR was comparatively quiet. At 9.30pm, it was too early for the alcohol-related accidents, and the main hustle and bustle of the day had died down.

About a dozen or so patients occupied the waiting area, a handful reading newspapers, the rest just staring vacantly into space. Sam had organised a wheelchair to bring me from the car. After I'd checked in, he wheeled me to the end of a row of connected red plastic chairs and took a seat beside me.

'How's the pain?'

Although my ankle was now throbbing like crazy, the rush of joy brought on by the sound of his voice had me smiling like a clown.

'Ah sure, it's not so bad. They'll probably think I'm some kind of hypochondriac wasting their time with something so trivial.'

'It's always better to get these things checked out.' He smiled. 'We don't want you going around with a permanent limp because of my negligence, do we?'

My heart flipped over. He felt responsible for me. He cared. Whatever was going on between him and that Welsh cow, there was no doubting that he was concerned about me. Wrapping myself up in that certainty, I settled in for a long wait, with Sam by my side. But only about 20 minutes later, my name was called.

Sam wheeled me through to the consulting area. And it was at that point, going through the swing doors, that the memories came back. Just five months ago, I'd been here, trembling with fear, submitting to the most invasive examination of my life, which in turn had followed the most dreadful trauma of my life. My body gave an involuntary shudder. Sam put a hand on my shoulder.

'All right, Beth?'

I nodded, the recollected horror robbing me of the power of speech. Then, a nurse came to take the wheelchair from Sam.

'Hi, Beth. We're just going to take you to a cubicle for initial assessment. Thank you, sir.'

'Don't worry, Beth. You'll be fine,' Sam reassured me. But by now, I was being pushed away from him, down a wide aisle hemmed in by cubicles all the way down its length, with medical staff, stethoscopes dangling round their necks, bustling in and out through partition curtains.

An hour later, I was wheeled back out again to where he was waiting. The X-ray was clear and my ankle was now in a support bandage. Official diagnosis: a bad sprain. But internally, I was reliving the night of April 24. The worst night of my life. Lying on a stretcher in that cubicle, the kindness of the nurse with the soft Donegal accent, the hospital gown with the straps that criss-crossed at the back, and the dreadfulness of having to open my legs to allow swabs and photographs of the bruising to be taken; it was all still crystal clear in my head. It was like the intervening four months had been concertinaed into nothing. I felt like it had just happened.

'Well?' Sam was on his feet immediately.

'I'm grand. Only a sprain.'

'Sure you're okay?'

'I'm okay,' I sighed. I looked at the floor and mumbled, 'I just have bad memories of this place.'

'Oh Beth. I didn't even think… You came here… after?

I nodded dumbly.

Without another word, he wheeled me outside and helped me into the jeep.

The drive home was filled with that ultimate oxymoron; noisy silence. Sam seemed to be at a loss on how to reach me. After an eternity, we pulled into my driveway, and the outside light came on.

'Elizabeth!' My mother appeared in the open doorway, her eyes squinting into the darkness. 'Where've you been?'

'I'm okay, Mam. Just had a small mishap.' I could see the shock spreading across her face as she saw me swinging my bandaged ankle onto the tarmac. Sam was already around at my side to help me out.

'Oh my God!' The anxiety was clear on her face. 'What on earth happened?'

'Beth had a fall, Mrs Maguire. She's sprained her ankle and needs to rest it for a few days, but she'll be fine.'

Sam's words didn't have quite the consoling effect he'd intended.

'Fine? Look at her! The poor lamb isn't able to walk.' She glared at him. 'I might have known these riding lessons would lead to trouble.' Her voice was like shards of broken glass.

'Oh, Mam, I'm all right. For God's sake, don't make a drama of it.' With Sam linking me, I hobbled towards the door.

'Thank you, Samuel.' She moved forward to take my arm, intentionally blocking his way. 'I can manage from here.'

He shot her a look of derision before striding back to the jeep. And with that, the doorway into what might-have-been between Sam and I was firmly closed.

'So,' Laurie grinned. 'No sooner do I turn my back than you fall at his feet. Literally.' She'd called over to sympathise but was having a hard time keeping a straight face.

'Yeah sure,' I grumbled. 'Of course you know I did it on purpose.'

'However you did it, honey, it worked. You know now how much he cares about you.'

'But I went to pieces in the hospital,' I wailed.

'Look, pet, I know it was bound to be tough on you going back there after what happened, but Sam would have understood that. And just think, if it had been any of the others in the class, do you really think he would have gone to the hospital with them?

I had to admit she was probably right.

'You know what you need, Beth?' She was on her feet, picking up my crutch. 'A break from here. Come on, I'll take you out for a coffee. My treat.'

'Ah, Laurie, I'm not really in the mood.' I was still mortified by the way things had ended last night, thanks once again to my beloved mother. I'd had a go at her afterwards and the atmosphere between us could only be described as Siberian.

'It'll be good for you. You can't sit around here feeling sorry for yourself all day. A cappuccino and cream bun are just what the doctor ordered.'

'Okay, okay,' I raised my hands in mock surrender. 'Anything for a quiet life.' I hooked the crutch in under my armpit and hobbled out.

When we got to the hotel in Ballymartin, there was a funeral party winding down. The stragglers hung around in clusters, reluctant to break up what was left of the gathering, their muted laughter being swallowed into an uncomfortable silence. Laurie went to the counter to order and I shuffled awkwardly down to the back of the lounge and claimed a corner table.

'Believe me.' Laurie slid onto the seat across from me with the coffees. 'Give it a couple of days and he'll be round to see how you're doing.'

It stood to reason that he'd want to check if I was okay. We were a lot closer to being friends again now. Maybe he'd see Gill for the shallow cow she really was; maybe he'd realise we should both have had more faith in each other and stood up to the whole damn world ten years ago; maybe he'd remember how wonderful we'd been together.

Laurie's face darkened.

'What? I followed the direction of her eyes. Sam and Gill were taking seats at a table directly in our line of vision.

'I don't believe it.' All my glorious maybes evaporated like snowflakes on lakewater. They were obviously much closer than I'd wanted to believe. And we were trapped. The only way for us get out was to walk straight past them.

'Beth, it could be about anything. It could be work related. Don't let it get to you.'

I was skulking in a corner, watching the man who meant everything in the world to me dating a girl half my age. How could I not let it get to me? I felt like the eyes of the whole of Ballymartin were on me, seeing the blush of embarrassment spreading across my cheeks. I closed both hands around the coffee mug and held it to my face, trying to disappear behind it. In the distance, the occasional remnant of laughter rose from the funeral-goers.

Mercifully, the geography of the lounge afforded us a clear view of their table while we remained out of sight to them. Sam, leaning forward slightly, seemed to be doing most of the talking. He looked earnestly at her, clearly waiting for a response to whatever he'd just said. Could he be proposing? I looked wildly at Laurie.

'Beth! You've no idea what it's about. Stop reading into it what's not there,' she scolded. No matter how hard I tried, it was a physical impossibility to drag my eyes away from their table.

'Oh no.' The words came involuntarily from my lips. He had just taken her hand in both of his, and was speaking in soft tones.

'I've got to get out of here,' I muttered. 'I just can't take any more of this.'

'Come on, so.' Laurie stood up and reached for the crutch. 'Just the briefest hello on the way past them, all right?'

Sam was so absorbed in his tête-à-tête, he only saw us as we brushed past their table. Confusion lined his face.

'Beth!' He removed his hand from Gill's as colour flooded into his cheeks.

'Oh, hi, Sam.' I hobbled on as fast as my injured ankle would allow. From the corner of my eye, I caught Gill shooting me an ugly scowl. On our way out, at the front of the lounge, the praises of the dead man were still being sung.

CHAPTER TWENTY-SIX

THE DELUGE OF self-pity washing over me sent me back to the pages of my old diary. It was a bit like poking at a loose tooth; although it hurt, I couldn't leave it alone. I had to relive those days when Sam and I thought we could take on the world. By immersing myself in times of happiness, I could somehow make them real again.

December 19, 1999

We've done it! In spite of his mother, in spite of mine, in spite of the disapproval of the whole of Carrigmore, we're engaged! I'm going to be his wife! Sam and Beth Butler. I can feel the happiness pulsing through my blood. And the way he looked at me when he produced the ring. Like in a fairytale, we'd ridden out into the forest and stopped at a clearing. He'd said he wanted to check a loose shoe on Bessie and asked me to dismount. And then, instead of picking up her hoof, he put his hand into the pocket of his body-warmer and pulled out a small box, the kind you see in a jeweller's window, with a blue bow on it. My first thought was that he'd gotten me a pair of earrings, like the ones I'd recently lost. The next thing, he'd opened the box to reveal a ring that flashed in the light of the evening sun. A solitaire; the princess-cut diamond embedded in a twist of gold. And then came the words that set the whole world dancing. 'Will you marry me?' I felt like I was in happy-ever-after land. 'Yes, of course I will.' He slid the ring onto my finger and drew me into his arms. His lips closed on mine. We both swore that whatever opposition we met with didn't matter. We'd face them all down and show them how little class difference really meant. Riding back through those same woods was like going through an enchanted forest. Evening sunlight filtered through the branches and a symphony of birdsong showered us with music. Not even the thought of having to tell my mother of our engagement can dim my happiness. Sam Butler and I are going to be married and nothing on earth will ever come between us.

Nothing but the slow corrosion of trust in each other and the inevitable pull of loyalties on both sides; the heartbreak of seeing him unable to stand up for me when his mother slighted me; all the shame I felt at not being able to bring him home without my mother treating him like something she'd picked up on her shoe. Hot, stinging tears prickled at the corners of my eyes. I shut the diary and placed it on the highest shelf.

'ISN'T IT WONDERFUL?' Rosemary's exhilaration filled the kitchen. She had arrived down to inform us that she'd just had her pregnancy confirmed. She was seven weeks gone. She was going to be a mother. She and David were over the moon. They'd spent hours on the internet last night looking at what names were in vogue and which were the most in places for a christening. And so on.

Mother was overjoyed. It would be her first grandchild. She'd be able to hold her head up in Carrigmore again.

'Of course I have to take care of myself. David's insisting I go for a nap in the afternoons, and we're switching to an all organic diet.'

Of course. Taking care of herself would be right up Rosemary's street. In fact, I couldn't ever remember a time when she hadn't been taking care of herself.

'We must have a little celebration down here, dear, just to break the news,' Mother suggested.

Rosemary positively purred with pleasure. She'd be delighted to share her news with Carrigmore. Of course she'd have to give the champagne a miss, but wasn't that only a small sacrifice to make when you thought about the miracle that was happening inside her.

It was at that point, mercifully, that Brian's car swung into the drive. Any more of my mother and sister wittering on about the joys of bringing a new life into the world and I'd need a bucket. As he stepped out, the passenger door swung open to reveal Laurie.

'Rosemary, nice to see you.' He came forward to give his sister a peck on the cheek.

'Well, Brian.' She preened herself, preparatory to the Big Announcement. 'I have a bit of news for you. Looks like you're going to be an uncle.'

'No way!' His smile would have done the Cheshire Cat proud. 'That's brilliant! Congrats, Sis.'

By now, Laurie had followed him in.

'Yeah, congratulations, Rosemary. You must be delighted.'

'We both are.' She was off again. 'I can't tell you how much we're looking forward to parenthood.'

'Actually,' Brian moved over beside Laurie and took her hand, lacing his fingers through hers. 'We've some news of our own.'

He exchanged glances with Laurie while the room crackled with tension. Oblivious to what he was detonating,

Brian carried on.

'You know Laurie and I have always been good friends.' He was now stroking her hand. 'Well we've become a little more than that.'

Mother's face had frozen in horror. For a few seconds, it was as if we were actors on a stage who had forgotten their lines.

'So you two are, like, going out together?' Rosemary looked askance at Mother.

'Yeah,' Brian grinned. I held my breath, waiting for the explosion.

'A married woman?' The words were like a hail of bullets. 'Have you completely lost your mind?' Now that she'd regained her voice, Mother unloaded a torrent of fury. 'And as for you…' She turned to Laurie, her voice rising. 'What are you thinking of, throwing yourself at a man who's taken Holy Orders?'

Brian's face had turned to stone. He moved in front of Laurie, as if to protect her.

'I thought maybe that for once in your life, you'd be happy for me.' His voice dripped contempt. 'I should have known better.'

'Happy!' she snorted. 'How would I be happy when my only son is bringing even more disgrace on the family? I thank God your poor father isn't around to see what you're up to.'

'If he was, he'd be the first to wish Laurie and me well,' Brian spat back at her. 'He always had my best interests at heart. But with you, the only thing that matters is being able to boast about the achievements of your family throughout the length and breadth of Carrigmore. Well I've had just about enough of your snobbery.' He settled his arm protectively around Laurie's shoulder and steered her towards the door. 'Come on, Laurie. Let's go.'

'Just a minute.' Mother's voice was sharp, each syllable cutting the air. 'There's something you seem to have forgotten.'

He paused, eyes glittering with disdain.

'What about the conditions of your "time out" as you call it? Do you really think the order is going to continue supporting you now? And you carrying on with a woman? In public?'

'Do you really think I'd go on accepting their money now that I'm "carrying on" as you so delicately put it? You can rest assured, Mother. I've already written to the Provincial requesting a meeting next week. I'll be making an official declaration of my decision to leave and putting in my request for laicisation. Happy now?'

Her face crumpled as her last shred of hope fluttered away. Brian, his hand still on Laurie's shoulder, turned back towards the door.

'Where are you going?'

'Do you honestly think I can stay under this roof after all that's happened?

'What are you saying, son?' Her voice was edged with panic.

'I'll be out of here as soon as I pack my stuff.' Every word was enunciated clearly, his anger slowing his speech. 'And don't even try to contact me.'

With Laurie in tow, he marched out of the kitchen and tramped up the stairs, leaving Mother and Rosemary staring in disbelief at empty space. The ball of anger that had been building up inside me pushed its way to the surface.

'What was it you were saying about trying to keep the family together? Well I hope you're happy now!'

'But, Elizabeth, he was supposed to be only taking a year

out to reconsider his position. Wouldn't you think he could at least have seen that through before getting involved with women. Especially ones that are still married.'

'Oh, for God's sake, Mam! You know Laurie is separated. Legally.' I threw in for good measure.

'In the eyes of the Church she's still married. And he's still a priest,' she sniffed.

It was that familiar sniff of disapproval that really got to me. The river of resentment I'd kept damned up for years came gushing out.

'You know something? I'm delighted for Brian and Laurie, and I really hope they make a go of things together. Of course I wouldn't expect you to be happy for them because all you've ever done is try to impose the pattern *you* want on *our* lives. Brian was right! It's always, always about doing things your way. You pushed him into the priesthood before he had the chance to make up his own mind. You ruined my chance of happiness with Sam ten years ago because he wasn't *your* idea of a good match. To hell with you and your ridiculous social-climbing notions. Just look at where they've gotten you! You're going to end up a lonely, bitter old crone.'

I was now on my feet, shaking my crutch at her like a madwoman. She was ashen-faced. I turned away and limped out.

BEFORE I REACHED Brian's bedroom, I could hear Laurie's voice raised in protest. I knocked and the door was pulled open.

'Beth, maybe you can talk some sense into him?' Laurie was clearly trying to dissuade Brian from his course of action. 'If he moves out now, it'll cause a rift between them that may never heal.'

'That rift is already the size of the Grand Canyon.' Brian was thundering around, flinging stuff into a hold-all. His bed was a riot of t-shirts, odd socks and cotton trousers. 'And she's the one who's caused it. Didn't you hear what she said. "Bringing more disgrace on the family." If I stay under her roof, I'll never have a life of my own. That woman is nothing to me.' His tone was flat and final, a denial of any bond of kinship. A wall had shot up around him and there was no way of breaking through it. He continued pulling stuff out of drawers while Laurie and I looked helplessly on.

There was a sharp rap on the door and Rosemary stuck her head in.

'Have you two any idea what you've done?' Her voice was like the whine of a food blender. 'Poor Mam's below crying her eyes out. You've really upset her.'

I looked at Brian. His face was still rigid with anger.

'I'd better go down,' I sighed.

'I'll leave you to it.' Rosemary's bleating barely registered with me. 'I just can't deal with all this now. I have to take care of myself. I'll come back later when you've sorted things out.'

'You do just that.' I scowled at her. 'You'd only be in the way.'

I was down the stairs and heading for the kitchen before she could retort. Mother was standing at the sink, staring out into the yard. I waited for her to turn around.

'Elizabeth?'

This wasn't the mother I knew. This was a woman who was struggling to maintain dignity while her face was crumpling. I didn't know what to say. I was thrown into unfamiliar territory, floundering for a new code of conduct.

'Can we talk?'

It was a question, not a command. She walked shakily over to the table, moving like a patient after major surgery.

'What is it?' I was still mystified.

'Beth,' she hesitated. I'd never before heard her using the shortened form of my name. 'I know we've had our problems, but I need you to know something.' Outside, Rosemary's Toyota growled into life. 'In spite of what you might think, I've only ever wanted the best for you.'

How helpful to know that now, when my life was in ruins thanks to her interference.

'Maybe what I saw as the best wasn't always right for you.'

I was speechless. For the first time in my life, my mother was admitting that maybe she'd been at fault. Brian and I had clearly made an impact.

'All that stuff about Samuel. I was only looking out for you, you know? I just didn't want you to end up unhappy. Their sort don't usually mix with the likes of us.'

'There are exceptions to every rule, Mam.'

'Yes, I'm beginning to see that now. And I think maybe, even though he's not of our persuasion, he could still be a good man.'

It was too late. But I had to admit it must have taken a lot for her to come out with such a statement. Her upbringing in working class Catholic Belfast had conditioned her to see all Protestants as the devil incarnate. I bit back the obvious retort that people could be good or bad no matter what their religious background.

'And as for that Scotsman. I can see now he was nothing but trouble. Sure the whole village was talking about his drinking habits.'

She really was backing down, big time.

'And I'm desperately sorry for what happened to you.'

Her voice wobbled. 'I thought at the time he was the perfect match for you, what with you being on your own for so long and all that. But I was so wrong.'

I couldn't hold out against her any longer. Her tacit acknowledgement that she had played a part in the whole Andrew debacle and her remorse over it melted whatever resistance I had left. Maybe losing Dad had taught her something about the frailty of human relations, and the importance of family. She moved into my open arms and held me properly for the first time since I was a child.

'I still can't believe he could have done that to you. My poor Beth.'

Now the tears were dribbling down her cheeks. I said whatever I could to make her feel better.

'Mam, I'm getting through it. Really I am. I've been to counselling. And look what happened to Andrew in the end. You wouldn't wish that on anyone. But maybe it was some kind of divine retribution for what he did. So, let's try and put it behind us, alright?'

It was at that point I noticed the door was ajar. There was a shadow in the gap. I heard a warning cough. How long had Brian been just outside? Long enough to register the transformation, I hoped.

'Brian!'

This was another first. Gone was the 'Fr Brian' bit. Even since he'd come back from Zambia, she still hadn't managed to address him by name. Until now.

'Mother?' His tone was devoid of forgiveness.

'Please, Brian. Let me explain.' Desperation was written in her eyes

'You said I'd brought disgrace on the family. Perhaps you'd like to explain that.'

He wasn't letting her off easily.

'I'm sorry I said those things, son. I just couldn't let go of the idea of you as a priest. That's why I got such a shock. I mean, you and Laurie. It seems so bizarre.'

Brian looked hard at her. 'What's going on between Laurie and I is our business.'

'Yes, you're right. But surely you can see how hard it is for me to think of you as a lay person, to accept that you're no longer living the religious life.'

'If you had any real regard for me, you'd accept me as I am, and stop trying to shape me into something I'm not.' Brian's voice quivered slightly. 'Maybe even be a little bit proud of me. What I had to do wasn't easy, you know.'

'I know that Brian, and I am proud of you.' She reached for his hand. 'And I don't want to lose you.'

His face finally softened. He looked across to include me in the new cordiality that seemed to have blossomed between them.

He half smiled at her. 'As long as you're okay with the new direction my life is taking.'

'Whatever makes you happy son, I'm okay with it.' She looked broken, but relieved.

A light footstep in the hallway reminded us of Laurie's presence. Mother crossed the room and opened the door.

'Laurie, would you mind coming in for a minute?'

I felt a squeeze of anxiety. After how Mother had treated Laurie just a short while ago, I wasn't sure how smoothly this would go. Laurie too was uncomfortable, trying to glean from our faces what was to come.

'I'm truly sorry for what I said, Laurie. You'll have to put it down to the ramblings of a silly old woman.'

Laurie looked at Brian, unable to conceal her amazement

'I know I've been very hard on Brian lately. I suppose

with him being my only son, I had all sorts of aspirations for him.' She held her hands in front of her stomach, fingers curling and uncurling. 'But maybe I was a bit pushy at times. And I only saw what I wanted to see.'

'That's all in the past now, Mother,' Brian beamed at her. 'Now we're all moving on.'

Minutes later, we were drinking a toast to Brian and Laurie, wishing them all the happiness in the world. Mother's face had lost its habitual pinched expression, and she was actually showing some interest in Laurie's work in the bookshop. Maybe there was light at the end of this particular tunnel. What a crying shame her endorsement of me and Sam had come too late.

I WAS JUST finishing breakfast when my mobile rang. It was Sam. I hit the reject key. Whatever was going on, I didn't want to know. Maybe if I stayed out of his way for a while, I'd gain some kind of distance. I'd be able to face him without caving in completely. But not now. I needed time.

But I couldn't resist checking the message he'd left.

'Eh, hi Beth. Sam here. Just wondering how you're doing? Hope the ankle is improving and that you're managing to get about a little better now. Maybe you'd like to come out for a drink, or maybe dinner?'

Could I have been wrong about him and that cow? I didn't think so. His interest in her the other day was too marked to ignore. He was just feeling sorry for me and I couldn't handle that right now. With a sinking heart, I deleted the message.

'COME ON, BETH. You're not thinking this through.' Laurie's

eyes burned with frustration. 'If he says he wants to see you, he wants to see you. Forget about what we saw. That tart could be out of the picture by now. Did you not see how pissed off she was looking? I'll bet he dumped her.'

'And suppose he didn't? No, Laurie. I'm backing off now, before I make a complete tit of myself.'

'He's asked to see you, Beth. Don't you think you owe it to him?' she said quietly. 'After all that's between you?'

I began to waver.

'I mean how would you feel if it was the other way round? Suppose you wanted to see him, for whatever reason, and he kept avoiding you. You'd be mortified.'

She had a point. Before I could change my mind, I unlocked my keypad and typed in a text message.

> 'Hi Sam. Yes, ankle improving and would love to meet up.'

A couple of minutes later, the message alert went off and his name flashed up.

> 'Great. Pick you up about 7.00pm to-night and we'll grab a bite to eat. Okay?'

I hadn't expected it to be quite that soon. I'd have to find something to wear, do something with my hair, shave my legs. I checked myself. I was fantasising again. This wasn't a date. This was a meeting of two old friends. I texted back that a bite to eat would be fine.

At exactly 6.59pm, the jeep swung into our driveway. I'd eventually compromised between dressed up and casual. I wore tailored black jeans with a cream top and a fuchsia scarf. With my ankle still strapped up, high heels were out of the question, so I had to settle for a pair of flats.

And wouldn't you know, I had a spot just coming up on my chin that the thin veneer of foundation I put on didn't quite camouflage. At least this time, Mother wasn't getting at me about Sam. In fact she was delighted. In spite of all I'd said to her about him being involved with someone else, I knew she was hoping for miracles. Once she heard the jeep, she was falling over herself to get to the door first, probably trying to make up for her rudeness in the past.

'Good evening, Samuel. Nice to see you again.' For the first time ever, she smiled at him.

'Oh. Mrs Maguire.' He stepped back, taken unawares.

'Please come in. Beth's nearly ready.'

I hobbled into the hallway as fast as my ankle would allow. The last thing I wanted was a different kind of awkwardness between them, the kind that spoke of unwarranted expectations. But in spite of the severest warnings to myself, at the sight of him, my heart filled with longing.

'Hi Sam.'

'Beth.' His smile reached out to me. In a couple of strides, he'd crossed the space between us and put a supporting arm under mine. 'I've booked a table in the Greville Arms. Is that okay with you?'

'That's great, Sam.' I turned to my mother. 'Right, Mam. See you later.'

'Have a lovely time, you two.' She stood in the doorframe watching us go, her eyes alive with hope. She was an old woman who seemed to have finally unshackled herself from the prejudices that had held her in their grip for so long.

THE MUTED LIGHTING in the dining room of the Greville Arms combined with the gleam of squat red candles on every table created the perfect environment for lovers. But of course, we didn't fit into that category. I wouldn't dare allow myself that hope. I steeled myself once again.

With impeccable manners, Sam held out the high-backed chair for me before the waiter could get to it. I lowered myself awkwardly, conscious of my bandaged ankle. The menu and wine list were produced and we were left to ourselves. Their roast lamb had always been my favourite. Succulent meat served with a honey orange glaze and port and mint dressing.

'I see they still have the lamb on.' He hadn't forgotten.

'Yes, I think I'll go for that.' I risked a tentative smile. 'For old time's sake.'

He placed the order and the wine arrived, an Australian shiraz we used to drink back then.

'Well, here's to old times.' He raised his glass to mine. 'And to rekindled friendships.'

Friendship. There was that word again. The one I didn't want to hear.

'To old times,' I muttered. 'Yes, and friendship.'

Even though I'd told myself not to expect anything, I was disappointed. This was going to be even harder than I'd anticipated. My smile must have wobbled just a bit because as soon as he put down his glass, his hand closed over mine.

'Okay, Beth?'

'Fine,' I lied, trying to turn the smile on again.

'It's just that, you seem a little down.'

My voice dropped to a hoarse whisper. 'I shouldn't be here with you. I mean it's not fair to Gill, is it?'

'Gill?' His confusion was unmistakable. 'What's Gill got to do with anything?'

'Well, I mean, you two are going out together, aren't you?' The question hung in the air between us.

'Oh, Beth. That was over ages ago. Not that it ever amounted to much in the first place. It was all pretty one-sided. What she was most interested in was the size of my wallet,' he smiled.

Relief washed over me.

'So you're not in love with her?'

'I've never been in love with her! There might have been qualities in her I admired, but it wasn't long before she began reading more into it than there really was. The next thing I knew, she was broadcasting that we were an item.' He stared into space. 'I was such an idiot to go along with it. Especially when it gave a misleading impression to others.' He looked directly at me.

The look was charged with meaning. An insane happiness began to spread all over me. I inched my fingers back towards his hand, still on the table. When we touched, it was like an electric shock. And then, suddenly, he was stroking the back of my hand, my wrist, my bare forearm. It was the most erotic sensation I'd ever felt. I reached deep into all my reserves of courage.

'Sam, I— I've missed you so much.'

I looked up at him, not daring to breathe, my heart banging in my chest. This was the moment I'd waited so long for, that so much depended on. He moved back a little, and removed his hand from mine.

'Actually, Beth. I've got something to tell you.'

With shaking hands, I reached for the glass of wine in front of me.

'It's just that, um, you know that show jumping yard I worked for in Kentucky? They're looking for someone to manage it. They've made me an offer I can't refuse. I get to bring on the young horses and compete at national level with the Grade A's. It's a heaven-sent opportunity.'

I took a deep gulp of the wine.

'And I've managed to find the right man to take over from me here. We'll be phasing out the livery horses so he'll just have our brood mares to look after.'

At this, the last shreds of hope that I'd been clinging on to broke free and scattered away.

'Beth?' His tone trembled with concern. 'Beth, are you okay?'

I nodded dumbly. The hum of background noise seemed to come from a long way off.

'When will you be going?' My voice came out hoarse.

'They want me to start in October.'

October. Just over a month away. And then I'd never see him again.

Sam shifted slightly, taking my hand in both of his.

'There's just one thing, Beth,' he paused. 'I can't do it without you.'

Again, the words hung, like disembodied spirits, somewhere over our heads. I tried to grasp them but they drifted just beyond my reach, as incomprehensible as hieroglyphics. I stared at him, confusion expanding like cotton wool in my head. And then I saw the little box with the blue bow he'd drawn from his pocket.

'You and me, Beth.' He swallowed. 'Don't say it's too late. I can't bear to lose you again.'

Was that 'you and me' I heard in the same sentence?

His fingers fumbled with the box and finally got it open to reveal the princess-cut diamond embedded in a twist of gold that I'd given back to him ten years ago.

'Please, Beth.' His eyes were alive with hope. 'I need to know if there's still a chance for us.'

His voice had dropped to a whisper, the sweetest whisper I'd ever heard. This was no illusion. This was Sam, my Sam, telling me he wanted to be with me. I looked at him, at his eyes filled with the agony of uncertainty.

'Say you'll marry me. We can start our new life together out there. Get away from all this,' he waved a hand dismissively, 'all the things that have kept us apart. And when we come back, it'll all be different.'

He wanted me to go to Kentucky with him. To be his wife. To a world far away from all the frustrations of small village life, where I always seemed to be swimming against the tide. Even with my mother now finally on my side, I'd still be facing all the obstacles that went with the territory of a mixed marriage in a small community. All the foolish pride that got in the way of the acceptance of anything that wasn't the norm. Mother could always come and visit us. In fact she'd only recently been talking about her ambition to travel. I was sure Laurie and Brian would jump at the opportunity to come with her. But as for the rest of my acquaintances. My mind skated across Carrigmore's host of characters; from Miss Maloney in her corner shop, and her pitiful pursuit of the sleazy Frank Moran; to Fonsie Kelly with his lewd banter and his unwelcome attentions; to Jennifer Muldowney, who, after 40-odd years of teaching the village children, now had nothing to look forward to but a solitary retirement with only her cats for company. On reflection, this had to be what they called 'a no-brainer.'

'Beth?'

It took just the slightest squeeze of my hand to give him his answer.

'Yes. Yes, Sam, Yes,' the words tumbled out. The distance that had once stretched between us was obliterated in an instant. He eased the solitaire out of its box and slid it onto my finger. The patrons of the restaurant broke into scattered applause as Sam grinned at me, before getting to his feet and pulling me into his embrace. He gently stroked my face as he leaned forward, his lips closing on mine, giving me the sweetest kiss I'd ever experienced. I looked into his eyes, certain that this time nothing could keep us apart. In one of those sudden moments of clarity, I saw all the happiness that had seemed to be so far out of my grasp was really only a heartbeat away. All I had to do was reach out for it.

EPILOGUE

"WHO CAN BE in doubt of what followed? When any two young people take it into their heads to marry, they are pretty sure by perseverance to carry their point, be they ever so poor, or ever so imprudent, or ever so little likely to be necessary to each other's ultimate comfort. If such parties succeed, how should a Captain Wentworth and an Anne Elliot, with the advantage of maturity of mind, consciousness of right, and one independent fortune between them, fail of bearing down every opposition?"

– Jane Austen
Persuasion

ACKNOWLEDGEMENTS

I WOULD LIKE to thank the many individuals who have contributed in no small way to the success of this novel. For his early encouragement when the story was just beginning to take shape, Limerick author, Michael Collins. For her invaluable feedback on an early draft and ongoing support, Alison Walsh. For his expert advice on legal matters, Sean Corrigan B.L. and on medical matters, Dr Pat Kelly. For her discerning eye where babies are concerned, Teresa Maguire. For their guidance on issues around the priesthood and religious education, Rose Moran and Margaret Horan. For sharing with me her insights gained from working with survivors of sexual assault, Angela Keaveney of Longford Women's Link. For their attention to detail in reading the manuscript, Sally Pybus, Jean Rogers and Majella Reid. For their constant encouragement, the Ballymahon Writers Group and the Longford Fiction Writers Group. For all their tips on editing in the later stages, Caroline Barry and Neil Richardson. And for continued support of all of my literary endeavours, the Longford County Librarian, Mary Carleton Reynolds.

It goes without saying that writing a novel is only the beginning of the journey. Bringing your work to the public requires teamwork. And that's where Book Republic came in for me. They paid me the courtesy of an amazingly swift response to my submission, and the progression from acceptance to publication was equally fast. My heartfelt thanks go to Karen, John, Claire, Jean and all the team who have made my journey into print so painless and enjoyable.

And of course, from the very beginning, the voice of Jane Austen and her story of Anne Elliot and Captain Wentworth was whispering at my side, urging me on.

-Anne Skelly
June 2011.

ABOUT THE AUTHOR

ANNE SKELLY IS originally from Dublin and now lives in rural Longford with her husband and their three dogs. She has been writing short stories for about ten years and has been short listed in a number of literary competitions, most recently the International First Writer Award. *Foolish Pride* is her first novel.

Since moving to Longford, Anne has been deeply involved in local literary activities. She has served on the committee of the Goldsmith International Literary Festival and directed the Longford Writers Group Festival. She worked for three years as Creative Writing Development Officer for Longford County Council, during which time she worked with writers groups throughout the county to provide support and organise inter-group events and edited Longford's literary website, *Virtual Writer.*

She currently facilitates writers groups in Ballymahon and Longford and delivers introductory courses in Creative Writing for Westmeath and Longford VECs.